T

# The Conversations

**By**

# John Duncklee

Lovingly Dedicated to
"Comma Momma"

Wolfpack Publishing LLC
48 Rock Creek Road
Clinton, Montana 59825

ISBN 978-1-62918-120-2

Cover & Book Design L. J. Martin

# THE CONVERSATIONS

by

**John Duncklee**

## Part One

"Mom, will you tell me a story about when you were a little girl?"

"I can't right now, Tommy," Blanche Holmes said. "I have to leave for a lunch meeting with 'The Ladies Of Westchester' at the Shore Club."

Tommy Holmes turned away and went to his room. He was used to both his mother and his father not talking with him. Again, he would be left with Lisa Marie, the girl his mother hired to watch him. But, as soon as his mother drove away from the farmhouse on the edge of town, Lisa Marie would put the headphones in her ears to listen to her favorite music. One time she had put the headphones on Tommy, but he thought the sounds that Lisa Marie called music was just noise. He had given the headphones back to her quickly.

Tommy waited in his room looking out of the window through which he could see when his mother drove off to her social life. As he waited he thought about his father's life in the city as a Wall Street banker. That was what his father had told him about his job. After being at his job all day, Jason Holmes came back to his old refurbished farmhouse that had been in the family for five generations, and sat with Blanche drinking his before dinner cocktails that made him talk funny. Whenever Tommy tried to talk with his parents when they were having their "Happy Times", as they referred to their drinking times, they would always say to him, "Why don't you go play with your toys in your room, Tommy?"

By the time Tommy had his sixth birthday, he had become so used to his parents not talking with him that he stayed by himself when he was home. When he was in school he rarely talked with anyone except when he had to answer a question from his teachers.

However, Tommy had found a favorite place close to the small stream that wound through the woods beyond the farmhouse. Tommy had been escaping to his favorite place for a year, sitting on an old log at the edge of a clearing overlooking the stream. He liked listening to the water gurgle through the rocks and boulders until the current ran smoothly, at times carrying fallen leaves from the trees and bushes in the woods.

Now it was September, and the stream carried leaves of different shades of orange, red, brown and yellow. Tommy relaxed as he sat on the log. Thoughts about his parents vanished from his mind as he gazed into the stream. There were times when he found talking to himself a pleasant pastime. Today was one of them.

Above all the subjects in school, Tommy liked Arts and Crafts the best. He enjoyed drawing, making things out of wood, but most of all he liked ceramics. His teacher, Miss Clara Anson, taught her students all about clay and how to make things using clay. She started the boys and girls with moist clay that she kept in buckets covered by lids. She showed them how some things took more clay than others to make. The most difficult part of the process for most was what she called "centering" the glob of clay on the potter's wheel. It took most students many tries before they could bring the sides up to form a vessel or bowl. But, once they got the feel of that, they found it easier and easier as they added greater and greater amounts of clay to be centered and formed into what they wanted to make.

Tommy took to throwing pots like a duck takes to water. He soon wanted to make other things from clay, and asked Miss Anson how to make statues. She taught him how to make frameworks for his figures out of wire that she unwound from old coat hangars, and then showed him how to plaster the clay onto the framework. She was surprised how well Tommy was able to carve different parts of the figures so that they looked like what he said they were.

One day as he sat on the log in the clearing next to the stream out in the woods, Tommy had an idea. "I think I will make a friend out of clay at school and bring my friend out here," he said out loud. "Then we can talk to each other, and I will not feel so alone."

All this happened a week after his mother had gone off to her meeting with "The Ladies of Westchester" at the Shore Club. He went to school and asked Miss Anson if he could make his friend out of clay. Miss Anson crinkled her brow as she looked at Tommy.

"Why do you want to make a friend out of clay, Tommy?" She asked. "Don't you have any friends near your house?"

"My house is an old farmhouse and there are no other houses near mine."

Miss Anson shrugged her shoulders and proceeded to show Tommy what he needed to do in order to make a friend out of clay.

It took Tommy two weeks to finish his clay friend. He had wished that he could spend all day on it instead of in the other classes that he did not care for. Finished with his clay friend one afternoon, Tommy stood it on a table and looked it over. The other students gathered around to see Tommy's creation. They had all been interested in Tommy's progress as he made the figure.

"How did you make the eyes?" one of the boys asked.

"Marbles," Tommy said. "I made thumb marks before I fired it and then glued the marbles into the thumb marks with "super-glue".

Miss Anson was quite impressed with Tommy's accomplishment and told him he would be getting an "A" in art for the year. She gave him permission to take his clay friend home to show his parents.

Tommy left for home carrying his creation. But he did not go straight home. He carried the figure out into the woods to his special place by the stream. Arriving at the clearing, He brushed away the fall leaves to make room for his sculpture on the opposite side of the clearing from the log he used to sit on. Tommy stood the clay friend on the cleared spot. Then, he sat on the log and looked at his friend.

"I am going to call you 'Ralph' ", he said. "Do you like that name?"

"That is a good name," Ralph said. Only it was Tommy speaking for his clay friend.

"I like talking with you, Ralph," Tommy said.

"I like talking with you, too, Tommy," Ralph said.

The two friends continued talking back and forth with each other, Tommy always talking for Ralph as if Ralph was alive. Soon, Tommy felt like what he said for Ralph was really coming from Ralph's mouth, not his.

While Tommy had been making Ralph's face, he had formed Ralph's mouth into a broad smile. As the two sat talking with each other in the clearing, both Tommy and Ralph smiled at each other. Tommy felt happier than he had ever been before. He had finally found someone who would talk with him.

Talking to Ralph made Tommy forget the time. Suddenly, he realized that not only had he not been home since school let out, but he was probably late for supper. He turned to Ralph.

"Ralph, you are my best friend," Tommy said. "I wish I could stay with you all night, but I have to get home to supper or I will be in deep trouble."

Tommy rose from the log, gave a short wave with his right hand toward Ralph, and started trotting along the trail that would lead him to the old farmhouse. As he approached the house he noticed that the garage doors were closed. That meant that both of his parents were home. He wished he had taken his wristwatch with him to the clearing. He knew that his parents would have finished their drinks and were probably in the dining room either eating or waiting for Bertha, the cook, to serve them supper. He climbed up the steps leading to the front door, opened it and walked in. He went directly into the dining room where he was not surprised to see his father and mother sitting in their chairs with their heads turned in his direction, staring at him with looks that seemed like daggers flying at him. He knew his mother would be the first to ask him where he had been.

"Where have you been, Tommy Holmes?" Blanche asked in a stern voice.

"I just got back from the woods," Tommy said. "I forgot to take my wrist watch."

"What in the world were you doing in the woods at this hour?" Blanche continued her questioning.

"I was talking with my friend."

"Who is this friend?" Blanche asked, raising her left eyebrow.

"Ralph," Tommy said.

His mother hesitated, then reached for her glass and took a sip from it. Tommy pulled out his chair and sat down. He saw his mother take the brass bell, lift it and shake it so that it sounded the signal for Bertha to start bringing in the supper. Tommy sighed, hoping that the questioning would be over.

"Who is this Ralph you are calling your friend?" Jason Holmes inquired.

"Ralph is my best friend," Tommy answered, as he heard the door to the kitchen open and the sound of Bertha's footsteps coming into the dining room.

"You have never mentioned this Ralph before, Tommy." His father continued. "Does he live around here?"

Tommy felt himself getting nervous at his father's questions. He reached for the spoon in the bowl of mashed potatoes, took a spoonful and put it on his plate.

"I asked you if this friend, Ralph, lives around here," Jason Holmes said with his impatience showing in his voice.

"Ralph lives in the woods," Tommy said. "He is my friend."

"What is his last name?" Jason asked.

""'He doesn't have a last name, Father. May I eat my supper?"

"All right, you may eat your supper, but when we are finished I want to know Ralph's last name."

Tommy began eating his supper, all the time trying to think what he could do about Ralph's last name. The entire situation had upset him so much that he could not think what he could do. When he had just about finished the meal he looked across the table to the vacant chair and before he knew what he was doing, blurted out, "What is your last name, Ralph?"

He kept looking at the chair across the table, realizing he should not have said what he had said. His parents looked at one another with obvious quizzical looks, but they didn't say anything. Finished with the supper, Tommy asked to be excused, and left the room before getting an answer. He went directly to his room, happy that the questioning about Ralph had stopped. At least he hoped it had stopped. He cringed as he thought about his father or mother coming to his room with more questions. Suddenly, he felt it was his turn to ask questions.

"Ralph, why are they talking to me so much just because I have a friend named Ralph. They never talked much to me at all. They were always too busy talking about their days and drinking their before dinner cocktails."

"I don't know," Ralph said. "Why ask me? They are your parents."

Realizing what he had been saying, Tommy laughed, but put his head into his pillow so that no sound of laughter would escape his room. Within a half hour Tommy had fallen asleep lying on his bed with all of his clothes on. His parents stayed at the dining room table sipping their after dinner drinks and talking about Tommy, trying to understand him.

"Jason, I am concerned about Tommy talking to himself and to this invisable friend Ralph," Blanche said.

"I find his story of Ralph quite strange. He doesn't even know Ralph's last name," Jason said.

"I do not remember talking to myself when I was his age," Blanche said.

"I know I never talked to myself, I was always talking to my brother and sister, arguing about one thing or another."

"I wish I could forget all the fights I had with my brother. He was a monster. He still is half the time when he comes to visit."

"Tommy's lucky he doesn't have to put up with what we dealt with," Jason said.

"I suppose we will just have to go along with Tommy and Ralph and see what happens. I don't know anything else to do," Blanche said. "I am tired after that meeting with the Garden Club. I think I'll go to bed."

"I am with you. I want to get to sleep and not think about Tommy and Ralph, whatever his name is."

The Holmes retired for the night without further discussion about their wayward son. Neither parent checked on Tommy, who was sound asleep fully clothed with a smile on his face.

Tommy opened his eyes to a new day earlier than usual. He shook his head slightly when he saw that he had gone to bed with his clothes on. Bertha was starting to make breakfast for the Holmes family when Tommy pushed open the swinging door to the kitchen from the dining room.

"What you doing so early?" Bertha asked.

"I guess I must have slept a long time," Tommy said.

"You wants to wait for yo Momma and Daddy fo breakfast?"

"I'll just have some cereal for me and Ralph, and then we will go to school."

"Where be Ralph and who is dis Ralph?" Bertha asked.

"Ralph is my best friend. He is already sitting at the table. I will take a bowl of cereal to him."

Bertha got two bowls from the cupboard, put them on the counter and filled them both with cereal. Tommy took the milk carton from the refrigerator, carried it out to the dining room, and put it on the table. That done, he went back into the kitchen and got the cereal bowls.

"Thanks, Bertha. Ralph thanks you, too."

"You welcome, Tommy. Jes leave da bowls on da table. I get dem later."

"Thanks, Bertha," Tommy said and went back into the dining room.

He got silverware from the buffet and sat down telling Ralph to eat his breakfast.

Finished with his cereal, Tommy went outside, and walked to school without waiting for his parents to come downstairs for breakfast. He walked slowly, carrying on a conversation with Ralph as he went. He told Ralph about going to the clearing after school so that they could watch the stream as it flowed along from wherever it came from and to wherever it was going.

Jason and Blanche arrived in the dining room just as Bertha was setting the breakfast table.

"Where is Tommy?" Blanche asked.

"He and Ralph came in early and they already went to school," Bertha said.

"Did you get a good look at Ralph?" Blanche asked.

"No, Ma'am, I was getting yo breakfasts. Tommy come in and got cereal for both a dem. When I went to get da bowls, Dey was both empty. Maybe he drinks da lass a da milk holdin da bowl ta his mouth likes ma boy does."

"Did you see them start for school?"

"I's in da kitchen, but Tommy tole me dat dey was goin to school when he come in fo da cereal."

Bertha went back to the kitchen to get the plates full of scrambled eggs and bacon, with English muffins. She served the breakfast, and returned to the kitchen.

"Jason, what do you make of that?"

"What do you mean?" Jason asked.

"Don't you think it odd that Tommy and his friend, Ralph, were here for breakfast?"

"I suppose that is strange, but what are we to do? They are off to school. That's what Bertha said."

"I wish we had come downstairs while they were eating their cereal. We could have seen what this Ralph looks like. Maybe we know his family."

"All right, Blanche, I have to catch my train into the city. I need to finish my breakfast. Why don't you go to Tommy's school and ask Miss Anson about this Ralph character. We have an important bank acquisition today, and I need to think about some details, not about this Ralph, whose last name we don't even know."

Mid-morning found Blanche in the principal's office at Tommy's school. She had requested Miss Anson's presence for a short conference that she, Blanche, considered very important.

Miss Anson appeared through the door of the principal's anteroom.

"Hello Missus Holmes, it is nice to see you. What can I do for you?" The teacher said, knowing that something must be on Tommy's mother's mind to make her visit the school.

"Miss Anson, my husband and I are concerned about Tommy's behavior. Lately we have noticed that he talks to himself a lot, but he also carries on conversations with a friend of his named Ralph. We are wondering if Ralph is in Tommy's class and what his last name might be."

"I don't have a Ralph in Tommy's class, but I have noticed that Tommy seems somewhat distant in spite of his intense interest in working with clay."

"He never speaks about working with clay," Blanche Holmes said.

"Did he show you the sculpture he made?"

"I don't know anything about a sculpture."

"That's strange because I told him he could take it home to show his parents," Miss Anson said, and crinkled her brow in consternation.

"Well, thank you, Miss Anson. I will talk with my husband when he comes back from Wall Street tonight. You have been very helpful."

"I wish I could tell you more, but to me, Tommy is exploring his creativity better than most students I know. It was nice to see you, Missus Holmes, and I will see if I can observe Tommy more closely."

Blanche left the school and drove back to the old farmhouse, still befuddled about her son's behavior talking to his invisible friend, but she was especially puzzled about the sculpture Miss Anson mentioned that Tommy had brought home to show her and Jason. She clenched her teeth as she thought about confronting Tommy when he got home from school. Then she realized that she would not be at home at that time because the Woman's Club directors were having a short meeting to talk about getting more women to join their club.

As she was getting dressed for the Woman's Club meeting she decided that she would wait to pursue the "Tommy situation" until Jason came back from Wall Street and they were having their "Happy Time" drinks.

By the time Tommy arrived home from school, Blanche had already left for the Woman's Club meeting. Tommy went inside the house, gave a short wave to Lisa Marie who was lounging in the living room on the sofa gyrating to the music blasting into her ears from the earphones. He left his lunch box in the kitchen, said hello to Lisa Marie and left the house to follow the familiar path to his clearing. He sat down on the log when he arrived.

"Hi Ralph," he said. "How are you today?"

"I am fine," Ralph said. "I have been waiting for you all day."

"I have to go to school, Ralph. You are lucky. You can stay out here in the clearing and listen to the stream all day."

"I did not mind school while I was there," Ralph said. How is Miss Anson?"

"She is fine. She is helping me to create a lot of stuff with clay. When I get something finished that I like, I will bring it out here to show you."

"I would like that," Ralph said.

They chatted for a while until Tommy got tired of sitting on the log and rose to go look at the water. His back was toward the clearing as he stood looking at the stream so he didn't hear Lisa Marie approach until she arrived inside the clearing and spoke.

"Tommy, so this is where you go every afternoon after school," she said.

Her earphones were not in place and nowhere in sight.

"What are you doing here, Lisa Marie?" Tommy asked.

"Your mother was about to leave when I got to the house today. She told me to follow you and find out where you are going," Lisa Marie said.

"What are you going to do now that you have found me?" Tommy asked.

"I don't know. Tell me why you come out here."

"I come out here because I like this place. Nobody talks to me at the house, so I come out here and talk to Ralph. This is Ralph. Meet Lisa Marie, Ralph."

"Wow, that's a far out sculpture, Tommy. Who made it?"

"I made it in school and brought Ralph out here where we can talk."

"I think you and I have the same problem with our parents," Lisa Marie said. "My Mom and Dad hardly ever talk with me either. That's why I am always listening to music."

"I notice that you listen to music all the time," Tommy said.

"I guess it has gotten to be a habit. But, I love my music."

"I like talking with you.

"Where are your ear phones now?"

I took them off because I knew I would have to talk with you. Now that I have, I think I like talking with you, too."

"Sit down on the log," Tommy said. "There's plenty of room for both of us."

Lisa Marie stepped over to the log and sat down. Tommy did the same.

"This is a nice place, don't you think?" Tommy asked.

"It sure is. I wish I had a place like this to go to near where I live, but there is nothing but houses."

"I guess I am lucky to have a place to go that I like."

They chatted a while until Lisa Marie looked at her wristwatch.

"It's time for me to get back because your mother will be home soon and she would be mad if I am not there."

"I'll go back with you. Then you won't have to tell my mother about the clearing or Ralph."

"I will not say anything about either. I will tell her you stayed home so I couldn't follow you anywhere."

"That should work," Tommy said.

"How come you haven't said anything to Ralph since I got here?" Lisa Marie asked.

"I had you to talk with. I had fun talking with you."

Tommy and Lisa Marie arrived at the old farmhouse ten minutes before Blanche Holmes drove into the garage and entered the kitchen through the door from the double garage that had been added after automobiles became common.

Tommy and Lisa Marie were sitting and talking in the living room when Blanche walked in looking surprised at what she saw.

"You two look like you are enjoying yourselves," she said. "Now that I am home, Lisa Marie, you can go, but I would like a few words with you before you leave. Tommy, would you please leave us for a few minutes?"

Tommy didn't say anything. He rose from the chair he had been sitting in while talking with Lisa Marie, and climbed the stairway to the second floor where he went to his room. He talked with Ralph as he went up the stairs.

"Well, Lisa, were you able to follow Tommy and find out where he goes all the time?" Blanche asked once Tommy had gone out of earshot.

"Tommy came home from school and we have been talking."

"It is too bad he didn't go to the woods so you could follow him. I was hoping we could get to the bottom of why he is acting so strange."

"I am sorry, Missus Holmes, but I have no answers for you. Why don't you try talking to Tommy?"

"You can go now," Blanche said, annoyed by Lisa Marie's juvenile advice.

Lisa Marie inserted her audio equipment into her ears and left the house nodding her head to the beat of the music. Blanche sat in her favorite chair in the living room for a few minutes until she rose, went to the bar against the wall, and made herself a drink to swallow as she contemplated the dilemma with her son. She dreaded the time when her husband returned from Wall Street because she had no results to give him. She knew that he wanted her to solve any problems with Tommy. She had always known that Jason became almost angrily impatient when anything came up that involved Tommy's behavior or needs. Jason's only interest seemed to her to be associated with the Wall Street bank that demanded most of his thinking. She sometimes felt that Jason loved the bank more than anything in the world, including her. However, divorce never entered her mind because Jason's income was so enormous that she would have trouble dealing with life without it.

The first drink made her think she was relaxing so she returned to the bar and made another. She was glad that Tommy had remained in his room because she felt uncomfortable about ordering Lisa Marie to follow him when he got home from school.

Jason arrived as she finished the second drink. He rushed into the living room with the news that he had single handedly pulled the acquisition deal together and his bank stood to make several million dollars just on the rise of its stock price on the "Big Board" of the New York Stock Exchange in a single day's trading.

"I bought a thousand shares myself so we could benefit on the price rise," he said. She handed him the drink she had made as he gave her his good news.

Blanche knew little to nothing about the transaction Jason had spoken about. In spite of her family's banking history, financial business held little interest for Blanche Holmes. She was more than content with her social life in Westchester County, "The Home of New York Executives".

"I hope your day was as good as mine," Jason said.

"I can't say much for my day except the Woman's Club directors thought my ideas for recruitment were good and they appointed me head of the recruiting committee."

"Did you get the chance to go to Tommy's school and talk with Miss Anson?"

"Yes," Blanche said. "Miss Anson could not contribute anything. She said that there was no student named Ralph in her class. But she did mention something that I have been thinking about all day. She said that Tommy had made a sculpture out of clay and that he had brought it home to show to us. I do not recall him bring home a sculpture, do you?"

"Beats me. I have never seen anything that Tommy has made in school. I wonder what happened to it"

"Another thing that bothered me was that I told Lisa Marie to follow Tommy when he came home from school. I told her to find out where he went, but she and Tommy were talking in the living room when I got home from my meeting and he had not gone anywhere so Lisa Marie couldn't follow him."

"Blanche, I think we need to turn Tommy over to a good child psychiatrist and get to the bottom of all this talking to a Ralph and disappearing without telling us where he is going. The sculpture matter is another thing that puzzles me. I hope you understand that this is what I think is best for Tommy. I am far too busy to attempt to straighten this all out. I believe that a good child psychiatrist will be our best answer."

Blanche rose from her chair, and made two more drinks. After handing one to Jason, she sat down again.

"I am afraid that I have no idea about how to go about getting a child psychiatrist for Tommy," she said. "Do you have any ideas?"

"You know Bruno Weber at the club. His wife is Helga. I think she knows you from the Garden Club. I play golf at Winged Foot with Bruno sometimes. He swings a good driver and is not bad with a putter. I have heard that he is good with children. Both he and Helga are from the same town in Germany. Their parents brought them here as babies before Hitler invaded Poland. Bruno's father was a noted psychiatrist in Manhattan during and after World War II."

"Will you make the arrangements for Tommy?" Blanche asked.

"For heaven's sake, Blanche, you can do that easier than I can. His office is here in town. Look up his number and call for an appointment. I have far too much going on at the bank right now to be dealing with doctors."

"I am busy, too, Jason. I have one meeting or another almost every day. I also have the shopping to do."

"All right, Blanche," Jason said. I will make an appointment and you can see that Tommy goes to Bruno's office. I'll call him tomorrow from the bank."

"Make the appointment as soon as possible, Jason. I want to get all this cleared up and stop worrying about Tommy talking to a Ralph who seems to be invisible."

"All right, I will take care of that tomorrow. I will call to tell you when to take Tommy to Doctor Weber.

The next morning Jason left for the city. Tommy ate a hurried breakfast and went off to school. Blanche sat in the living room by a window looking out into the fields beyond the old cedar fence that once kept livestock from wandering near the garden and landscaping near the old farmhouse.

Jason telephoned Blanche just before noon to tell her that Bruno Weber would see Tommy the following day at ten o'clock in the morning.

"I'll have to take him out of school, Jason. Can't you have the doctor see Tommy after school is out?"

"Blanche, I was lucky to get an appointment for tomorrow. Bruno is fully booked. Because we play golf together he said he could re-schedule one of his patients in order to see Tommy sooner rather than later. I told Bruno that I considered Tommy's behavior somewhat of an emergency. Look, Blanche, we can talk about this when I get home. I have a lunch date that I must hurry to right now. Bye."

The day seemed to pass sluggishly for Blanche. She could not get the problem with Tommy off her mind. For a time she wanted to forget all about the situation. Then she dwelt on what she deemed a bother and interruption into her own life in order to deal with her son who talked to himself and some ghost named Ralph. By the time Jason arrived home from his busy day on Wall Street, Blanche had already drunk her first "Happy Times" Scotch-on-the-rocks.

After listening to Blanche's complaints about the inconvenience of taking Tommy out of school, Jason suggested firmly that she should keep Tommy home and call the school to inform them that Tommy would not be in school until the afternoon.

"I didn't think of that, Jason," Blanche said. "What a good idea. When I think about it, having Tommy's appointment in the morning will not interfere with my book club meeting at three o'clock tomorrow afternoon."

She rose quickly from her chair and poured another drink to celebrate her relief. She rose her full glass toward Jason.

"Here's to tomorrow," she said, and took a gulp from the glass.

Tommy came in from his visit to the clearing and headed for the stairway to his room talking with Ralph.

"Just a minute, Tommy," Jason said. "We need to talk to you. Come into the living room."

Tommy turned away from the stairs, walked into the living room, and stopped in between Blanche and Jason.

"You will not be going to school in the morning because your mother will take you to see a man named Bruno Weber. He wants to talk to you about some things. Do you understand?"

Tommy nodded his head, turned around and went back to the stairs. Halfway up to the second floor he began talking with Ralph again.

Jason and Blanche turned to one another.

"I sure hope Bruno can find out who Ralph is and put a stop to all that nonsense," Jason said.

"I hope you are right about your friend, Bruno. This entire thing is getting to me. I wonder if Tommy realizes what trouble he is causing."

"This Ralph business is becoming a distraction to both of our lives," Jason said. "If you get the chance when you see Bruno, tell him we need to know about Ralph in order to deal with Ralph."

"I wish you were taking Tommy to see this Bruno friend of yours. I have no idea how to tell a 'shrink' that I want to know all about a ghost."

"Well, Blanche, you are taking Tommy to see Bruno tomorrow morning, and you need to accept that responsibility."

Jason filled their glasses again, and they retired to the dining room for Bertha's dinner. Tommy joined them, but remained silent as usual. Jason and Blanche glanced at one another occasionally, but did not carry on a conversation.

Finished with his meal, Tommy asked to be excused and left the room for the stairs. As he started from the table he muttered, "Come on, Ralph."

Jason and Blanche remained silent with looks passing between them under raised eyebrows.

The following morning, Tommy went to his room after breakfast to wait for his mother to tell him it was time to go. He talked with Ralph, expressing his curiosity about what was going to happen with this man called Bruno Weber. Once in the car with Blanche, Tommy stopped talking with Ralph and looked out of the window to try and find out where his mother was taking him. He had heard his father tell her that Bruno's office was located in the Stringer Medical Center on the road to the Manor, the part of town where the wealthy people lived close to the Shore Club. Blanche slowed down and turned in to a parking lot, half of which had signs reserving places for various doctors.

"Okay, Tommy, let's see what Doctor Bruno Weber has to say," Blanche said, as they left the car and started walking to the entrance to the building. Inside, as they entered a lobby, there was a girl in uniform that inquired which doctor they had an appointment with. The girl also asked for Blanche's name. She pushed a button on her telephone and when Bruno's receptionist answered, she told her that Missus Holmes and Tommy were in the lobby.

"Missus Holmes, please go down the hallway to the fifth door on the right," the girl said.

"Thank you," Blanche said. Tommy smiled at the girl when she winked her eye at him. Blanche did not see that exchange.

Passing through the door to Weber's office, his receptionist greeted them.

Good morning, Missus Holmes and Tommy. Please have a seat. Doctor will be with you shortly."

Blanche hated the way receptionists always referred to their bosses as "Doctor". She would rather hear, Doctor Weber or whatever the doctor's name was instead of Doctor will do this or Doctor will do that.

Five minutes later a soft sounding buzzer sounded at the receptionist's desk and she looked up at Blanche and Tommy. She pointed to the door on her left.

"Doctor will see you now," she said, and rose to open the door for Blanche and Tommy.

Bruno Weber came out from his private office and met Blanche and Tommy with his hand extended to welcome them both.

"It is a pleasure to see you both," Bruno said. "Jason filled me in so Tommy if you will follow me, we can get started with our talk. Missus Holmes, I need to see Tommy alone, so if you will go back to the waiting room I will appreciate it."

"Doctor Weber, Jason wanted me to emphasize that we need to know about Ralph so we can better deal with Ralph," Blanche said.

"I am aware of Ralph, Missus Holmes, " Weber said. "Please do as I have requested."

Blanche abruptly turned around; angry at the way Weber had ordered her to go back to the waiting room. Weber took Tommy's hand and led him into his office.

"Have a seat, Tommy," Weber said kindly.

Weber sat in his chair behind the desk.

"Your father tells me that you have been talking with yourself and also with someone named Ralph. Is that true?"

"Yes," Tommy said.

"Can you tell me why you stay by yourself most of the time and talk to yourself?"

"Nobody talks to me so I talk to myself and Ralph. I don't get what the big deal is all about."

"That is interesting," Weber said. "Do you have any idea why nobody talks with you?

"Everyone is too busy. My mother is always going to some meeting and doesn't have time to talk with me. My father is at his bank all day. When he comes home he and my mother sit in the living room and drink their "Happy Times" drinks. They are too busy talking with each other to talk with me so I talk to Ralph and myself in my room. Lisa Marie listens to her music all the time so she doesn't talk. But she told me that her mother and father don't talk with her eiither. That is why she always listens to her music. I listened for a second once and it is just noise."

"And who is Lisa Marie?"

"She is the girl that my mother has to come in and stay when I get home from school."

"All right, Tommy, you are doing quite well with my questions. I have a few more. I hope you can give me the answers I need. Your father mentioned a sculpture that your teacher said was very well done and sent it home with you to show your parents. Your father said that neither he nor your mother have ever seen the sculpture. Can you tell me why they have never seen it?"

"I never showed it to them."

"Are you proud of the sculpture?"

"I guess so. Miss Anson liked it and she knows all about clay and sculptures."

"I take it that Miss Anson is your teacher?"

"Yes. I like her very much. She talks to me a lot."

"I am talking to you a lot. Do you like me?"

"I like that you are talking with me."

"Perhaps you can tell me what happened to the sculpture after you brought it home."

"I didn't bring it home. I took Ralph to the clearing by the stream where I go every day when I get home from school. Ralph and I talk a lot out there. Ralph is my best friend."

"What is Ralph's last name?"

"He doesn't have a last name. My father asked me the same question. I don't think my father believes me, but it is not my fault that Ralph doesn't have a last name."

"Of course it isn't," Weber said. "Who named Ralph?"

"I did. I made Ralph so I can give him any name I want to."

"Tell me if you can, how you like living in that old farmhouse. Are there any ghosts there that scare you at night?"

I like my house and I like my room. I have never seen any ghosts there. I like my clearing better than my house because I have fun there talking with Ralph."

"Tommy, can you tell me why you don't want your mother and father to see Ralph?"

"Ralph is my friend, not theirs. They would not talk with him either."

"Well, Tommy, I have enjoyed our talk and you have done well answering my questions. I think we can continue next week."

With that Weber led Tommy back to the waiting room, where he told Blanche to arrange for another appointment for the following week.

It seemed to Tommy that all the way home his mother never stopped asking him what he and Doctor Weber had talked about. Tommy finally became impatient with the "cross-examination".

"Mom, Doctor Weber asked me a bunch of questions and I answered them. He said I did well with his questions. His questions were for me and my answers were for him, so please don't ask me any more questions."

Blanche did not reply. She drove straight to school where she left Tommy off. Then she drove home to the old farmhouse where she got ready for the meeting of her book club.

When he arrived at his classroom Miss Anson asked him how his morning had been.

"My mother took me to talk to Doctor Weber and he asked me a lot of questions. He wanted to know all about Ralph, but I didn't tell him everything," Tommy said. "I have to go back next week. Miss Anson, do you know what all this fuss is about?"

"I have an idea, but I think it is best if I let you and Doctor Weber talk things over. I am sure he will turn out to be a good friend of yours."

After school was out, Tommy went straight to the clearing where he told Ralph about going to the doctor's office and all of the questions.

"He wanted to know all about you and why you didn't have a last name. I told him that I made you and could give you any name I wanted to. I liked Doctor Weber, and I think he understands me better than my parents do. I am going back to see him next week."

"Why?" Ralph asked.

"I suppose he thinks he can learn more from me about you and this beautiful place we share."

The following Friday morning Blanche drove Tommy to the Stringer Medical Center for his appointment with Bruno Weber. She remained seated when the nurse ushered Tommy into the examining room. Doctor Weber met Tommy promptly and they began their talk session.

"How did your week go, Tommy?" Weber asked.

"Everything was good. I had a lot of fun talking with Ralph. I told him all about our talk and how I think you understand me better than my father and mother do."

"I am glad you think that I understand you, and that is because you answer my questions without hiding anything. I am glad Ralph and you had a good time talking with each other. By the way, where did you say you and Ralph meet and talk?"

"We go to a clearing out in the woods next to a stream that runs through a lot of boulders and makes nice noises."

"You also told me that Ralph is with you in your room in that old farmhouse."

"Oh, yes," Tommy said, and smiled. "Ralph is with me whenever I feel like talking. I think I told you that Ralph is the only one who talks to me except Miss Anson, my teacher."

"Yes, I remember that," Weber said.

"I have been thinking a lot about what we talked about last week, and I have thought a lot about the way my father and mother are. The way they ask me questions about Ralph and other things, even the sound of their voices when they talk to me seem stupid. All of a sudden, after all the years of them being too busy to talk with me, they are now bombing me with questions just because I now have a friend to talk with. It really seems stupid to me."

"I know what you mean and I must tell you that I agree with you that your parents getting upset about Ralph is what you say, 'stupid'. I am not telling you to call your parents stupid, but I am telling you that sometimes people seem stupid when they do not understand someone else."

"You really do understand me, don't you?"

"I am doing my best to understand what you are faced with so that I can help you through your situation. Try to remember this. When you let yourself get involved with stupidity, you own the stupidity."

"What does that mean?" Tommy asked.

"When you see something stupid going on, do not let yourself get involved with it or you become stupid as well. So when stupid things are tossed your way, don't try to argue, just ignore it and find a way to get away from it."

"That makes sense to me. That is why I go to my clearing with Ralph and we watch the stream gurgle over the boulders. We have fun talking. We have escaped the stupidity of my parents. They seem strange to me. They are always too busy to talk with me, but they have plenty of time when they get home from what they have been doing all day to sit and drink their 'Happy Times' with each other before Bertha tells them to come and eat supper. Once they are sitting at the table, they talk to each other, but never with me. That's probably because their voices get sounding funny after they have had a few 'Happy Times'."

"What do you do when this happens?" Doctor Weber asked.

"Ralph and I go upstairs to my room and talk."

"I see that you already know to not get involved with stupidity," Weber said. "However, Tommy, I don't think it would help your situation if you told them they were stupid. That is something that you need to keep to yourself. Do you understand?"

"Oh, yes," Tommy said. "If I called my father and mother stupid they would get really angry with me. I do know pretty much to keep my feelings to myself so they cannot have something to question me about until the sun goes down."

"Well, Tommy, I think you are doing well considering the circumstances. I will give your mother a prescription that will help you deal with the stress you are confronted with. I will discuss our talks in part with your father tomorrow when we play golf. He called and invited me to an early 'T' time. That means an early start."

"I was hoping this was all between us and not with my parents." Tommy said.

"I will only tell him things so that he can better understand you and hopefully make life easier for you."

"I suppose that is all right, but you might not know my father like I do."

"I have played golf with him many times, Tommy."

Weber reached for a pen and wrote out a prescription, rose and went to the door and opened it. Tommy followed the doctor to the waiting room where he saw Weber hand the paper to his mother. Weber and Blanche chatted for a few moments until the doctor told Blanche that he thought that unless something drastic happened he didn't need to see Tommy again. Blanche and Tommy left the building and drove away toward Tommy's school.

After I get you back to school I need to go to Arnold Constable and get your cousin Heather something for her birthday. You do remember that you are going to her birthday party Sunday afternoon?"

"I remember," Tommy said.

"I will stop by Hughes Drugstore and get your prescription filled that Doctor Weber gave me. He didn't tell me what it was for, so I guess we just have to trust that he knows what he is doing."

Tommy didn't say anything more and neither did his mother. When they got to school, Tommy left the car and went into the building. Blanche drove away to do her errands.

After school ended for the day and before he left for home, Tommy stopped in front of Miss Anson who was seated at her desk at the front of the room.

"Miss Anson, do you know Doctor Weber?"

"I know of him, Tommy, why do you ask?"

"My mother took me to see him last week and today. That is why I missed mornings."

"What did you do at Doctor Weber's office?"

"He asked me a bunch of questions about Ralph, but he told me one thing that he said I might not understand."

"What was it that he said?"

"When you let yourself get involved with stupidity, you own the stupidity."

"That's interesting, Tommy. What stupidity was Doctor Weber referring to?"

"I think it was my parents," Tommy said, and smiled. "I think he understands me and all about Ralph."

"I have heard that Doctor Weber is very good at what he does."

"I just wanted to tell you, Miss Anson. I am glad that you are my friend."

"Yes, Tommy, I am your friend, and I think I understand you like Doctor Weber does."

"Good, I am going home now. Ralph and I will go out to the clearing and listen to the stream gurgle through the boulders."

"Okay, bye, Tommy, and bye, Ralph."

When Tommy arrived home from school his mother had not yet returned from doing her errands. Tommy went quickly to the clearing to sit on the log and talk to Ralph.

"I feel much better here than where I have been, Ralph."

"Where were you?"

"My mother took me to see some doctor, a Doctor Weber, who asked me a lot of questions about you and me talking with you."

"Why did he do that?" Ralph asked.

"I am not sure. But, I think my father and mother think there is something wrong with me because I talk to you and you talk back to me. I wonder if all parents are like that. I think I will ask Lisa Marie when I see her next. Her parents seem weird, too."

"What did you tell the doctor?"

"I told him about us talking and being here in the clearing next to the stream where the water gurgled over the boulders. He said that what I tell him is between him and me only.

"Do you think he is telling you the truth?"

"I am not sure, because after he was done asking about me and you, he said he was going to play golf with my father tomorrow and he would explain things to him that would help me. If I had known to begin with that the doctor was planning on talking about me to my father I would never have told him anything about you and me or where we are now in this clearing. This is our place, not anyone else's place."

"I guess you will just have to wait and see what happens," Ralph said.

Tommy and Ralph chatted for a while before it was time for Tommy to go home for supper. When he arrived home his mother handed him a square cardboard box.

"Tommy, this is a pretty dress I bought for you to give Heather at her birthday party. Open it and look at it."

Tommy handed the box back to his mother.

"I don't want to give Heather a dress. You bought it so you can give it to her. I would rather give her a baseball because she likes to play baseball," Tommy said, and started for the stairs.

"Why can't you cooperate, Tommy?"

"Why can't you let me choose what I want to give Heather for her birthday? Everybody there would laugh themselves silly if I gave her a dress."

"That means I will have to go back to town for a baseball," Blanche said, with a touch of "poor me" in her voice.

"No you won't. I will give her my baseball. It is almost new and has no scuffs on it."

"All right, Tommy, be difficult. Get me your baseball and I'll wrap it."

Tommy went upstairs quickly, wanting to get his baseball before his mother changed her mind. He was relieved that he would not have to give his cousin the dress for her birthday.

Jason and Blanche drank their "Happy Times" until Bertha announced that dinner was served. Hearing Bertha's call, Tommy came downstairs and took his seat at the dining room table.

"How did it go with Bruno Weber?" Jason asked Blanche.

"I have no idea. He had me wait in the waiting room while he talked with Tommy."

"Tommy, how did it go with Doctor Weber?"

"Okay," Tommy answered.

"What happened?"

"He asked me a bunch of questions. We talked."

"What about?" Jason persisted.

"Just stuff," Tommy said, and started eating.

"Bruno and I are playing golf tomorrow morning, so I will ask him my questions," Jason said, and began cutting the filet with his knife and fork.

Tommy wanted to flee so his fear wouldn't show. Again, he hoped that Doctor Weber would not tell his father what they talked about, especially about Ralph and how he enjoyed talking with him in the clearing. Tommy lost his desire to eat and picked at the meal without lifting any food to his mouth.

"What is the matter, Tommy?" Blanche asked. "You aren't eating."

"I am not hungry," he said.

"You should clean up your plate, Tommy," Jason said. "Think about all the starving children in Africa."

Tommy pushed away from the table and went to the stairway. He felt that if he tried to eat any of the supper he would throw it up. Once in his room and talking to Ralph, he felt better.

Back in the dining room Jason and Blanche looked at each other with quizzical expressions on their faces.

"I went to Hughes Drugstore and got Tommy's prescription filled, that your friend Bruno Weber gave me. I have no idea what it is for because the name is not familiar to me. I am planning on starting Tommy on the pills after breakfast, tomorrow."

"I am hoping to find out what is wrong with Tommy as I play a round with Bruno in the morning"

The following morning Tommy was awake early, and made his way down the stairway toward the dining room. Before he reached his destination he heard his father talking with his mother. He stopped, turned around and went back up the stairway to his room. He told Ralph that he did not want to hear his father talk about his plans with Doctor Weber. He waited in his room until he heard his father's Mercedes Sports car leave the garage and drive down the driveway to the road into town. He returned to the stairway and went down to the dining room where his mother looked up and said, "Good morning, Tommy."

"Morning," he murmured, and sat down in his chair.

Bertha brought him his breakfast of scrambled eggs and bacon with a generous piece of the sour dough bread that she was proud of.

"Thanks, Bertha," Tommy said.

Blanche took the bottle of pills from her pocket and opened it. She shook out a single pill and handed it over to Tommy.

"This is what Doctor Weber prescribed for you. It says to take one a day with a meal. So, we might as well start it out this morning."

Tommy took the pill and put it into his mouth, swallowing it with three gulps of water.

"What are these pills supposed to do?" he asked.

"I have no idea, Tommy, I am just following Doctor Weber's orders."

Tommy shrugged his shoulders, and began eating his breakfast. He was anxious to get through eating in order to slip away to the clearing and talk with Ralph. The weather had turned colder because winter was approaching. Tommy liked summer better because he could do as he pleased all day without thinking about school. However, as he sat on the log he thought about Miss Anson and hoped she would always find time to talk with him. As he sat there he thought about the days ahead when his mother would spend time with her clubs where she talked to all of her women friends but rarely to him when she was home. He told Ralph about his thoughts concerning winter.

Suddenly, he remembered that his father would probably get home from golfing around the middle of the afternoon. Tommy wondered what Doctor Weber was telling his father as they hit the little round white balls over the grass at Winged Foot Country Club. His father had taken him there once, but Tommy never asked to go back because his father talked only to the men playing with him and told Tommy to be quiet when the men were swinging their clubs at the balls.

"I will tell you, Ralph, I cannot understand what pleasure men find hitting the little white balls around trying to end up hitting them into a small hole in a lawn that looked like it had had a very short haircut."

"Maybe they do that to keep from thinking about their work," Ralph said.

"My father always comes home from playing golf slurring his words. He probably thinks he is having fun with his friends. I wonder if Doctor Weber slurs his words when he gets home."

Tommy started feeling drowsy and thought about going home for a nap. He wondered why he was getting so sleepy when it was only morning. He told Ralph about the pill his mother had given him that morning.

"I wonder if that pill is making me sleepy," Tommy said.

Mid-afternoon brought clouds that traveled toward the land from the ocean. Still feeling sleepy, Tommy walked over to the stream and looked up at the clouds and felt a raindrop hit his cheek.

"Well, Ralph, I think it is going to rain, so I am going back to the house."

Tommy, with a quicker pace than usual, walked back to the old farmhouse. As he arrived he noticed that his father had not returned from playing golf, and his mother's car was not there either. He surmised that his mother was attending some social meeting. He went upstairs to his room and sat down on his chair that he liked a lot because he could adjust its angle to fit his mood. He reached down and grabbed the lever handle, pulled it upwards, and leaned back. The chair responded by tilting, resulting in a reclining position almost into a bed. The sleepiness he had been experiencing since taking the pill made him close his eyes, and he fell asleep within minutes.

Jason and Blanche arrived at the same time, almost as if they had planned to meet at that particular hour. They drove their cars into the garage and stopped them in their usual spaces. After getting out of their cars Jason motioned to Blanche to follow him outside.

"Blanche," Jason said as they walked toward the garden that had an old wooden bench overlooking a small pond holding a dozen goldfish. "At first Bruno was reluctant to talk about Tommy, saying that Tommy was his patient and ethically he could not discuss his condition. But, by the time we were about to tee-off for the third hole, I had convinced him that I had sent Tommy to him in order to find out how you and I could help him change his habit of talking to himself and with this character, Ralph, who has no last name.

"What did Doctor Weber tell you?" Blanche asked.

"He said that Tommy spoke about a clearing in the woods that is located next to a stream. I remember that clearing. When I was Tommy's age I used to go there and fish in the stream. I never caught many, but once in a while one or two fish would bite my bait. It is a nice spot, but not a good place to fish. I went there anyway because I liked the way the water in the stream gurgled over and around the boulders. It sounded musical. Bruno told me that Tommy had expressed that the clearing and the stream were important to him, and that he seemed to spend a lot of time there."

"Did the doctor offer any solution to Tommy talking to himself and with Ralph?"

"Not really. Bruno thinks that we need to talk with Tommy more than we do so that he talks with us instead of with Ralph. Bruno was pretty vague, and I don't think he really knows what is going on with Tommy.

However, didn't you tell me something about your niece's birthday party tomorrow?"

"Yes, Jason, I told you I am taking Tommy to Heather's party," Blanche said.

"Then, tomorrow, while you are taking Tommy to your niece's birthday party, I am going to walk out to that clearing that I remember so well to try and discover why it's luring Tommy."

"Be sure to let me know what you find out," Blanche said. "Let's go in and have a drink. The League of Women Voters meeting came close to putting me to sleep."

Tommy remained asleep when Bertha announced that supper was ready. Blanche went upstairs to see why Tommy had not responded. Finding him asleep, she contemplated leaving him alone, but after pausing in his room, looking at him, she touched his shoulder to awaken him. Tommy blinked as he came out of the deep sleep. Blanche left to go downstairs, and Tommy followed after he finished waking.

While eating his supper, Tommy was glad that his parents were not questioning him about Ralph. He remembered that a rainstorm had started while he was with Ralph in the clearing. After supper, he walked outside to see if the ground was wet from the storm, hoping that Ralph was all right. He recalled his question about the pill Doctor Weber had prescribed that had put him to sleep. He came close to walking out to see Ralph and sit on the log, but chose not to so that it would not get his father started questioning him. He went back inside and went up to his room to read a book about ceramics that Miss Anson had lent him.

The following morning, Tommy saw Jason sitting at his desk in his office that adjoined the dining room. He had a cup of coffee within reach and was reading the Wall Street Journal. Tommy looked away quickly and went to his place at the table. The door to the kitchen was open so Bertha could see anyone coming for breakfast.

"Good morning, Tommy," Bertha said. "I have some scrambled eggs and bacon for you. Are you ready?"

"Thank you, Bertha. Yes, I am ready."

Blanche arrived and sat down at her place at the table. Bertha brought Tommy's plate and put it down in front of him.

"Is there anything else you would like with your eggs and bacon, Missus Holmes?" Bertha asked.

"Would you bring my coffee first?"

"Right away, Missus Holmes," Bertha said.

"Tommy, before you finish your breakfast, you need to take your pill," Blanche said, and reached for the prescription that was on the silver centerpiece. She opened the plastic container, shook out one pill and handed it to Tommy.

"Bertha, please bring Tommy a glass of water so he can take his pill," Blanche called to Bertha in the kitchen.

When Blanche turned to call to Bertha, Tommy reached down and put the pill into his pants pocket. When Bertha brought the glass of water, he took it in one hand and made believe that he had put the pill in his mouth with the other hand. He took two swallows of water from the glass and continued eating his eggs and bacon.

"Heather's party begins at one o'clock this afternoon, so we should start from here at twelve-forty-five," Blanche said.

Tommy looked at her and nodded his head. When he finished his breakfast, he went back upstairs, into his bathroom and flushed the pill down the toilet.

"I am not taking that pill that puts me to sleep, Ralph."

Tommy wondered if he could go to the clearing without his mother or father noticing him leaving the house. He decided that if he hurried out there and didn't spend much time talking with Ralph, he could probably get there without his parents seeing him. They were always too busy to notice what he was doing anyway, he thought.

Arriving at the clearing, Tommy said hello to Ralph and went over to the stream to listen to the gurgling water. He turned toward Ralph.

"The water going through the boulders is like music," Tommy said, and went back inside the clearing to sit on the log.

I can't stay long today because my mother is making me go to my cousin Heather's birthday party, but that shouldn't take all afternoon. I'll come back to see you when I get home."

Tommy continued his conversation with Ralph and told him about his mother buying the dress for Heather and how he was taking his baseball for a birthday present.

Suddenly, Tommy realized that he had overstayed his time at the clearing.

"Ralph, I need to get home and in a hurry. See you later."

Tommy trotted along the path back to the old farmhouse. A glass of milk and sandwich on a plate was at his place at the table. He sat down and devoured it and the glass of milk. Finished with his lunch, Tommy hurried upstairs and saw what he called his "Dress Up" clothes on his bed, evidence that his mother was close by. Just as he finished changing his clothes and putting his baseball into his pants pocket, Blanche came into his room.

"Are you ready? Where have you been? Hurry up or we will be late," Blanche scolded.

They went to the garage and got into Blanche's Chrysler Town and Country. Blanche retained a scowl and neither spoke the entire way across town to her sister's house.

Jason had been watching from his desk as he sipped the drinks while he waited for his wife and son to leave for the party. In spite of having consumed several drinks of single malt scotch he had noticed everything, including Tommy's hurried arrival from the woods and his wife and son hurrying to the garage. When he saw the car turn out of the farm and onto the road to town, he turned off his computer, put on his expensive Stetson hat, pulled on his high-heeled cowboy boots, the remnants from a banking conference held at a resort in New Mexico he had attended the year before. Then, he left the house heading for the woods. It had been many years since he, as a teen-aged boy, had gone into the woods and along the well-worn path that led to the clearing by the stream. As he entered the woods following the path through the trees he looked from side to side. He felt the effects of the single malt scotch, and looked straight ahead. He had gone fifty yards before he realized that the path was still damp from the rain the day before that had sent Bruno Weber and him to the Winged Foot Club House after the thirteenth hole.

As he walked along the path he felt something telling him to turn around as his legs began to feel heavy and slightly cumbersome. He stopped to look at the path. He turned and saw that the high heels on his cowboy boots had been sinking into the damp soil. *That's what is slowing me. I wonder why there are no puddles like there used to be after rainstorms.*

He started off again looking forward, thinking that the clearing and the stream should be coming into sight soon. A branch from a hemlock tree was bending over, almost blocking his way. He lifted his left arm and pushed the branch to the side. Beyond the branch he saw the clearing. He tried to speed up, but he found that he could only maintain the pace with which he had been walking since entering the woods.

He had gone another thirty yards when he caught a glimpse of the stream just beyond the clearing. He stopped and took in the view that was familiar even after the many years he had not been there to see it. As he entered the clearing he saw the log on the right side, just where it had been when he was a boy. *Hmm, is that the same log that was here when I came to fish in the stream?* He passed through the clearing and stood on the bank of the stream. He listened to the rushing water gurgling through the boulders. He turned and looked downstream and saw the small pool in which he once cast his baited hook attempting to catch a fish to bring back to show his father and mother. He remembered that there were only a few times he was able to bring a trophy back to the old farmhouse.

He stood pondering and remembering those days that seemed so far in the distant past. Yet as he stood there, he suddenly felt like it was just a short time before that he was there with his bamboo fishing pole.

Suddenly the spell was broken when he remembered why he had returned to the clearing and the stream. He turned and stepped back into the clearing and went over to the log where he sat down. He looked down at his cowboy boots and saw that there was dirt from the path stuck on the heels.

He sat up straight on the log and stretched. He looked straight into Ralph's eyes.

“So you are Ralph, the boy with no last name,” Jason said aloud. I am told that you and Tommy are friends and that you talk with one another, is that right?”

Jason kept staring at Ralph’s round eyes made from marbles.

“Why don’t you talk to me like you talk to Tommy? Don’t you realize that you are not good for Tommy? You are making him into a zombie. He only talks to you. Why don’t you tell him to talk to me?”

*Good grief, what am I doing?* Jason thought. *Here I am out here to see this ceramic statue that talks to Tommy and now I am talking to Ralph-Without-a-Last-Name.*

He looked down at the ground and shook his head slowly. Looking up again, he shook his fist at Ralph.

“You are ruining Tommy, and everyone seems to think you are just fine and dandy. Well, Ralph, or whatever your name is, I don’t agree. I think you are bad for Tommy. You are turning Tommy against his mother and me. He won’t talk to us. Are you some kind of monster?

Jason kept shaking his fist at Ralph and almost yelled at the sculpture.

“You are nothing but a chunk of clay! Tommy will be better off without you to influence him.”

Jason rose from the log. Stepped across the clearing and grabbed Ralph in both of his hands and shook him.

“I am not going to let you ruin Tommy!”

He picked up the sculpture, carried it to the stream and threw it onto the boulders. It hit one of the larger boulders that stuck up above the current and broke into hundreds of pieces. The head split in half, one half landing between two smaller boulders where the water ran almost smooth. Jason could see the marble eye as if it was still looking at him. He turned around and walked across the clearing onto the path through the woods. As he walked back to the old farmhouse, he decided that he would never return to the place that he had enjoyed as a boy.

Arriving at the old farmhouse, Jason made himself another single malt Scotch on ice and carried it outside to the front porch where he sat down on the old fashioned swing. He continued thinking about what he had just accomplished. He took a deep sip from the glass, put it down on the side table and leaned back in the swing. *That Ralph character won't be messing around with Tommy now. Tommy might be upset, but he will understand after I explain things to him. I did what is best for him. After all, I am his father and I know what is best for my son. Maybe I need to talk to that Miss Anson and get her on the right track toward Tommy. He seems to like her.*

Instead of lunch he made another drink, and returned to the swing. It was not long before he finished the drink and put the empty glass on the side table. He yawned, looked over at the woods. He lifted his cowboy-booted feet up onto the swing, and fluffed up the canvas-covered pillow to put his head on and closed his eyes. Thoughts of Tommy and his companion Ralph vanished from his mind as the single malt Scotch pushed him into a deep sleep.

Blanche drove home from the birthday party and left Tommy at the old farmhouse while she went to a board of directors meeting for the Garden Club. Tommy saw his father asleep in the swing on the front porch with his high-heeled cowboy boots still on. Jason was on his back and snoring slightly as Tommy passed by on his way into the house. He hurried upstairs to his room and changed out of his "dress up clothes" into his blue jeans and blue chambray shirt. He hurried changing so he would not have to talk to his father before leaving for the clearing.

As he walked through the front door, he glanced over to make sure his father was still asleep in the swing. Breathing a sigh of relief when he heard him still snoring, Tommy headed for the path at the edge of the woods that led to the clearing. He had not traveled twenty yards when he noticed the tracks of his father's high-heeled cowboy boots in the still damp path through the woods. He stopped walking and inspected the tracks closely.

"I wonder what he was doing out here in the woods." He said aloud. "What did Doctor Weber tell him about me?"

He quickened his pace and reached the clearing in less time than usual. He stepped into the clearing and looked around. Ralph was not standing where he usually stood.

"Ralph, where are you?" He asked. "Ralph, is there something wrong? Are you all right?"

Tommy looked around the clearing and followed the boot heel tracks that Jason had made earlier in the day. He followed the tracks to the stream. As he looked around at the stream he saw the broken pieces of Ralph, some under water, a few on the boulders. He saw half of Ralph's head with one marble eye looking at him from the top of one boulder in the middle of the stream.

"Oh, no!" he screamed into his hands that he had brought up to cover his eyes. "Why did he do this?"

Tommy turned around and ran to the log to sit down with his head in his hands. He commenced crying and sobbing and uttering, “Why, why, why?”

Occasionally he dropped his hands from his face and looked over to where Ralph had once been as they had carried on their conversations. The loss of his friend sent him into another session of crying and sobbing. Tommy sat on the log for over an hour before the sadness ebbed enough so that he sat in silence without crying. An occasional sob escaped as his mind wandered from sadness to pure anger directed toward his father for killing Ralph. There were a few times when his anger reached a climax and he wanted to run back to the old farmhouse, throw his father off the swing and kick him in the ribs. Then, as quickly as the anger reached that pinnacle, his mind changed to remembering the friendship that he had shared with Ralph and the fun and joy that he had felt when he was in the process of making the sculpture. At one point he wondered what Miss Anson would say when he told her what had happened. The sun had set and darkness was beginning to invade the land as his thoughts about Miss Anson crossed his mind. It was then that he decided to walk to Miss Anson’s house rather than go home and be forced to look at his father. He rose from the log, stepped over to the stream and stood there for a few moments.

“Good night, Ralph,” he said. “I wish I could have been here and stopped my father from killing you.”

Two things passed through his mind as he turned to leave the clearing. The first was that he didn’t want to leave Ralph in pieces among the boulders. The other was he wanted to see Miss Anson to tell her what had happened. He knew that she would be more likely to give him comfort than his parents would, especially since his father had caused all the sadness and grief. He started back on the path, not stopping at the old farmhouse, but walking through the neighborhoods until he reached Miss Anson's house on Myrtle Lane. He entered the small front yard on the flagstone walkway to the front door. He rang the doorbell and waited.

Clara Anson came to the front door and opened it. She looked down at Tommy, who was looking up at her when he started to cry.

"What's wrong, Tommy?" she asked. "What happened? Are you all right?"

She reached down and took Tommy's right hand in hers.

"Come in, Tommy," she said. "Come in, and tell me what happened."

Tommy followed her into the house. She led him into the small living room and told him to sit on the sofa. She went to the kitchen, filled a glass full of apple juice, and brought it in to him.

"Here, take a sip of this and you might feel better," she said, handing the glass to him.

Tommy took the glass and brought it up to his mouth. He took a small sip and put the glass down on the coffee table in front of the sofa. Miss Anson sat on a padded footstool opposite the sofa.

"Now tell me what happened, Tommy. We are friends and you can trust me."

"My father killed Ralph," Tommy said and began to cry again.

"My goodness, what do you mean?"

Tommy stopped crying and wiped his nose on the sleeve of his chambray shirt.

"I know it was my father because there are tracks of his high-heeled cowboy boots on the path that goes out to the clearing where Ralph was. I went out there and saw Ralph all broken into pieces in the stream among the boulders. Half of his head was on one big boulder and had not fallen into the water. I came here because I don't want to see my father again, ever."

"I am having trouble understanding your father doing such a thing to Ralph," she said. "I am glad you came here instead of just running away. However, I think I should telephone your mother to tell her that you are safe here with me."

"I guess that is all right, Miss Anson, but don't talk to my father because he might call the police. He is that kind."

"All right, Tommy, if he answers the phone I will hang up and try again."

Clara Anson took the telephone book, opened it to find the Holmes number and dialed it. The Holmes phone rang three times.

"Hello," Blanche said.

"Missus Holmes, this is Clara Anson, Tommy's teacher."

"Why are you calling on Sunday, Miss Anson?"

"I am calling to tell you that Tommy is at my house and that he is safe here," Clara said.

"For heaven's sakes, I thought Tommy was in his room. He did not come downstairs for supper, but Mister Holmes and I thought he must have had a snack in the kitchen when I brought him home from his cousin's birthday party. But, come to think of it, I had supper alone because Mister Holmes had gone to bed before I got back from an errand. I suppose I should have gone upstairs to check on Tommy."

"I think it is best if Tommy stays here with me tonight. I will see that he gets to school tomorrow. He is quite upset after he saw what your husband did to his sculpture that he calls Ralph."

"Who are you to tell me, Tommy's mother, what is best for my son?"

"Missus Holmes, I am only thinking about Tommy. He is here and I can see how upset he is. I have talked with him, and frankly I know what I am talking about. He and I have talked before."

"All right, I suppose Tommy will be fine in the morning. Tell me, what did my husband do to the sculpture?"

"He threw it into the stream and it broke into pieces. It is the same sculpture Tommy made in school that I sent home with him to show you his accomplishment."

"That's odd," Blanche said, "I have never seen such a sculpture. I don't remember Tommy bringing anything like that home from school."

"That is too bad," Clara said. "It was an interesting sculpture and very original. Tommy shows a lot of artistic talent. I hope you realize that."

"I am afraid that I have been much to busy to pay that much attention to artistic talent," Blanche said.

"That could be one of Tommy's problems," Clara said, and before Blanche could comment further, Clara said goodnight and hung up the telephone.

Tommy and Clara spent a couple of hours talking about the entire situation, recalling their previous conversation when Tommy told Clara about his parents lack of talking with him and how they were always talking about their own projects; Jason with the bank, Blanche with her many social activities. Tommy expressed his anger toward his father, and Clara tried to be sympathetic and at the same time realistic that his parents were his parents, and there was little he could do to change them. She didn't tell him her deepest thought about what terrible parents the Holmes were and how his father was addicted to money and power that consumed most of his attention.

When it came time for Clara to go to bed, she brought some bedding out to the sofa and arranged a bed for Tommy. She took him into her arms and hugged him, and kissed his forehead.

"Goodnight, Tommy," she said. "Have a good sleep. I am sure you will feel better in the morning."

"Goodnight, Miss Anson," Tommy said. "Thank you for being my friend. I wonder why my mother never hugs me when I go to bed. I suppose she is too busy either drinking with my father or thinking about the Woman's Club, The Garden Club or whatever other club she is a member of. I would like to stay here and live with you, Miss Anson. You like me more than they do."

"Tommy, you will feel much better in the morning. Good night."

Clara Anson almost wept after listening to Tommy express his feelings to her. She knew that what he wanted was impossible, but she wished she could somehow make Jason and Blanche Holmes aware of what they were doing that was driving their son a long way away from them. She spent time thinking about Tommy's situation before finally falling asleep.

The following morning Tommy was still asleep when Clara went to the kitchen to make her coffee. He stirred as the noise from coffee making reached the living room that was next to the kitchen. He sat up and rubbed his eyes. Thoughts about the previous day flew through his mind. Clara saw that he was awake and told him where to find the bathroom. She started making breakfast. When Tommy came back from the bathroom, Clara pointed to the breakfast nook that was beside the kitchen. He sat down and watched her getting breakfast.

"My mother never makes breakfast. In fact, Bertha does all the cooking," Tommy said. My mother is too busy with all of her clubs to do any of the work in the house."

"That's the way some people live, Tommy," Clara said. "Has your mother ever made breakfast?"

"She did once when Bertha had to go to see her daughter in the hospital."

"What did she make for breakfast?"

"I remember that it was a piece of toast and a bowl of puffed wheat. My mother has said that she doesn't like to cook."

Clara put two plates of scrambled eggs, bacon and English muffins on the table in the nook and brought her coffee over. She sat down and began eating.

"This is good," Tommy said. "Bertha is a good cook, but for some reason these scrambled eggs taste better than hers."

"I put a little chile powder in the eggs. That may make the difference. I lived in Arizona for a while and learned to like chile in just about everything."

"Is Arizona far away?" Tommy asked. "Is it easy to get there?"

"Arizona is over two thousand miles from here, and it costs quite a bit to get there," Clara said.

"I think Arizona would be a good place for me to go because I really like these eggs."

"Come over here any time, and I will make scrambled eggs with chile for you."

Clara wondered if Tommy was thinking of running away from his parents. She also thought that she should express her fears to the Holmes so that they could keep an eye on Tommy.

Clara felt relieved when she walked into the school with Tommy. But, she was determined to watch him closely to see how he was reacting to the crisis that his father had brought about.

It was ten-thirty when Loring Lincoln, the principal and Clara's boss, knocked on the window of her classroom door and beckoned her to come out into the hallway. Clara looked around and saw that the class was well occupied and went out into the hall to find out what the principal wanted to tell her.

"Miss Anson, Missus Holmes is in my office and wants to take her son, Tommy out of school for the day," he said. "She says that Tommy ran away from home yesterday and spent the night at your house."

"That is right, Mister Lincoln. Tommy had some disturbing experience at home and came to my place. I am glad he did that rather than run away and hide in some dangerous place where he could have gotten hurt."

"I think you should bring Tommy to the office and turn him over to his mother. We cannot afford to have any trouble from the Holmes family. He is a prominent banker on Wall Street."

"Just a minute and I will get Tommy and take him to the office."

Lincoln waited at the classroom door as Clara went to Tommy's desk to tell him that his mother was waiting for him in the principal's office. Tommy slid out from his desk and followed Clara out of the classroom into the hall. Clara held Tommy's hand as the three of them walked down the hallway to the school's office. Blanche was seated in the waiting room at the entrance. When she saw Tommy coming toward the office, she rose from the chair she was sitting in and came to greet them. Lincoln excused himself and went into the office. Clara held Tommy's hand as Blanche greeted them.

"Miss Anson, I want to take Tommy home for the day. After yesterday I think he needs some time with us to think over what he did," Blanche said.

"If that is what you think best, here he is," Clara said. "Tommy, it was nice talking with to you last night. I hope you can get things straightened out."

Clara dropped his hand and turned to Blanche.

"Will Tommy be in school tomorrow?"

"I'll see how he feels in the morning. I want to talk to him before his father gets home from the city."

"I hope you will try to understand what is bothering him," Clara said.

She almost regretted saying that to the woman she thought didn't spend enough time with her child to even start to understand him.

"Miss Anson, I am sure I will understand my own son."

"I must excuse myself, Missus Holmes. I have a class that needs supervision."

Clara turned and started back to her classroom. On the way she couldn't help think how cold Tommy's mother was to both her and him. *She didn't even say hello to him when we got there.*

Blanche drove silently home. Tommy sat looking out of the passenger side window at all the different houses. He noticed some that he passed every day on his way to and from school. He hoped he could escape from talking with his mother because he knew that she would ask too many questions about why he ran away to Miss Anson's house and spent the night. He was glad that his father was still in the city because he didn't want to say a word to the man that threw Ralph onto the boulders in the stream and broke him into all those pieces. Just before they reached the driveway leading to the old farmhouse he remembered that he needed to go to the stream and rescue all the ceramic pieces of Ralph that were on boulders and under water.

Driving up the driveway to the walk leading to the front entrance of the old farmhouse, Blanche braked the Chrysler Town and Country to a stop. Tommy opened the passenger side door immediately and got out of the car. He began trotting toward the tool shed that was on the outside of the small barn that was once used for teams of horses that pulled various conveyances for the families. Through the years the various families of Holmes kept the barn and tool shed in good repair.

Blanche got out of the car quickly, wondering what Tommy was doing in such a rush.

"Tommy, where are you going? What are you doing?" She asked, calling after him.

Tommy didn't answer. He continued his trot to the tool shed and opened the wooden door. Once inside he looked around and saw a wooden box that held odd parts for some machine that he was not acquainted with. He dumped the parts in the corner of the shed, grabbed a medium sized shovel called a "spade" and went out of the shed, closing the door behind him. His mother remained standing by the driver's side of the Town and Country. As Tommy approached carrying the wooden box in one hand and the spade in the other Blanche waited until she knew he could hear her.

"Tommy, what are you doing and where are you going with that old box and that spade?"

Tommy stopped abruptly, and without putting the box or spade down he answered his mother's questions.

"I am going to get Ralph's pieces out of the stream, put them in this box and bury them next to the clearing." He started out again.

"Why are you doing this, Tommy?" Blanche asked.

"Because my father killed Ralph and Ralph deserves to be buried where he once was and where he talked with me," Tommy said walking away from the old farmhouse.

"I will have to tell your father about this when he gets home from the city," Blanche said.

"Go ahead and tell him anything you want to. I am going to do what I have to do."

He started to trot again and continued until he had reached the path to the clearing before he slowed to a walk. The wooden box and the spade were too much of a burden to carry at a trot. When he had reached the halfway point, Tommy stopped, put down the spade and wooden box onto the path, and sat on the box to rest. He thought about what he had said to his mother about his father killing Ralph. He was sure that she would repeat what he had said to his father. Tommy smiled for the first time since he had seen the shattered Ralph on the boulders in the stream and under the water. Rested, he picked up the spade and wooden box and walked to the clearing.

Sitting on the log he looked around as he determined the best place to dig Ralph's grave. After looking around the clearing for a few minutes Tommy suddenly realized that the best location for the grave would be where Ralph had stood at the edge of the clearing while the two had carried on their conversations. He grabbed the spade and held it vertically over the place he wanted to dig and with his right foot on the bent-over top of the blade, he pushed down with his right leg. The blade entered the sandy loam soil. Tommy pushed harder and the blade sunk deeper. He took his foot off the blade and pushed down on the handle of the spade. The blade held about a square foot of soil. Tommy lifted the spade and dumped the load aside to start making a pile as he continued making the hole for the grave. Placing the wooden box in and out of the hole as he dug to make sure the box would fit snugly. After digging what Tommy figured would be the last spadefull of dirt from the hole, he wiggled the box down until it came to the bottom and left about four inches from the top of the box to ground level. He left the box to go to the stream and gather the pieces of Ralph that he had seen on a couple of boulders and underwater where they had fallen after the smash. Tommy took off his shoes and rolled up his pant legs to begin gathering pieces of Ralph.

As he gathered the pieces from the stream and carried them back to the wooden box in the grave, he decided to lift the box out of the grave and take it to the edge of the stream. That way he reduced carrying time from the stream to the box.

He left the piece with the marble eye still in its socket on the boulder that was three feet from the stream bank. About halfway through the gathering of the pieces he found the other side of Ralph's face with the other eye still in the socket. It was between two small boulders that were about two feet in circumference. He reached down under the surface of the stream, grabbed the other piece, and placed it next to the other that was still on its boulder. Tommy was happy to see that Ralph's face could be placed together in the box once he had all the pieces gathered that he could find.

Once he had all the chards in the box and put into the grave, he put the two pieces with the eyes together on top of the rest. He squatted over the box looking at the eyes for a long time and talked to Ralph as always.

The next stage of the burial was getting rocks from the stream and placing them on top of all the chards. Tommy took a great deal of care choosing the rocks and placing them so that they fit as closely as possible to cover the chards in the box. That accomplished, he took the spade and covered it all until it was at ground level. He looked at the spot in the clearing and returned to the stream where he brought larger rocks to place on top of the grave. He put some rocks in another pile in order to make it look as natural as possible. Tommy began to sob as he put his shoes back on and rolled his pant legs down. He continued sobbing as he grabbed the spade, put it over his shoulder as he had seen workman do with shovels, and started back down the pathway that led to the old farmhouse. He had no idea what time it might be. He had been too busy to think about lunch.

As it turned out, it was mid-afternoon when Tommy arrived home from his labors on Ralph's grave. He went to the kitchen where Bertha was busy preparing supper.

"Hi Bertha," Tommy said. "Am I too late for lunch?"

"Yo Momma tol me you was gone ta da woods an you be back fo lunch. It close to suppa now."

"Can I have some supper?" Tommy asked.

"I can gives you whats I got ready, but it be only a slice o meat."

"That's fine. I don't need much."

Bertha went over to the oven, opened the door, took out a pan holding a standing rib roast. She lifted it onto the counter, and with a butcher knife made from an iron rasp, she sliced a generous piece off and put it onto a plate. From one of the drawers under the counter she took out a steak knife and fork, and put hem on the plate with the slice of beef.

"You wants to eat heah o in da dinin room?"

"I would rather eat here in the kitchen so we can talk," Tommy said. "I like talking with you, Bertha."

"Ah likes talkin' wid you, too, Tommy boy. In fac dis be good time ta ask ya'll what be goin' on wid Ralph?"

Tommy started to explain about what happened to Ralph, that his father had killed him by throwing him onto the boulders in the stream. He also told about running away to Miss Anson's house and then about how he gathered the pieces of Ralph from the stream and buried them in the wooden box.

"I doan know whats to say bout all dat, Tommy." Bertha said. "I spose yo Daddy doan know nuthin bout spirits. He doan unerstan how you can talk wid Ralph and how Ralph can talk back wid you. Dere's some peoples dat caint unerstan spirits an deres some dat can. You unerstan Ralph an yo Daddy doan unerstan. I gotta tell ya, Tommy boy, I unerstans spirits good. Dey tells me all da time dat ah is Bertha an I is good. Ah is lucky cuz I doan knows no bad spirits. You may be white boy and Ah is black, but you and me knows spirits an dats good. We's also frens. Dat means a whole lots to me."

Tommy dropped his knife and fork onto the plate next to the half eaten slice of beef, scrambled out of the chair by the kitchen table and trotted over to Bertha into her outstretched arms. She took Tommy into her arms and hugged him a long time. When she released him, she put her chubby hands on his shoulders and bent over so that their eyes met.

"Tommy, ah know sumthin's wrong tween yo folks and y'all. An I knows y'all needs ta be alone. I jes wanna tell ya that you ever needs ta talk at me, jes come ta da kitchen an I stop whats I doin an we can talk bout anathin'. Ya gots ta knows I luvs ya, Tommy boy."

Tommy put his arms around Bertha as far as he could reach.

"Bertha, I love you, too. And, thanks for being my friend."

Releasing Bertha, Tommy went back to the table and finished the slice of rib roast.

"Bertha, if my parents ask you if you know where I am, please tell them that I have already eaten supper. Maybe that will satisfy them so I can stay in my room and finish the book I am almost done reading."

"I do dat fo y'all, Tommy. I hope dey leaves ya lone."

"I hope so, too," Tommy said, and left the kitchen for his room upstairs.

He didn't open the picture book. He stretched out on top of his bed and thought about what Bertha had said. He also thought about Miss Anson. He felt a sense of happiness when he thought about those two women that had hugged him. Then, as he had done many times, he wondered why his mother never came upstairs to hug him before he went to bed. "I guess she doesn't want to leave her drinks and my father long enough to say good-night to me," he said out loud, but quietly. All of his thoughts and feeling tired from digging Ralph's grave, as well as wading in the stream looking for the chards that were once Ralph, gave him reason to close his eyes intermittently. His thoughts turned to what Bertha had said about him and her understanding spirits until he fell asleep with all his clothes on.

A loud knock on his bedroom door awakened him. Before he could focus his eyes and sit up, he heard the door latch. Swinging his body around to sit on the edge of his bed he came face to face with his father.

"Tommy, come downstairs to the living room," Jason said. "Your mother and I want to talk to you."

Tommy scowled and crinkled his nose at his father's distasteful order. He waited sitting on the bed, but did not answer. Jason hesitated for a moment, then turned and left the room. Tommy stood up stepped over the door threshold and stopped. A thought rushed into his mind; *I will answer their questions without being afraid of them because they do not understand spirits like Bertha and I do. Therefore, there is no point in arguing with either of them.*

He left his door opened as he went downstairs to the living room. He saw them sitting in the same chairs with their drinks on side tables as always. He walked into the room and sat in the middle of the sofa.

"I am here. What do you want to talk about?" Tommy asked, surprising himself at his own abruptness.

Jason lifted his drink and took a sip. Tommy could see that his father was nervous in spite of the gruffness of the order he had given him in the bedroom.

"Your mother tells me that you told her that I killed Ralph," Jason said.

Before his father could finish what he was trying to say Tommy spoke.

"You did kill Ralph. I saw all of your tracks that you made with those cowboy boots."

"I didn't kill Ralph, Tommy." Jason said, trying to be calm, yet defensive. "Nobody can kill a bunch of clay, and that is what Ralph was."

"That might be how you felt about Ralph, but Ralph was my friend. We talked with each other."

"And I suppose you will try and tell me that a bunch of clay talked back to you."

"I will not try to tell you anything because you do not understand what I understand. Is there anything else you want to talk about?"

"I don't think I like the sound of your voice, Tommy," Jason said, perturbed. It does not sound respectful."

"Did you respect me when you threw my friend, Ralph onto the boulders in the stream?"

"We are not getting anywhere," Jason said, and waved his right hand in disgust. "Blanche, what do you have to say?"

"This is all too complicated for me to unravel. I think I will make myself another drink"

"If you are finished with me, I would like to finish sleeping," Tommy said.

"I am not finished yet," Jason said. "I am still curious about the way you think I murdered your friend, Ralph, when Ralph is nothing but a bunch of clay that has been molded into a figure and heated to get all of the water out. I am not enjoying being called a killer by my son."

"I think you should have thought more before killing Ralph. Or, did you think at all before you picked him up and threw him onto the stream boulders?"

"You are close to being insolent, Tommy, and I am afraid I cannot accept your behavior. You are not behaving like a Holmes should behave. I think it best for me to end this conversation and send you back to Bruno Weber. You might as well go back to your room."

Tommy lifted his head and bent it backwards as he gave out a sigh of relief that the session with his parents was over. As he climbed the stairs back to his room, he thought about Bruno Weber. Before he reached the top of the stairway, he almost said aloud that he would rather talk with Bruno Weber than with his father who failed to understand him. Tommy thought a little about running away again to Miss Anson's, but then he realized that such a move would give a victory to his parents. As it stood after the last discussion, he, Tommy Holmes, was winning by several lengths. He remembered Lisa Marie's descriptions of horse races that they watched on television one afternoon when she took off her speakers and turned off her "Noise Machine" as Tommy called it.

Two weeks later Blanche drove Tommy to The Stringer Medical Center for his appointment with Doctor Bruno Weber. Blanche had not said much to Jason about Tommy's so-called disrespect since that day when Jason got so frustrated while talking to Tommy that he got so drunk he spent the night on the sofa in the living room.

Doctor Weber greeted them in the waiting room where he again insisted that Blanche wait for Tommy because Weber wanted to talk with him alone without any intrusions from a parent.

Weber questioned Tommy with deeper questions than during their first conversation. After an hour Weber had reached into greater clarity about what bothered Tommy and how serious Tommy's feeling of being unloved were affecting his behavior patterns.

"What would your mother and father have to do to make you feel that they really loved you?" Weber asked at one juncture.

"I don't understand," Tommy said. "If they don't love me, they wouldn't know what to do and if someone told them, they would not know how to do whatever that was."

"Tommy, I don't know why or how, but your answers tell me that you understand yourself better than anyone."

"That should not surprise you. Don't you know yourself better than anyone else?" Tommy asked.

"You have a good point there, Tommy," Weber said. "Do you think your father and mother understand you?"

"No. And they never talk to me so how can they understand me? I think they had me to carry on the name of Holmes and so that they will have someone to live in our old farmhouse after they are gone. I heard my father tell that to someone once as he was saying good-bye to them after a visit."

"Tommy, thank you for being open and honest with me. I think I might have a solution to the Holmes problem that you might approve of when you hear it. Next time I am going to insist that both of your parents are present for the appointment."

They left the consultation room and went to the waiting room where Weber told Blanche that he wanted to see all three of them on Thursday at ten o'clock in the morning, three days away.

"I don't know if I can get Jason to skip a day at the bank," Blanche said.

"Then tell him that if he does not skip a day at the bank for his son, I will charge him triple for this visit."

Blanche drove back to the old farmhouse. Tommy left the car as soon as it stopped and made his way to the clearing next to the stream. Blanche went into the living room and made herself a drink. She sat in her usual chair to sip the drink as she contemplated what Bruno Weber had ordered her to do. She had forgotten that Tommy was supposed to return to school.

Tommy sat on the log looking at Ralph's grave. He turned to look at the stream and only then remembered that he should be in school. *She must have forgotten to take me back to school. I will wait until she remembers, and maybe she won't, and I will have time to talk with Ralph. I wonder why Doctor Weber wants the three of us together in his office.*

Blanche felt exhausted from just the time at Doctor Weber's office waiting for him to finish the session with Tommy. Before realizing that she needed to return

Tommy to school, she climbed the stairs and went to bed. She slept until Jason came home from the city and walked into the bedroom to find her snoring.

"Blanche, wake up," Jason said. "Get up and tell me about Tommy's appointment with Bruno Weber."

Blanche groaned as she opened her eyes and realized that she had been fast asleep the entire afternoon.

"I'll meet you in the living room," she said. "I didn't know I was so tired."

What she had missed was Tommy arriving home a half hour before Jason came in the door. Tommy had gone to his room and had seen his mother sleeping on her bed. He had gone into his room quietly and had closed the door. When he heard Blanche's footsteps going down the stairs he opened his door slightly because he wanted to hear what his parents were going to say about the Thursday appointment with Doctor Weber. After opening his door enough to catch their conversation, Tommy went over to his desk and sat down.

Blanche walked into the living room. Jason had already made himself a drink and was sitting in his favorite chair.

"Make yourself a drink and tell me all about what happened at Bruno Weber's today," he said.

"I'll pass on the drink. Doctor Weber wants all three of us in his office at ten o'clock Thursday morning. That's three days from now."

"I have a bank to run, Bruno knows that. What is he thinking of?"

"He might have been joking, but he said he would charge you triple for today's visit if you will not give up a day at the bank for your son."

"I can pay his bill any way he wants me to. I wonder what goes through that shrink's head at times. He should know I have a bank, and a real big bank, to run during the week. I sometimes, as you know, have to go to work Saturdays."

"Jason, please stop arguing with Bruno Weber when he isn't even here," Blanche said.

"All right, Blanche, if you think this is what we should do. I must admit we need to do something about all the weird things that are happening around here."

After listening to his father complain about going to see Doctor Weber, Tommy's anger flared. He came out of his room and down the stairs. Bouncing into the living room he stood in front of his parents and began his tirade.

"If you don't want to go to Doctor Weber on Thursday, don't. Go to your bank," Tommy said, stomping his feet, first one and then the other. I will go by myself. I like Doctor Weber. He talks to me and he also listens to me when I am answering his questions. We get along fine. Go to your bank and count your money that you are always talking about to Mother. Doctor Weber understands me. He likes me and I like him, so there. Go to your bank on Thursday. I will go to see Doctor Weber. It is not far. I can walk."

Tommy stomped his feet again, turned and went up the stairway taking two stairs at a time. Jason and Blanche turned to one another and just looked, mouths opened with amazement at what their son had just hit them with in his tirade.

Twenty minutes later, Bertha came out of the kitchen and announced supper. Jason took his and Blanche's drinks into the dining room while Blanche went upstairs, and knocked on Tommy's bedroom door to tell him that it was suppertime. She returned to the dining room and sat down. A few minutes later, Tommy came down from his room with a scowl on his face. He sat down at his place at the table, and said nothing as he ate his supper that Bertha brought to him.

Jason and Blanche, their minds lubricated with single-malt Scotch, bantered nervously back and forth as if Tommy was not in the room. As soon as he had cleaned his plate, Tommy left the dining room without asking to be excused and went back to his room. Jason and Blanche stopped talking until they heard Tommy's bedroom door close upstairs.

"Bruno Weber really has befriended Tommy," Jason said. "I am wondering what he has in mind to say when we are all in his office. I will do my best not to raise my voice at him in spite of him being a golf partner."

"I have never talked with Bruno Weber, so you will probably have to do the talking while we are there in his office," Blanche said.

Jason and Blanche were nervous at breakfast Thursday morning. Tommy, as usual, did not speak during the meal, but he could sense the tension between his mother and father. Tommy finished his breakfast and went back to his room to wait for the time to go to Doctor Weber's office. He thought about Miss Anson at school and in some ways he wished he was there instead of having to accompany his parents to see Doctor Weber. He sat at his desk and escaped into a picture book with a story.

His mother's call grabbed him away from the story, and he went downstairs and out to the garage where he climbed into the middle seat in the "Town and Country".

Blanche drove, seeming to ignore Jason's remarks about how she was handling the automobile. Weber's office was a mile and a half from the old farmhouse. Blanche parked and the three of them left the car for the entrance to The Stringer Medical Center.

The receptionist in Weber's office greeted them and told them, "Doctor will be right with you."

They sat down in the chairs that were lined up against the walls of the waiting room. Five minutes later, Bruno Weber poked his head out of the door to the inner rooms.

"Good morning," he said. "Come with me."

Weber held to door open for the Holmes family and they followed him down a hallway to a room with an eight-foot diameter table with several upholstered chairs around it. A manila file folder was in front of one of the chairs. Weber went to that chair, held the back with both hands, and waited until each member of the Holmes family had chosen a chair.

"Please sit down and relax. Jason, I am sorry to make you miss a day at your bank, but I feel this is important for all of you, especially your son, Tommy."

"I guess the bank will be there tomorrow without me there today to hold up the walls," Jason said, and chuckled at what he deemed humor.

"All right, let us tackle the problem and see what we can do to solve it. I have seen Tommy twice and both times he has been very open with me and that has helped me think about solutions. First of all I can tell you that I look at your situation as something that has been going on for too long to have an easy solution. The gap between you, Blanche and your son, Tommy is the result of a definite lack of communication between you two adults and your child. Tommy not only feels left out of this family, but also has developed some deep feelings of being unloved. He has acquired these feelings because there has been a lack of communication. He has mentioned that you, Jason, and Blanche carry on conversations between the two of you, but never include Tommy. He has come to dread when you do talk to him because what you say seems like orders or admonishments. You talk to him, instead of with him. Don't feel guilty about that, because there are more people than not that talk to a person rather than with them. The human ego is quite far-reaching believe me. Have I been clear, thus far?"

"So far, I think I understand," Jason said. "How about you, Blanche?"

"I suppose I understand, but I thought I talked with Tommy a lot."

"That is one reason we are here today," Weber said. "Sometimes we don't realize what we have created, either by too much of something or not enough. We seem to forget that there needs to be some sort of balance. A single person in spite of living alone needs to discover balance in their life. This may sound simple, but it can be a difficult and lengthy process. Perhaps I can put it this way. Everyone is different with different psyches and perspectives. It would be a different world if we all knew ourselves. Knowing all of our depths makes it easier to deal with these depths. Then, once at peace in an inward sense, we are in a better space to deal with others no matter to what stage of understanding the others may have arrived."

"What does all that have to do with us?" Jason asked.

"I am not completely certain that the gap between you parents and your child can be closed by you adults undergoing therapy to help you discover yourselves. However, I have thought about a sort of solution that will alleviate the tensions caused by the gap even though my ideas will not be a total solution. But, in my practice I have found that simple partial arrangements can help make intolerable situations far easier to live with than remaining in the same rut of neurosis."

"I am anxious to hear what you have been thinking about," Jason said.

"I haven't spoken about this to you, Tommy, so listen carefully so that you can agree or disagree with what I am proposing."

Tommy nodded his head affirmatively. He had not understood all that Weber had said, but enough so that he knew the doctor understood what things were like between him and his parents.

"Tommy has no problem with his school situation. One of his teachers has taken an interest in his artistic ability and Tommy has made good progress. He made a sculpture of a boy and brought it home. He took it to his favorite spot by a stream and enjoyed talking with this sculpture that he named Ralph. He told me that both of you were concerned about his talking to himself and then later with Ralph. Tommy has made it clear that when you threw Ralph into the boulders in the stream to destroy Ralph he came close to regarding you as a murderer."

"I did that for his own good," Jason said.

"Obviously what you thought was for Tommy's own good was quite different than what he thinks," Weber said.

Jason flushed with embarrassment, and squirmed in his chair.

"I think that the best partial solution to your family situation is to give Tommy the chance to go to a good boarding school where he can develop his creativity and become a part of a school community. He seems to get along well at his current school so by living at a school where the emphasis is on creative development instead of rudimentary education, he could find a compatible environment where he could feel as an integral part instead of as an outsider. Put a different way, he could feel like he belonged somewhere. One of his problems about living at home is that he feels very much like an outsider, not as member of the family."

"Is there such a school?" Blanche asked, finally speaking up.

"The Escalante School is a unique boarding school that was started by a wealthy Spaniard eighty some years ago where children can learn how to live together in a harmony that includes inner personalities as well as being able to pursue creativity in a wide variety of venues. It is a school for boys with special needs. They have been known to hire a specialist for one student so that the student could learn all the ins and outs of weaving. They also offer curricula of the basics of education without overdoing the time spent on them. All the meals are served in a family setting with the boys changing tables weekly in order to be able to have different exchanges of ideas."

"This all sounds different and interesting to a point," Jason said. "But, Bruno, how will Tommy get accepted at The Wharton when he finishes at this Escalante School?"

"I assume you are referring to The Wharton School of Finance at the University of Pennsylvania?" Weber asked.

"Yes," Jason said. The Wharton is a tradition for male members of the Holmes family."

"Well, Jason, I think The Escalante will prepare Tommy well for life and that might be a good opportunity for him to break tradition. He seems to be more bent on creative endeavors than gambling with finances."

"I have done quite well as you are well aware of," Jason said.

"I am talking about Tommy's life, not yours. Come now, my friend, doesn't your Wharton teach something besides manipulation of numbers?"

"I suppose they do. It has been quite a while since I graduated. And, by the way, I graduated *cum laude*."

"I think it would behoove you to visit The Escalante School and see if you like it. Tommy needs to find out if he would like to go there. I will call and arrange for your visit. When would be convenient?"

"Bruno, you know how busy I am with my bank. We are negotiating a major transfer of mortgage paper with several European banks at this time, and I need to be there to make approvals and disapprovals. This is very tricky business. Can Blanche take Tommy for the visit? Whatever she decides is fine with me."

"I suppose that will be satisfactory with the Escalante Head of School. I will ask him when I call. You really don't understand what this situation is all about yet, do you, Jason?"

"I'm afraid I don't understand what you're getting at, Bruno."

"That is a major part of the problem. Maybe I can explain further on Saturday on the front nine if I don't tee off the sixth hole into that pesky pond."

"I may not make it Saturday. European banks keep different hours than we do. I'll call you Friday if I cannot make it Saturday."

Bruno showed them to the door to the waiting room and the Holmes trio left for home. Jason did not go inside. Before arriving at the old farmhouse he informed Blanche that he needed to get to his office in the city and that he would have to spend the night at the bank's hotel room in the hotel off Grand Central Terminal.

"If Bruno calls about that school, you can answer any of his questions and make all the arrangements for you and Tommy to pay the school a visit. I won't be able to go there because I am far too busy with this European deal to spend any time away."

"All right, Jason. I wish you would come with us to visit this school."

"Now, Blanche, you know I would love to go there, but too much depends on the success of this very complicated deal. It is all in Euros and that is bad enough."

He got into the Mercedes Sports Car and headed for the city. Tommy went inside, joined his mother for lunch and then wandered out to his favorite spot by the stream. He sat on the log and pondered what he had understood during the meeting with Doctor Weber.

The idea of going to a boarding school intrigued him. He had no idea what it would be like to live with an entire school full of boys, but the thought of being away from his parents, who didn't seem to care if he was in the room or not, was a pleasant thought. He sat there trying to imagine what the place might be like, wondering if there might be a ceramics shop where he could make more sculpture. Then he began thinking about what kinds of sculptures he wanted to make. It was not long before he came close to sleep and falling off the log.

Bruno Weber telephoned Blanche the following afternoon. He told her that he had made an appointment with George Moser, the Head of School, for the next Tuesday for her and Jason to take Tommy to visit The Escalante School that was located north of Newburgh near the Hudson River. The appointment was for ten o'clock in the morning. When Blanche told Bruno that Jason would not be going Bruno sighed into the telephone.

"I am disappointed to hear that, Missus Holmes. Jason doesn't seem to understand that he is a major part of the problem you folks are having. Be that as it may, enjoy your visit. I think you will like The Escalante School and their faculty, and I am sure Tommy will probably want to stay there instead of gong home. Please give my best regards to George Moser. He is an outstanding educator."

When Jason arrived home from the city, Blanche told him about her ten o'clock appointment with the Head of School in Newburgh.

"Jason, that is awfully early. I think I should drive Tommy up to Newburgh on Monday afternoon and get a hotel room for the night so we will be on time for the appointment."

"That sounds reasonable to me. Do what you must about all this matter and make the decisions for both of us. I am really far too busy to think about anything but bank business at this point in time."

Blanche had already poured her drink so Jason went to the bar and poured his to take to his chair. After sitting down and taking a sip of single malt Scotch, he reached into his jacket pocket and took out an envelope. Taking the contents from it he began reading the pages, occasionally glancing at the ceiling and back to the papers.

"What is so interesting?" Blanche asked. "Is this banking business so important that you have to bring work home with you?"

"Blanche, this is a letter we received from Zurich yesterday. Three of my vice presidents have read it and cannot understand what those people are demanding, so I brought the letter home so that I can read it and tomorrow morning I can explain it all to them. They are all smart fellows, but somehow they are lacking understanding about Swiss bankers."

The following Monday afternoon, Blanche and Tommy arrived in Newburgh in mid-afternoon and registered for a room at the Hampton Inn. After a snack in the hotel coffee shop, Blanche drove Tommy around the city to acquaint him the new surroundings should she and Jason decide to send him off to the Escalante School. While driving around she found the school and made a mental note of its location so that she would find it easily the next morning. They had supper in the hotel dining room. Back in the room, Blanche turned on the TV and they watched cable news until Blanche announced that it was bedtime.

The following morning after breakfast in the hotel, they went to the Escalante School, drove up the long driveway to a cluster of well-maintained brick buildings. A small sign announced where the office was, and Blanche parked the Town and Country in one of the spaces provided visitors on one side of the two-story structure. The October chill made Blanche shrug her shoulders and pull her fall coat tighter around her. Tommy followed quietly behind Blanche as they entered the building through a large hand-carved wooden door. They were met by a man with salt and pepper hair, of medium build wearing blue jeans, a plaid flannel shirt and a tweed jacket with leather patches on each elbow.

"Hello," he said. "You must be Missus Holmes and Tommy Holmes. Thank you for your promptness. I am George Moser."

"Nice meeting you, Mister Moser. I am sorry that my husband couldn't make it. He is swamped with business at his bank on Wall Street."

"Yes, Bruno told me about the situation," Moser said. "Please step into my office," he said pointing to an open door. "Have a seat and relax, I will be with you in a moment. I must see to a small problem with one of the students."

Moser left, walking down the hallway to a room at the far end. Blanche and Tommy sat down in two of the four leather upholstered chairs that had been placed in front of an oval desk made of dark walnut. Five short stacks of papers were on top of the desk. Behind the desk and off to one side a computer screen was on a small table. The screen saver was full of waving colored lines that seem to have no destination. Tommy glued his eyes on the screen.

Moser returned in less than five minutes and sat down at his desk.

“Sorry for the delay. One of the boys is having problems with a project. I just needed to motivate him to try a new approach.

Now, let me begin with telling you about The Escalante School. We are different. In fact you might say that people used to ordinary or traditional schools find Escalante methods quite unbelievable. So, should you have any questions as I proceed, please interrupt me with them, and I will do my best to clear up anything that might come to mind.”

Blanche nodded her head. Tommy kept his eyes on George Moser as if he was sizing him up.

“First of all I will tell you that we have no grades here. There is no first, second, third or fourth grade, and there is no such thing as grammar school, junior high school, middle school or high school. Our students graduate when they feel they have been in this environment long enough to have learned what they have wanted to learn. We do not grade our students’ creations with anything like grades A,B,or C. There is no such thing as “flunking or failing. Nobody is kept back because there are no grades or levels.”

“Mister Moser, I am not sure what my husband will say to all this. As for myself, I am quite excited to hear your methods.”

“We do not have examinations. On this idea you may ask, ‘why not?’. Well, I can answer that by saying that since we do not have grades we don’t have any use for examination to establish them. We feel that placing a student’s projects on a level means literally nothing to the student because we do not encourage competition here. Everything is personal to and for the students on an individual basis.

It is basically this idea that was the basis for the foundation of The Escalante School. Each person is different with different personalities, talents and desires. Everyone is multi-talented. Therefore, we believe that students should be free to explore anything that intrigues them. Most of our faculty are men with many interests so that the students may call on them for help toward their goals on their projects."

"I have a question, Mister Moser," Blanche said. "How do your students learn reading, writing, and math?"

"We do have these subjects as requirements. All students must become proficient in these three subjects. It is obvious that without developed skills in these three subjects, it would prove difficult for them to get involved in their personal projects of inquiry. These subjects are taught on an individual basis to a level from which the individual may progress to top proficiency at his own pace. Incidentally, we call math "arithmetic" because it is rare that any of the students want to go further than addition, subtraction, multiplication and division. Those who wish to pursue advanced science projects are given the opportunities to make further progress. We can offer various mathematical disciplines."

"I know my husband will want to know if after finishing Escalante, will Tommy be able to pass the entrance exams for The Wharton School of Finance. "

"That is all up to Tommy. We had one student enter Wharton and when he graduated he elected to become a lobster fisherman in Maine."

Graduation from The Wharton, as my husband's family calls it, is almost a prerequisite to life for the

Holmes clan," Blanche said. "By the way, is that Escalante student who graduated from The Wharton still a lobster fisherman?"

"Actually he was a lobsterman for two years and then he sailed on freighters in the Atlantic and Pacific for three years. He has been a best selling author of maritime novels for almost a decade."

"That's quite a recommendation for The Esacalante School," Blanche said.

"You are quite right, Missus Holmes. Now, if you don't object, I would like to chat with Tommy alone. If you will relax in the waiting room in the foyer, we should be ready for your tour of the campus shortly."

Blanche rose from her chair, smiled and left Moser's office without a word, closing the door behind her. Moser turned to Tommy.

"Since you will be a resident student here, I would like to get to know you better so that I can advise you before you begin. I know more about you than you may realize. Doctor Weber told me all about the conflict you are having with your parents. Such conflicts are not uncommon among our students here. The story about Ralph, your sculpture that your father threw onto the boulders in your stream tells me that you have an active and promising imagination, a quality that we hope to enhance here at Escalante. We feel that candidates for the school that lack imagination do not derive much from our philosophy."

"What do you mean, philosophy?" Tommy asked.

"The way we think about education, the method we employ and what we hope for in general results of the Escalante experience," Moser said. "We have a different philosophy about education than most. We also believe that prospective students that some people regard as strange, more often than not have broader imaginations than those that conform to society's models. We have no models here because we stress individuality and give total respect to it. You can expect to be free to pursue just about anything that intrigues you. I already know that you have talent and interest in working with clay. You have already made one sculpture so you might find interest in sculpting using a different medium. Then again, you may decide to create poetry or paintings. For that matter you may wander through our garden and find that learning all about plants is an avenue that is of interest to you. You will discover that we are here to encourage differences, not discourage exploration in the mind.

Doctor Weber is part of The Escalante School. He visits occasionally because we have some of his patients here. They come here with his recommendation just as you have. Doctor Weber is one of us although he comes here of his own accord without compensation.

One thing you need to know is that once you arrive to begin your Escalante experience, you are encouraged to remain here at least two months before going to your home for a visit. This reasoning comes from what we have experienced with some who become upset with a change that some call "homesickness"."

"You don't have to worry about me getting homesick. I am already excited about moving here. The way I feel about where I live is that I either come here or I will run away to somewhere else where people will talk to me."

"Doctor Weber told me about the situation you have at home. Perhaps it will make you feel better to know that you are far from being alone with such parents. We have seen some boys arrive here that have been told to be seen and not heard all their lives. After a week or two of mingling with everyone here, they have to learn that others want to speak, too.

Do you have any questions about The Escalante School?"

"I don't think so," Tommy said.

"Then I think it is a good time to give you and your mother a tour of the campus."

Moser and Tommy left the office, and walked to the waiting area. Blanche rose from her chair and joined them.

"Well, did you two have a nice time talking?"

"As a matter of fact we did. I am pleased to tell you that I am accepting Tommy as one of the students and he should start next week, preferably Monday morning if you can have him here Sunday to give him time to get settled in his quarters."

"Good heavens," Blanche said. "I think I need to talk with my husband."

"That's understandable. I suggest that tonight, while this visit is still fresh in your mind, would be an appropriate time to discuss The Escalante School with your husband. I will give you a packet of information to share with him. Everything you need to know is included in the packet, including financial arrangements."

"Your packet will certainly help. That is if Jason is not too busy with his bank stuff to read it."

"I am sure, from what Bruno Weber has told me, he will understand what is in the packet. I think he will appreciate the way we have made our tuition charge a tax-deductible item."

"I have heard him talk about taxes for many years, Blanche said. "I am sure Jason will also be interested in your athletic program."

"Missus Holmes, I am afraid he will be disappointed because we do not have an athletic program. We do not support any organized sports. However, should the students want to play baseball, we have a diamond and a field where they can play. We do not encourage football because of the violence to which it seems to give birth. Another thing we stress is an anti-war attitude. Jason might not like that because Wall Street bankers always see opportunities to make huge sums of money when the country is waging war. We often have discussions about what Eisenhower called "The Military/Industrial Complex". There seems to be frequent discussions among faculty and students about prominent men and women that stood for peaceful solutions to world problems rather than jumping into armed conflicts that the industrialists count on the middle class to wage and die from."

"I am not sure if Jason will approve of all that you have been saying," Blanche said.

"You might remind him that it is his son that will attend The Escalante School, not him.

I think you might be interested in the way we learn at Escalante. We admit all ages within reason. There are youngsters like Tommy and those who might be old enough to be in college, but for one reason or another stay with us. The faculty is not the only group that teaches. In fact we don't use the term "teach" here. We don't believe that anyone teaches, they motivate students to learn. Learning, we believe, is totally personal. Just look at the curricula of our traditional schools. Much of it is irrelevant and far too boring to hold interest. Here we encourage investigation into choices and the pursuit of interests rather than require this or that, most of which encourages memorization to be able to pass examinations. We never give examinations here at Escalante. Memorization is just what the word says. It is not learning. We feel that memorization is only useful in such cases as multiplication tables and some other things to do with math so that calculations can be rapid without wasting valuable time on such trivia. By the way, that white building over there is a general use center," he said, pointing to a two story building with a long porch extending over the length of one side. "Students use rooms for their projects and there is a large living room where students can visit and hold discussions. We encourage students to get involved with motivating other students. Sometimes it is difficult to distinguish the faculty from the students."

"What about social activities, Mister Moser?"

"I am glad you asked. We have a sister school outside of New Windsor, a short distance from here, just beyond that large stand of trees. We get together for occasional dances, picnics and even river activities. The sister school, Mujeres del Mundo, meaning Women of the World in Spanish, was established at the same time as we were by the Spanish Count, José Escalante y Heredia. He was interested in advancing women into activities that were not necessarily considered feminine at that time. He was an iconoclast in those days. Now the Women's Liberation Movement has become popular and quite common."

Escalante was also very forward in his thinking about mankind, and insisted that our bi-laws include that we must never discriminate for reasons of race, color or religion. We do not emphasize religion here, but if a Muslim or Shinto meets our criteria for entrance, they will be as welcome as anyone. We encourage applicants from all over the world and from all racial backgrounds. Count Heredia was a worldly sort of man and thought that the more different races mixed, the more peace would have a chance to survive."

"Do you have such things as parents visiting weekends?"

"No," Weber said quickly. "Parents can visit any time as long as they notify us and the student so that we can inform them if there is a conflict with their visit and the student's project schedule. We call it a "schedule" in spite of having no schedules because parents are used to the word. We strongly feel that schedules chain thought and limit inquiry."

They approached a one-story building, painted white like the others.

"This is what we call "The Eatery" where meals are served cafeteria style. There are no specific times for meals. Students can enjoy their food at most all hours. The place closes at eight o'clock at night and opens at six o'clock in the morning. The students and faculty do all the work preparing meals and cleanup, on a rotation basis. I even take my turn. The students and faculty do all the work on campus. We have no servants or gardeners. Most students here are from wealthy homes and have grown up with servants that wait on them in myriad ways. The Escalante experiences weans them away from being waited on and gives them a sense of pride in taking care of their surroundings with their own hands and minds. Would you care to share a meal with us?"

"Thank you, no, Mister Moser," Blanche said. "I think I should get back as soon as possible to be sure Jason is planning to come home tonight. I have a lot to discuss with him, and that is never easy."

"Fine, Missus Holmes, suit yourself. I will leave you here because I am hungry. I will await your call about Tommy's arrival. I hope you and our pamphlet will help your husband understand what we are all about. I would be happy to talk with him if he has any questions about our way of educating and our financial structure. It has been a pleasure meeting you and Tommy. And Tommy," he said extending his right hand, "I am looking forward to seeing you move in. I think you will fit in perfectly."

"Thank you for showing me around, Mister Moser. I hope I see you again soon."

Blanche drove the Town and Country home without saying much to Tommy. Tommy was used to that so he spent the time watching the landscape along the way. Arriving home an hour before Jason generally returned from the city, Blanche put the Escalante School Pamphlet on the side table next to Jason's chair in the living room where he would have to see it before putting his drink on the table and sitting down. Tommy went to the clearing and sat on the log, thinking about the new school and all the things that Mister Moser had told him alone and with his mother. He found himself excited at the prospect of moving to the new school, where life appeared to be far different than in the old farmhouse. It suddenly dawned on him that if he went to the Escalante School he would no longer be able to see and talk with Miss Anson. He pondered that for a few minutes until his thoughts scurried back to what she had told him about the freedom that The Escalante School strived for. He also thought about taking his turn at the various tasks that needed doing at the school. He wondered what meals would be like there with no Bertha to prepare everything. He thought momentarily about Lisa Marie even though she had not been to the house after his mother told her she was no longer needed to look after him. He had missed Lisa Marie slightly after she had said good-bye to him with a hug around his shoulders. He wished that she had stopped listening to her music long enough to get better acquainted. After the time she told him that her parents were the same as his, he had felt closer to her than before.

As he sat there he chatted with Ralph, telling him all about the new school and how he hoped that his father would not say no to sending him there. He cut the conversation short to get back to the old farmhouse before Jason drove in from the city. Tommy planned to be in his room with the door opened enough to hear the conversation between his mother and father concerning The Escalante School.

Tommy got back in plenty of time to get everything arranged in his room so that he could hear what his parents were saying about the new school. As he passed the living room, he glanced in and saw his mother sitting in her chair watching a news program on the television as she sipped her drink. As he walked softly up the stairs he hoped that she would not drink too much before his father arrived from the city. He also hoped that his father would read the pamphlet that Moser had given his mother before he had had too much to drink so that he could concentrate on The Escalante School.

Inside his room, Tommy pushed his door so that there was about a foot opened to the hallway. He went to his bed and grabbed his pillow so that he could rest his head on it as he listened to what his parents said about him moving to The Escalante School. He whispered to Ralph that he was ready and he wanted his parents to think about him for a change.

Jason arrived through the front door. He had parked the Mercedes in the driveway in front of the house. He left the evening newspaper on the table in the front hall and walked into the living room.

"How was your day, Blanche?"

"I had a very good day today and yesterday. I liked The Escalante School very much and I think Tommy did also. They sure are different there. The Escalante is a lot different than where I went to school."

"It's a boarding school, Blanche. Those are all different."

I know that, Jason, but this place has some very modern ideas. I found them interesting. Sit down and read their pamphlet. I'll get up and pour you a drink."

Blanche got up from her chair and went to the bar where she took a glass and the bottle of single malt Scotch down from the shelf above the counter of the bar. Jason sat in his chair and took the pamphlet from the side table, opened it and began reading. Blanche put the drink on the side table, hoping her husband would read it before he drank too much Scotch. Blanche watched Jason as he turned the pages of the pamphlet and skimmed what was written. Finally he found what he was looking for.

"Here it is," he said. "The financial crap. Good grief, did you read this page, Blanche?"

"I didn't read any of the pages, Jason. I saved them all for you. After all it is you who will make the decision."

"Bruno called me to tell me that he thought this Escalante School is a perfect place for Tommy. But does that rascal think I am made of money? Ten grand a year, and then they are asking for additional donations. What do they feed those kids, lobster and filet mignon?"

"Come now, Jason. You told me your income from being president of the bank last year was six million dollars. Ten thousand a year for your son's education will not come close to putting you in the poor house. I'll bet you will find that Tommy will get a better education at The Escalante School than at any other school in the country."

"You are talking with a hole in your head, Blanche," Jason said, and sighed. "I had a helluva tax bill to pay on that six million."

"Mister Moser told me that you would like the way the school had made it possible to write off all their charges from your taxes if you follow what they have done."

Jason opened the pamphlet again and read over the financial pages without speaking further. Finally, he closed the pamphlet and put it back on the side table. I think you are right. What they are doing sounds perfectly legal and will actually save on taxes. I'll have the bank's accountant look this over and send Moser a check for the rest of the year. When will Tommy start?"

"Moser wants him by next week. I will drive him up there on Sunday, this week, so he can start Monday morning."

"They don't waste any time, do they?"

"I think that Mister Moser was impressed with Tommy," Blanche said, and rose to get another drink. She stopped at Jason's chair and took his half full glass with her. "You deserve another drink, Darling."

"Good Lord, you haven't called me Darling since before you got pregnant with Tommy."

"Just relax and enjoy it, you never know when I'll call you Darling again."

## Part Two

Tommy got up from the floor of his bedroom, took his pillow back and put it on his bed. He sat down on the edge of the bed and smiled. He was glad that his father had agreed to send him to The Escalante School, and without a big argument with his mother. The thought that his mother wanted him away from the house never occurred to him. He was just content to know he would no longer have to live where nobody talked to him.

The following day, Tommy went to school to tell Miss Anson the good news and to say good-bye to her.

"That is excellent, Tommy. I have heard about Escalante and they have an amazing philosophy. I am sure you will enjoy the freedom they offer. I hope you will come and visit me here when you come back for holidays."

"I will, Miss Anson. I will always appreciate your friendship and when you let me stay at your house the night I ran away. Who knows where I might be right now if you had not been there to help?"

"Did you see their ceramic studio?" She asked.

"No, and I didn't ask."

"I understand that they have a full ceramic studio with both an electric and a gas kiln. I met one of their faculty members at an art show a couple of years ago and he told me all about their equipment. His name is

Harold Cooper. I think he is still there. I think you will like him because he also does sculpture besides pottery."

"I will tell him that you are my ceramics teacher," Tommy said. "Mister Moser, the head man there told my mother and me that they don't teach, they motivate students to learn."

"Harold explained all that to me and I must agree. Remember how I showed you how that chunk of clay acted when you pushed it into different shapes?"

"That was great. Then you left me alone to make what I wanted to from that chunk. I hope your friend Harold is still there."

The children in her class began wandering in before the bell rang. Clara Anson gave Tommy a hug good-bye and watched him go out of the classroom door into the hall. She smiled and was happy with the good news that Tommy would now escape the parents that probably should never have had a child. She greeted her class more enthusiastically than usual that morning.

Blanche took Tommy on a shopping spree to replace worn out and outgrown winter clothes. The school pamphlet supplied her with ideas of what to purchase with regard to the seasons. She paid a lot of attention to selecting felt-lined boots to keep his feet warm while working outside doing snow removal from the pathways and sidewalks on the campus.

In spite of the short notice, Blanche scurried around getting Tommy's "school clothes" together and packed in a canvas duffel bag she had once ordered from L.L. Bean when Jason had promised a Caribbean Cruise, but cancelled a week before boarding. His bank had been threatened by a major withdrawal.

Sunday noon was Blanche's departure time. She got Tommy out of his room, and tossed the duffle bag into the back of the Town and Country. Jason had not returned from Winged Foot so she started the car and headed for Newburgh. Neither Blanche nor Tommy spoke as she drove along, glad that there was not much traffic to deal with. She looked over at her son and the thought passed through her mind that she would leave quickly after arriving at the school so that he would have time to get settled in to his new surroundings. Tommy kept looking out of the passenger side window as he usually did. His thoughts were about the clearing, his favorite spot, and that he hoped nobody would go there to disturb Ralph's grave.

Blanche pulled in to the parking area at the office building. Before she or Tommy left the car, George Moser came out of the door to the building and walked over to Blanche's window.

"Good afternoon, Missus Holmes," he said leaning over to face Blanche through the driver's side open window. "If you drive up this road," he said pointing with his left hand, "you will come to a long white building with brown trim and shutters. That is the boy's quarters. You can leave Tommy there with his belongings. One of the boys there will show him around and he can choose an available room in which to move."

"Thank you, Mister Moser," she said. "Should Tommy need anything that I have forgotten, please have him call me."

"We try to encourage our students to take care and solve their own issues without relying on parental assistance," Moser said, and turned around to go back to his office.

Blanche drove Tommy to the living quarters, and left him at the entrance with his duffel bag.

"Tommy, I hope you will like it here," she said through the open window on the passenger's side of the Town and Country.

Just as she started driving away, the door to the living quarters opened and a man came out and spoke to Tommy.

"Hi there," he said. "You must be Tommy Holmes. I am Harold Cooper. Clara Anson, your teacher told me to expect you. I saw your mother drive up and leave you off. I came out to welcome you to Escalante and give you a hand with your luggage."

"Miss Anson told me about you. You are the one that is interested in ceramics like I am," Tommy said. "I said good-bye to Miss Anson last week."

Yes, she told me when she called to tell me about you starting here. I have been keeping a lookout for you."

Cooper picked up the duffel bag and led the way into the building. He walked in front of Tommy down a central hallway onto which individual rooms opened. About thirty feet down the hallway, Cooper stopped, turned to the right and opened the door to the room with the numbers 1001 painted on it. Tommy followed Cooper into the room.

"Here's where you sleep and as you can see, there is a desk for study if here is where you choose to study. Most students find the large activity room in the building next to this one a better place because they can get together with others for discussions."

Tommy reached over to the duffel bag that Cooper had put on the bed. He opened the top and began taking the clothes out.

"I'll let you get settled. When you are ready for something to eat, go back down the hallway to the last room on the right and knock. I'll take you to the dining hall."

"Thanks, Mister Cooper. Thanks for meeting me and showing me to my room," Tommy said.

"We are pretty informal here, so just call me Harold or Hal, Cooper said.

Tommy looked up toward Cooper. "Thanks, Hal."

Tommy felt good. He had already met someone he liked. He also thought it was nice that Miss Anson had called Hal about him coming to Escalante.

The dining area was a combination kitchen, cafeteria-style counter and twenty round tables with six chairs each. The room was a third occupied when Cooper and Tommy entered. Cooper led Tommy to the beginning of the line where they picked up plates and silverware. Cooper showed Tommy what was what, and when they had filled their plates he went to one of the tables where two students were eating and conversing. They sat down and Cooper introduced Tommy to the two students that were older than Tommy, but they showed hospitality toward him in spite of his young age. They called Cooper "Hal".

Hal had made sure he had told Tommy to take only as much food as he could eat because waste was frowned upon at Escalante. As they dined and talked, Tommy asked questions about how the work was assigned because he saw students working in the dining room carrying food to the cafeteria line and dirty dishes out to a back room where Hal said there was a mechanical dishwasher.

The two students at their table asked Tommy where he was from and what he liked to learn. He answered their questions and the answers seemed to satisfy their curiosity. Finished with their meal, Tommy and Hal went back to the sleeping quarters where they sat in the room where students went for discussions and occasional games. There were two boys intensely involved in a game of Monopoly. Tommy and Hal sat in one corner and talked back and forth about Clara Anson and ceramics. Hal told Tommy that Clara had told him about Ralph and how Ralph had ended up in the stream.

"I am already happier here than I was at home with my mother and father. You have probably talked to me more in a couple of hours than my father has in five years," Tommy said.

"Clara mentioned something about that problem. No wonder you talked to yourself and to Ralph. It sounds to me like there was no one else that would talk to you."

"Miss Anson talked to me a lot. I like her a lot. She seems to understand me better than anyone."

"Clara is a very understanding person. We are both lucky to know her," Hal said.

"Who were those two boys that were sitting at our table?" Tommy asked.

"They are cousins from Jamaica. The darker of the two is Charlie Rosas. The other boy with oriental features is Tack Sing."

"They look too different to be cousins," Tommy said.

Races are not given as much thought in Jamaica as they are here. There are many families made up of mixed races.. I have found those two quite interesting, especially when I get them talking about what it is like to live on an island like Jamaica.

Hal and Tommy talked until it was time for bed. Tommy welcomed the chance to tell Hall about what his home life was like in addition to describing the activities he enjoyed most. The following morning, Hal accompanied Tommy to the Head of School's office after the Monday morning meeting that was held each week so that any questions or problems could be aired and discussion would start in order to solve whatever the situations might be. Tommy, looking back at the almost total lack of communication in his family, thought that such an event was a helpful occasion for everyone.

George Moser spent a half hour explaining general aspects of Escalante to Tommy and told him that Hal would be his mentor to answer any specific questions that Tommy might have that Moser had not covered.

After the chat with Moser, Hal suggested that they get acquainted with the ceramics workshop so that Tommy could discover what equipment was there and all the other details about what Escalante expected as far as the use of equipment and supplies. Hal explained that there were seven students that had interests of varying degrees in ceramics and told Tommy that he would have no problem working on the potter's wheels or firing his creations in the two kilns. Hal also showed Tommy some of the items he had been working on. Tommy was impressed at Hal's fine workmanship.

"I wish I had been as good as you are when I made Ralph," Tommy said.

"But, look what happened to Ralph. Now you can practice and become better with your efforts. And, you won't have to fear that someone will destroy what you have created."

"I already like it here," Tommy said, and smiled.

"Good," Hal said, and patted Tommy on his right shoulder. "We should probably talk about what other avenues you would like to travel on while you are here. There are other subjects that you may not have a great deal of interest in, but you might consider them anyway."

"I love reading, but not everything. I liked a couple of Will James' books and a few other authors. I also am interested in writing. I guess I get that from Will James' stories."

"Writing sounds like an interest to explore well. I will take you to Joe Eager, and you can talk about writing with him. Joe has written twenty books and goodness knows how many short stories. I am sure you will find Joe interesting to talk with as well as studying writing with. He has an office over in the Language complex beyond the dining hall."

"What else do you mean about other subjects to study?" Tommy asked.

"Writing is one and you have already spoken for that. You should consider math in order to figure all sorts of things."

"I don't like math," Tommy said.

"You don't have to like math, but you might try learning some of the so-called essentials like addition, subtraction, multiplication and division. I remember when I was forced to take algebra and I hated every minute, mainly because I was forced to take it. I don't like being forced to do anything. However, math is essential when preparing glazes for ceramics. You might keep that in mind."

"All right, I will try to study math, but I already know how to add.

Hal took Tommy to Joe Eager's office and introduced him.

"Joe, Tommy is interested in writing. I told him you're the one to talk with. I'll leave him here with you while I go trim some pots that I know are ready."

"Thanks, Hal. I have been wondering when I would have a new writer show up," Eager said.

Hal left for the ceramics workshop. Joe and Tommy began talking about writing.

"What makes you want to be a writer, Tommy?"

"I like the way Will James writes his books. He makes me feel like I am with him in a corral or on a horse."

"James is definitely a good writer. I have read some of his work. He tells it like it is and doesn't use anything fancy to tell it. Let me explain the way I take on students that want to learn about writing. I am in this office most of the time. I do not schedule my students or myself. I suggest writing projects and you can do them on your own time. Then, when you think you have finished, stop by here and I will read what you have written, then tell you what I think. You may want to change something or you may think I am full of baloney. At any rate, by the time you have been writing for a while, I will suggest places that might accept what you have done for publication. Depending on how well you learn, that might take a few months or a few years."

"That sounds good to me. I need to start from the beginning," Tommy said.

"I am glad you realize that," Eager said. "A lot of boys think they are already writers when they first sit down here in my office. I know I am a writer, but I am still practicing and striving to write better all the time."

"Hal told me you have written twenty books and lots of short stories."

"But, I have been writing for quite a long time," Eager said. "Let's get started by me telling you what I think writing is all about."

Tommy sat listening to Joe Eager talk about writing until they both decided that it was time to have lunch. They went to the dining hall and joined Hal at one of the tables. Tommy enjoyed listening to the two teachers, and the more he became acquainted with them the more he was glad that his parents had sent him off to Escalante, even though he knew their purpose was to get him out of their way. At one point in the conversation, Tommy realized that he had not thought about Ralph and his father smashing his friend in the stream all day. That afternoon, Joe Eager gave Tommy a project to work on that Joe said would give him practice with opening a story and grabbing the reader. Joe called it "The Hook".

The week passed quickly for Tommy. He had gotten settled in all the way around and was working on things he enjoyed doing. Hal had started him on making some bowls. By the time he had thrown a dozen he had become used to the wheel and wondered why Miss Anson did not use the potter's wheel more often. He asked Hal about that.

"Clara enjoys hand building more than throwing," Hal said. "Once you get good at the wheel, I will show you some of the things about hand building that will be useful to you when you do a sculpture."

Tommy's first week at The Escalante School went well. He had become acquainted with several teachers and fellow students ranging from his own age to twenty years old. Several of the older students were also instructors in various subjects. Tommy liked the way The Escalante School was organized, yet maintained more or less a unique freedom. He was curious about the sister school, Mujeres del Mundo. Back home his school had both boys and girls in the same classes.

Fall arrived with an abundance of color and a definite chill in the air. Tommy looked forward to the first snow, hoping that enough would fall so that he could make snowmen. A week after Thanksgiving that first storm arrived and left a foot of white puffy snow on the ground. Tommy had a lot of fun making several snowmen before going around to the different men who were giving him ideas about various subjects. Tommy asked about Thanksgiving and what might be in store for the holiday. Hal told him that The Escalante School did not celebrate holidays because there was such a variety of religions and backgrounds at the school. Hal also told him that the same was true for Mujeres del Mundo. Tommy shrugged his shoulders.

"I am glad there are no holidays here so I can stay and not have to go home to watch everyone eat and drink too much."

Another storm added six inches of snow to the previous layer. Some of the boys took their skis and climbed the hill at the end of the school property. Tommy watched from afar, but had no desire to have skis. Winter melted into spring. Tommy had made a few friends and had joined in several discussions from time to time. He spent a lot of time in the ceramics workshop, but also began writing short stories. He also took advantage of the books in the school library, and read some of the works of several authors besides Will James. He liked "Old Man and The Sea", by Hemingway more than the rest of that author's work. He inquired of Joe Eager what he would recommend for adventure stories because he yearned for adventure. Tommy had read a substantial part of the list Eager had given him. Tommy had also begun to write a few short stories, but mostly just their beginnings and parts containing dialogue.

One weekend, after he had been at the school for two months, Hal offered him a ride home because Hal was going to visit Clara Anson. Tommy looked forward to seeing her, but he was not sure he was ready to visit his parents. He rarely thought about them after being away for so long a time. He thought about Ralph and sometimes walked out into the woods and talked with him.

He enjoyed seeing Miss Anson, but when he got to the old farmhouse he hesitated before going inside. Neither parent was at home, but he had a nice chat with Bertha who welcomed him with loving hugs as if he was her own son. Tommy told Bertha about all the things he had been doing and how much he liked the school and the people there. He was still in the kitchen when his mother drove in and came into the house. She was surprised to see Tommy and stood looking at him as if he was some sort of ghost.

"Good heavens, what are you doing home?" she asked.

"Hal Cooper gave me a ride. He came to see Miss Anson. I will be going back to school tomorrow morning," Tommy said.

"It is too bad that your father had to go to Chicago on bank business," Blanche said. "He will be upset that he missed you."

Tommy did not answer. The only thing that went through his mind was that his father would probably give a sigh of relief that he had not been here while he was home on the visit.

"Come into the living room and tell me all about school," Blanche said, and started down the hallway.

Tommy followed, although he wished he had just gone up to his room when she took a glass from the bar and filled it with single malt Scotch. Tommy had no idea what single malt was, but he knew that after a few drinks of it his mother and father no longer made much sense when they talked. He stood in the living room for a few minutes before excusing himself to use the bathroom. Tommy went to his room. He reclined on his bed until he was sure that his mother had finished her supper before returning to the kitchen where Bertha filled a bowl full of beef stew for him. Not wanting to see his mother, he ate his supper in the kitchen and talked with Bertha about all that he was doing at The Escalante School. Escaping to his room for the night, Tommy hoped his mother wouldn't decide to seek him out for a drunken conversation.

Tommy hurried through his breakfast the following morning before his mother awakened, said good-bye to Bertha, and hurried out of the house to walk to the clearing. Stopping at Ralph's grave, Tommy looked down at the rocks that covered the spot that was special to him. He wiped the tears that eased out from his eyes.

"Ralph, I miss you a lot. I think about you every day, at least once. I know you can't talk back with me anymore, but I do talk to you when I am alone. I am trying to figure out where I want to be. I have this feeling of not belonging both at the old farmhouse and at The Escalante School. I wish I could feel differently about the school, but I know I would rather be somewhere else. I just don't know where that is."

***

For Tommy, the years seemed to vanish into some sort of vacuum. Life at The Escalante School became more or less routine. However, In spite of Hal Cooper trying to have him work on throwing pots on the potter's wheel, Tommy cared only for sculpturing. Hal accepted his stubbornness especially when he saw Tommy's various sculptures that showed a different sort of imagination than Hal was used to seeing by students and in his own creations.

When he turned sixteen, Tommy was spending less time in the ceramics studio and more time reading or writing stories. It was not because he was losing interest in sculpting, it was because he wanted to spend time on other things in order to try and grasp what "made the world go round", as he once had read.

He also spent time thinking about girls, and one girl in particular. Julie Bronson had been at Mujeres del Mundo since she was ten years old. Tommy didn't pay much attention to her or other girls at that school when the two schools got together for dances and other social activities until he found himself attracted to them as they, too, grew older and began looking more like women than flat-chested young girls.

For several years he did not attend the dances but when he finally decided to go, he found it enjoyable. Once he met and danced with Julie Bronson, he made sure he didn't miss a dance with Mujeres del Mundo.

It was during the second time after they had met that Julie had pulled him in closer as they danced to a slow piece of music. He felt her roundness and almost panicked. Julie had a strong hold on him around his waist.

"Tommy Holmes, I like the way you dance, and I like dancing close to you," she said.

Tommy was speechless. He was at a complete loss for words because of his surprise at Julie's forward approach. In spite of feeling his manhood grow and knowing that she could not help but feel him, he continued dancing until the song was over. He stopped dancing, but kept her in his arms.

"That was a nice dance," he said. "You are a good dancer."

She leaned into him and whispered in his ear.

"You got me all excited," she said. "I never felt that way with other boys."

"I must admit the same. I hope they put another slow song on the player so we can do that again," Tommy said.

"I like the slow dances, too. The music fits my mood better than the fast rock and roll songs."

They continued dancing and carrying on a conversation by leaning closer toward each other and whispering. At the end of the session, they sat at a small table for two in the foyer of the recreation hall.

Look at all those old biddies with their eagle eyes watching all the girls to make sure none of us slipped outside with a boy," Julie said.

"There are three of our so-called mentors that must be here to check out the boys. Maybe we should head for a door to the outside and run away," Tommy said, and smiled.

"Believe me, there are many times when I think about doing just that. I feel like I am in some sort of prison here at Mujeres del Mundo. My parents sent me here so that I would grow up to be a 'Lady' and not some wild animal. Why did you get sent to The Escalante?"

"I suppose for much the same reason that you were sent here. I have been at Escalante since I was seven-years old. I guess that had I not been sent here, I would have run away from home long ago. My parents don't talk to me and they drink every night to the point where they have trouble talking and sometimes walking. I talked to my friend, Ralph."

Tommy continued telling Julie all about Ralph and how his father had smashed Ralph on the boulders in the stream.

"Wow, that is quite a story, Tom. Do you mind if I call you Tom?"

"I like the sound of Tom better than Tommy. Tommy makes me feel like I am still seven-years old."

"Well, I must say, my father and mother don't drink much, but they are so religious that they squeak."

"What do you mean, squeak?"

"It seems to me that all they talk about is the Bible and Jesus, or Jesus and the Bible. Before they sent me off to this place, I had to listen to my father read from the Bible every evening after supper. I was so bored that I fell asleep most of the time. In fact I would fall asleep as he was reading and when I woke up he was still reading, but I had not heard anything while I slept. He caught me a couple of times and chewed me out big time and told me I would grow up to be a heretic if I didn't listen to 'God's Word'. I am damn sure lucky they thought this school would straighten me out. Otherwise they were thinking about sending me to some holy-roller school. They chose this place because they didn't want me to tarnish their reputation as religious zealots at the holy-roller school. Here, with these girls from all over the world I learned quickly that all that crap my parents were trying to feed me is total bullshit."

"My father has a Wall Street bank and I think he is more married to his bank than he is to my mother. His business is about all he thinks about even when he is home and drinking his single malt Scotch. I have read about drinking alcohol and what that can do to a person. I wonder how long he will have a functioning liver."

"Tom, it sounds like we both have crazy parents. But, they seem like opposites. My mother and father would both birth jaguars if I ever drank alcohol in front of them. Like I said, they squeak."

Tommy looked up and saw that the girls and boys had started to leave the recreation hall. The female teachers of the school herded the girls and the boys were walking out to the buses to return to The Escalante. Tommy took Julie's hand and they rose from the chairs at the table. Most of the crowd had left. Charlie Rosas walked by and said, "Hello, Julie."

"Hi, Charlie," she replied. "Nice seeing you."

Tommy and Julie stopped outside of the entrance and stood facing one another.

"I have never done this before and I don't give a damn who sees me, but I am going to kiss you goodnight," Tommy said.

He put his arm around her waist and pulled her in close to him. For a moment he looked into her eyes and saw her happiness. Then he kissed her like he had seen men kiss women in the movies. After they separated he looked around to see if anyone had seen them. The front entrance was empty.

"I had better get my butt into the bus," he said.

"Good night, Tom. You are really special," Julie said, and quickly stepped to him and kissed him again.

"I'll see you at the dance next month," Tommy said.

"I wish it could be sooner, Tom," Julie said, right after Tommy turned away to get to the bus.

He heard her, and turned back as he walked. "Me, too," he said, and threw her a kiss with his right hand.

The following weekend Hal gave him a ride home as he did at least once a month when he visited Clara Anson. Tommy spent most of his at home weekends in the clearing, either talking with Ralph or reading books that he brought with him. He did see his parents occasionally, but those moments were short at best. They had not changed their habit of "Happy Times" so Tommy did his best to avoid them during that time of day. As he grew into adolescence the drinking habits of Jason and Blanche bothered him less and less. He accepted that they were determined to continue drinking so all he had to do was avoid them when that time of day arrived.

Jason was still far too involved with his bank to be able to sit down and have any sort of father/son conversation with Tommy. This was also something that Tommy had come to accept even though he was not pleased with the situation. However, by accepting his father's attitudes, Tommy was able to make his own decisions and have his own thoughts about what he wanted to do, not only at The Escalante School, but also in the future. At times when they were taking breaks from their work in the ceramic studio he and Hal chatted about different lifestyles.

He never mentioned Julie Bronson to his father or mother, but Hal had seen them dancing and asked Tommy who the girl was.

"Her name is Julie Branson," Tommy said. "Why do you ask?"

"I am just curious," Hal said. "But when I watched you two dance I could see that I should talk to you about those girls at Mujeres del Mundo."

"They are just girls, aren't they?" Tommy asked.

"They are girls, all right, but they are cooped up in that school just as you are cooped up in this school. When they have opportunities to be with you boys, they can become a bit lustful."

"What do you mean, lustful?"

"Let me say that they might want more from you than you should give, considering your and their situations. After all, you are still in what most call high school. You have a lot of living ahead of you. I know very well that in spite of all the rules against Escalante boys meeting up with Mujeres del Mundo girls except for dances, that is bound to happen. And, I might add, that boys can be even more lustful than girls at times.

So, when you meet Julie in the woods between the two schools and decide to take off your clothes and experiment with your bodies, remember that this can make babies. And, at your stage and age, I don't think you need to have a baby to support and care for when you haven't finished your education."

"Suppose what you are saying happens. I know how she made me feel just dancing with her. I kissed her and I felt a stronger pull toward her."

"I am glad we are having this talk. Obviously your father has never talked to you about girls and sex, and I think you need to know what can happen when you and Julie are out in the woods without your clothes."

Hal reached into his pocket, took out a small package wrapped in cellophane and handed it to Tommy.

"These are condoms. Do you know what they are for?"

"Yes, a couple of the guys in the sleeping quarters were playing with them, blowing them up like balloons. But they also told everyone watching what they were for and that they used them a lot with their girl friends."

Good," Hal said. "I am glad you know what they are. Just don't forget to use them. You don't need to become a father at sixteen."

After his conversation with Hal, Tommy went to his sleeping quarters and put the package of condoms in the dresser drawer. He came close to talking with Ralph to tell him about Julie Bronson, but decided to return to the ceramics studio instead. He had been working on a sculpture that included wood, clay and copper, and he wanted to add the copper according to the plan he had thought about. Hal told him that he was going to see

Clara over the weekend and he wanted to know if Tommy wanted a ride home.

"That will be fine," Tommy said. "I think I would enjoy talking with Bertha."

"She certainly seems to be a good one to be friends with," Hal said.

"Bertha is the greatest," Tommy said. "I don't think I would want to go home if it wasn't for Bertha being there."

The ride to the old farmhouse on Saturday morning was pleasant. Hal didn't say much, but Tommy talked a lot about Julie Bronson and how he enjoyed dancing with her, but on the other hand he wondered why she seemed to like him as much as she said she did. He couldn't understand how, in the time they had spent dancing, they could have become as close as he thought they were. They had talked some, but not much.

Arriving at the old farmhouse, Tommy hurried into the kitchen and found Bertha mixing something in a large bowl She dropped the spoon and gave him a long hug. "Tommy, boy, you is getting' 'most too big ta hug. I reckons I is gonna hafta grow my arms longa."

"Good to see you, Bertha. I've got lots to tell you," Tommy said.

"Well sit ya down and tell me all," she said.

Tommy sat on the metal highstool that was against the kitchen wall and began to tell Bertha all about Julie and the dance. He told her about kissing Julie and what Julie had said about getting together at the next dance. Bertha stood by her worktable and listened. When Tommy had finished talking, Bertha looked him in the eye.

"Tommy, ma boy, you is gettin' growed up and ya needs ta be ceerful. Sum a dem gals you be seein' might git ya in trouble. I knows ya think dem soft an cuddly, but be ceerful or you might end up makin' a baby. Ya doan needs that."

"I know what you're sayin', Bertha, and I appreciate your concern, but I know all about that stuff. I promise I'll be careful.

They talked for a while until Tommy excused himself to go out to the clearing to talk to Ralph. Bertha had told him that his parents had gone out of town on some trip. She couldn't remember exactly to where they had gone. Tommy was happy to hear about their absence so he would not have to talk to either one. He had a long talk with Ralph. He was glad that Ralph understood all the things he told him about Julie Bronson. But one aspect bothered him. He had told Ralph that he knew that Julie and he were going to "do it", as Tommy called having sex and he had never done that before and was not sure how to go about it.

"You'll figure that all out when the time comes," Ralph said.

"How do you know?" Tommy asked.

"I just know even though you didn't put one of those things on me when you put me together."

"I now wish I had thought of that so you could tell me what to expect."

"But, think back," Ralph said. "Your father tossed me onto the boulders of the stream before those thoughts ever passed through my mind."

Tommy laughed, then said good-bye to Ralph before returning to the old farmhouse and going into the kitchen to tell Bertha that he was going back to The Escalante School.

The large recreation hall at The Escalante was the site of the monthly dance. Tommy got there early, hoping to find Julie before the dance began. He had made sure to put the package of condoms in his pants pocket before leaving his room. As he stood at the entrance to the recreation hall waiting for the bus from Mujeres del Mundo to arrive, he reached into his pocket to make sure he had not forgotten the package. Thoughts about using them swam through his mind as he stood for a while, and then paced back and forth on the sidewalk in front of the building.

As the bus made its way toward the recreation hall, Tommy kept his eyes on it all the way. He felt himself taking a deep breath as the bus stopped and its door creaked open, spilling out the laughing crowd of girls. He spotted Julie at the same time she saw him. He stood still as she skipped over to give him a short hug and a kiss.

"Hi," Tommy said. "I am happy to see you."

"Me, too," Julie said, and they went into the hall to find chairs to sit upon before the music started.

"I have been thinking about you every day," Julie said, after they had sat down. "It has seemed like a year since that last dance."

"It sure has. I am just happy that you are finally here."

"Before the music starts making it impossible to talk, I want to make a date with you for some day next week," Julie said.

"What do you mean, a date for next week? The next dance is a month away," Tommy said.

"I know that,Tom. But I want to be with you before that. There is a path that goes through the thick grove of trees between the schools and an old shack about halfway through. Can you sneak away from this place on Wednesday afternoon?"

"I suppose so," Tommy said.

"Then let's meet at that old shack so we can get to know each other better than we can at these horrible dances where the teachers are always watching us to make sure we are behaving according to their rules."

The music from the sound system began with a gentle song. They rose from their chairs and joined the rest of the young people. Tommy put his right arm around Julie's waist and took her left hand in his. He leaned toward her and whispered in her ear.

"Wednesday's a date at the old shack. How far is it from here?"

"Probably two miles," Julie whispered back.

She pulled him closer to her and he felt her firm breasts on his chest. He sensed his manhood changing its mood, but did nothing to hide it from her. They continued dancing close until the music stopped. The next song to come from the sound system was a lively rock and roll piece that came as a surprise. Tommy wondered if some faculty member was running the sound system and had seen Julie and him dancing so close that only their clothes separated them.

They danced with one another for the entire evening. Tommy was happy that no boys tried to cut in. He and Julie had furtive conversations as they danced to the variety of songs that had been chosen by the faculty member in charge. Tommy caught a glimpse of Hal watching Julie and him as they danced, but could not figure out what he was thinking. Tommy just felt a bit uneasy that Hal didn't seem to watch any other couple on the dance floor. When the sound system stopped after the last song, which was a slow instrumental that brought the dancing couples close together, Tommy and Julie made their way quickly to an alcove between two of the buildings where they could spend a few moments alone before she had to board the bus to return to Mujeres del Mundo.

"I am looking forward to Wednesday," Julie said, as they held each other closely.

"That will be nice," Tommy said. "I hope I can get away from here without anyone seeing me go into the woods."

"Just look like you are studying trees for a botany project," Julie suggested.

"That would be great if I was interested in botany, but I have never expressed such an interest. I think that the only one I have to worry about seeing me is my ceramics teacher. He was watching us dance throughout the entire evening."

"Don't worry about it, just walk away and into the woods. I'll bet nobody will notice you. That's what I am going to do when I leave for our date together."

"I think we had better get you to the bus," Tommy said. "It would not be good to have you punished for missing that ride back to your school."

"All right, but give me your hand," she said.

Tommy looked downward as Julie took his right hand and put it onto her left breast.

"That really feels good," Tommy said.

"That is just something for you to look forward to on Wednesday when it will be bare," Julie said, and giggled.

They broke away and walked to where the bus waited for the girls to get aboard and take their seats. There were just two girls that arrived after Julie had entered and sat down. Tommy walked back to his room and sat on his bed. His thoughts centered on the feel of Julie's breast through her blouse and what she had said about Wednesday.

His visions of Julie kept Tommy from making any progress on the sculpture he had been working on. Giving up on his attempt to create the form that he had had in mind when he started, he began taking walks around the school property. Twice, he walked near the woods and found the path he would take to meet Julie on Wednesday. As he stopped to look at the path the second time, he wondered why he had not explored the woods before in all the years he had been at The Escalante School. After pondering the question for at least a half an hour he concluded that before he met Julie he had been too concentrated on his sculpturing and writing to wonder about the woods that separated the two schools.

Tommy was uneasy as he sat with Hal Cooper at Tuesday evening's supper. Their conversation was stilted, and Tommy ate as quickly as he could so he could leave the dining room and return to his room. Hal had gotten used to Tommy's various changing moods so his behavior at supper did not surprise him.

Back in his room, Tommy tried to work on writing the short story he had started, but found that he was unable to concentrate on what he was trying to write. He gave up and went outside for a walk around the campus that took him to where the path through the woods began. He stopped and looked at the opening, wondering what would happen between Julie and him the following day on their date. He pondered walking down the path to where she said there was an abandoned shack, but his hesitation led to his turning around and returning to his room. He finally settled down to reading a novel by Hemingway that he had started two days before. He had begun to like "The Sun Also Rises", but he still preferred "Old Man and the Sea" over any of the other works of Hemingway that he had read or perused enough to be able to pass a partial judgment. After an hour of reading, the book fell from his grip, and he fell asleep on the bed fully clothed. Nothing interrupted his sleep until he heard someone's door slam. That happened after sunrise. As he regained consciousness he remembered his date with Julie. Swinging his legs around so that he sat on the bed, he went over in his mind what he needed to accomplish before slipping away on the trail through the woods to meet Julie at the old abandoned shack. He wished he was in his clearing by the stream and talking with Ralph instead of trying to think of what was ahead that day. He looked forward to seeing Julie and holding her like he did at the dances. Other than that he had neither thoughts nor expectations. He had never been on a "date" before and hadn't a clue what might be in store for him.

After showering and taking care of other personal chores, he put on clean clothes and went to the dining room for breakfast even though he did not feel any hunger, only excitement and wonder. Looking around the room, he sat down at a table, glad that Hal was not there. He wanted to be alone, and rushed through his breakfast. As he rose from the table he hesitated. The thought came to him that his date with Julie was for the afternoon, not for morning as he had been thinking since he awakened to the door slamming. He walked outside enjoying the spring breeze that had started while he was eating his breakfast. He wished he could get in touch with Julie so that he could move their date to morning instead of afternoon because he had no ideas on how to pass the time as he waited to start down the path through the woods. After pacing around for a few minutes, he went back to his room and continued reading "The Sun Also Rises". He read a few pages, put the book down on the table by his bed and began talking with Ralph.

"Ralph, I am so nervous I'm shaking. Is this what girls do to you?"

"You just need to get used to being around girls," Ralph said as Tommy stood up and began to walk in a small circle in the middle of his room.

Tommy stepped over to his desk, opened the top drawer, took the package of condoms out and put it in the front pocket of his Levis.

"It is early, but I might as well wait out there as being here all nervous like a scared cat. Ralph, wish me luck on this date with Julie Bronson. I hope she knows what to do, because I have never done it before."

Tommy left the building, walked as aimlessly as he could to the path that opened out of the woods and began his walk to meet Julie. After a hundred yards he began to calm down and felt good to be walking toward the old shack that was the meeting place Julie had designated. Inside he still had feelings of wonder about what he knew would happen just by the way she had talked about meeting in the woods where they could be alone and not bothered by either school. He remembered how Julie's body felt as he had pulled her against his when he had kissed her after the last dance. He wondered what she would do when they met by the old shack in the woods. He patted the outside of his Levis pocket thinking that whatever might happen he was prepared, thanks to Hal Cooper.

He thought back to some of the conversations he had been privy to when groups of the boys at Escalante gathered in the reading room and told about their various exploits with girls. He never spoke during these sessions, because he felt that he was the only one there that had never been with a girl. However, some of the stories told by a couple of the boys seemed like tall tales, thought up to impress the groups. As he walked along he thought that he would never tell anyone about what might happen between him and Julie Bronson. As he thought about her, he felt his body tingle with excitement and desire. He quickened his pace for a moment, then, slackened it when he remembered that he was going to be early for the date. He wondered how long he would have to wait for her to show up at the old shack. He stopped walking, startled by a squirrel racing across the path in front of him. He watched as the squirrel leaped onto the trunk of a tall oak tree and climbed rapidly upward circling the trunk as it went. It finally chose a branch to rest upon as it took an acorn from it mouth and cracked the shell. Tommy continued looking at the squirrel as it dug out the nutty part to eat as it sat there looking around as if it owned the woods. Then Tommy realized that the squirrel was looking around in case some danger would appear within its territory.

As he walked along the path, Tommy looked into the woods to see if there was any other wildlife. The only other creatures were the birds that seemed eager to talk with one another with their various languages.

The path curved to the left so that Tommy could not see what might be ahead, but suddenly the gray, weathered logs of what Julie had called “the old shack” came into view. He stopped for a moment to study the structure from a hundred yards away before proceeding. He could not understand why Julie had called the building an “old shack” because from where he stood looking at it, the “old shack” appeared to be a small, but substantially built cabin. He commenced walking toward it again, and soon saw a door in the center of the wall facing the path. As he approached closer, the door looked like it had been closed for a long time. He was still looking at the cabin’s door when Julie jumped out from behind the far wall of the cabin and stood naked in front of him. Surprised to the point of coming close to falling over, Tommy stood with his eyes glued to her bare breasts and through his open mouth, he took a deep breath and exhaled it immediately.

With one exception, Tommy had never seen a naked woman before. Before he had gone to the Escalante School he had seen his mother emerge from her bathroom naked as she was heading for her bedroom. She had quickly wrapped a towel around herself. Tommy had looked away the moment he had seen her.

The naked Julie Bronson was nothing like Blanche Holmes. Julie’s young body had no wrinkles, nothing sagged, and as he glanced quickly to her face he saw an impish smile that came close to making him laugh. But, he looked away and again focused on her breasts. He had a tremendous desire to jump over the ten feet separating them to caress her breasts that blended from her shoulders and chest in a sublime symmetry. They were not exactly equal in size, but their shapes matched as the femininity of their curvature held him breathless with his mouth open and no words able to escape. Her nipples were dark pink jutting proudly from their areolae. He saw that they were hard and he felt a strong urge to approach them and let his lips engulf them as his tongue tasted their beauty.

"I knew you'd be early," Julie said. "Come here to me, Tom. I want you close. I want to take off your clothes so that I can see you naked as I am."

Tommy stood as if frozen in his tracks. He could not keep his eyes from digesting every inch of Julie Branson.

"We didn't come here to stand gawking at each other," she said, and clapped her hands.

The sound of Julie's hands clapping together jolted Tommy out of his trance. He stepped over to her. She took his right hand and led him to the rear of the cabin where he saw two blankets spread out on what had once been a patch of grass. He stood with his hands covering her breasts as she unbuttoned his shirt, took it off, and tossed it on the grass. His fingers danced over her breasts. Without reaching down, he shoved his sandals from his feet with his toes. In a short moment she had undone his belt, unbuttoned the fly in his Levis and let them drop to the ground. He kept his hands on her breasts as she shoved his undershorts down to his ankles. He stepped out of the garment without letting his hands leave her breasts. His hardened manhood did not embarrass him in the least. That was one thing he had been thinking of every day as he waited for this date.

"Julie," he said, finally able to speak. "I had no idea a woman could be as beautiful as you are."

"Thank you, Tom. I like hearing that from you. You are quite handsome, yourself."

She took his hand and as she dropped down to the blankets, she pulled him with her. They became entwined at once as their lips joined in a passionate kiss that made Julie arch her back. Then, with her arms around him, she pulled him as close as possible.

"I really don't know much about this," he said.

"Don't worry about a thing. Everything will work out fine. I will lead you to water and you can drink."

"That sounds good, but there is one thing I have to do before this happens, so I had better do it right now," Tommy said, and leaned away from Julie so that he could reach his Levis. He reached into the right hand pocket and took out the package of condoms. Undoing the wrapping, he took one in his hand and turned back to where Julie waited. She said nothing about what she was witnessing and Tommy went about putting it onto his stiffened manhood. He had a fleeting thought that Hal Cooper would be proud of him for remembering what to do.

Their foreplay increased until Julie took Tommy's manhood in her hands and directed it into her moist womb.

"Now just relax and don't be in a rush," Julie said. "I need a little time, but you will know when I am ready to explode with you. It won't be long because you have already got me where I need to be."

Embracing her as he proceeded, Tommy thought about how wonderful her beautiful breasts felt against his chest.

As she had promised, Julie began her climax shortly. Tommy could feel what was happening inside as well as outside as she began thrusting upward as if she was trying to swallow him with her womb. He heard her low sounding groans of pleasure as her arms tightened around him. It was time to experience what she had called their "explosion".

Tommy remained on top of Julie for a short while. Neither spoke until he had rolled off and onto his side when his wilted manhood slipped out.

"What do you mean that you have never done this before?" Julie asked. "You are a perfect lover. Just perfect."

"I am glad you think so," Tommy said. "It must be you that makes me perfect."

He kept his hands moving around and over her breasts.

"I wish I had a cleavage like some of the girls at school," she said.

"I like you just the way you are. A cleavage would hide the beauty of your beautiful feminine curves and deny your breasts their individuality."

"You sure have a way with words describing my breasts for someone who is experiencing his first love-making," she said, and kissed him on his lips. Then she pulled his head down to her breasts.

"Now, taste these, Tom Holmes. They are your reward for being a perfect lover."

Tommy did not hesitate to enjoy her "perfect breasts". He also ran his fingers over her smooth solid body as she closed her eyes and soon began breathing slowly and deeply. Tommy raised himself with his left arm and saw that Julie had fallen asleep. Tommy decided that it was time for him to put on his clothes. Before reaching for his undershorts and Levis, he removed the condom, and tied an overhand knot in the open end to keep the liquid inside. Then he grabbed his Levis and put the used condom in the right front pocket. With that accomplished he went about getting his clothes on and sitting next to Julie to wait for her to wake up.

"What are you going to do with that thing?" she asked. "Are you going to take it home and wash it so you can use it again?"

Thinking that she was asleep, her voice surprised him, and he was glad that he was not facing her as he felt his face heat with embarrassment.

"I am going to send it to my father and mother to make them wonder what I am doing at The Escalante School," he said, and laughed. "I hope I didn't wake you."

He turned around and faced her.

"You are just as beautiful asleep as you are awake," he said.

"Feast your eyes one more time before I put on my clothes," she said. "Unless you want to do it again?"

"That one time will last me quite a while, Julie. I still haven't recovered."

"Someday we should try doing it all day and all night just to see how long we can last," she said.

"You had better give me a month's notice before we try anything like that," Tommy said.

“I am kidding, Tom. What we just finished was more than enough for me. You are a great lover and sent me flying really high.”

“I was flying right next to you,” he said, and smiled. He rose to his feet and gave her a hand up to help her stand. She straightened her blouse and shook out her wavy auburn hair.

“We need to meet here again soon,” she said. “How about next week, same day, same time?”

“Sounds good to me. I will look for you here just after noon.”

“All right lover boy, gimme one more kiss to feel all the way back to Las Mujeres.

Tommy took her into his arms and they shared a long kiss. Releasing her, Tommy held her by gripping her near her armpits, then moved his hands over her breasts.

“You are just plain beautiful, Julie Bronson,” He said. “ I wish I could take you back with me and we could spend the night together.”

“That would be nice,” she said. “But I have to get back to that school full of young fillies. Bye, my lover.”

Tommy waved and turned around to walk back to The Escalante School. He didn’t feel any hurry about returning so he walked slowly, wondering if he would see the squirrel again. He also thought about what he had just shared with Julie Bronson, and wondered if his parents had ever discovered such joy and pleasure. He also realized that he would never know that answer.

His mind was jammed with thoughts and images of Julie Bronson. He forgot all about the squirrel and was surprised when he reached the end of the path leading to the vast amount of green lawn that demanded constant mowing from spring to fall by the students. He went directly to his room. Once inside his sleeping quarters, Tommy felt the hunger from not having had anything to eat since breakfast. Before leaving for the dining area, he took the used condom from his Levi pocket, wrapped it in a page of newsprint from the Wall Street Journal, and tossed it into the wastebasket. He put the unused condoms back into his desk drawer.

Arriving at the cafeteria-style steam table in the dining area, Tommy helped himself to a larger amount of food than he usually ate for supper. Looking for an empty table, he saw Hal at a small table for four with a cup of coffee. He walked over and stood by his mentor.

"Mind if I join you, Hal?" Tommy asked.

Hal looked up at the mention of his name.

"Sit down, Tommy, Glad to see you."

Tommy put his tray down on the table and took a seat across from Cooper.

"It looks like you are hungry," Cooper said.

"I sure am," Tommy said. "I haven't eaten since breakfast."

Cooper looked up and smiled at Tommy.

"Where have you been, out in the woods?"

"How could you possibly know where I have been?" Tommy asked.

"For one thing, there are some leaves stuck to your Levis, and I detect an unusual smile on your face."

"Dammit, nothing around here seems to happen without you knowing it," Tommy said.

"You have to realize that I have been at Escalante for quite a few years. You get to know a lot of what goes on, especially when you know a little about the students."

Tommy finished chewing a mouthful of the cheese casserole.

"You even predicted that I would visit the woods between the two schools. Then you gave me those condoms."

"Do you need more?"

Tommy dropped his fork onto the tray, and looked at Hal sternly.

"I have two left, thank you," he said. "Do you want them back?"

Hal laughed at Tommy's humor, and took a sip of coffee.

"I've been wondering if you have seen that cabin out there along the path through the woods," Tommy said.

"I pass by that cabin a lot because I take my walks along that path. I enjoy that woods, and love watching the squirrels and birds. I often wonder about who built that old cabin and what did they use it for."

My family has a similar cabin in the Adirondacks. It was once a part of a farm that had fruit trees and a field for vegetables. My uncle took me there when I was seven. It was during the time when my parents were all upset because I was talking to Ralph. My uncle took me to that cabin to try to figure me out. I just kept talking to Ralph. My uncle told me that our family had bought that farm before the middle of the eighteen hundreds, and they built the cabin for a hunting lodge."

"Do they still use the cabin?" Hal asked.

"Nobody has used it for many years and the grasses have grown up around it. I asked my uncle why the family didn't sell it if they didn't use it. He told me that our family never sold land because land is a limited resource. There will never be any more land so it will always be valuable."

"That is interesting," Hal said. "I have read about wealthy families holding on to their land even though they have sold everything else. It makes sense because there are more and more people that occupy the land, but the area of the land never changes. Sounds to me like the wealthy are wealthy for a good reason; they know how to manage their wealth."

"We got away from what we were talking about," Tommy said. "Does Mister Moser know about everything that happens here at Escalante?"

"He doesn't concern himself with small things that happen here. He depends on me, but I am very careful what I tell him. For example, I think that knowing that you and your pretty girl friend meet each other in the woods is no business of George Moser no matter what his title at the school is. What he doesn't know about the students' personal lives doesn't hurt a bit."

"I am glad I can trust you, Hal. For some reason I don't feel the same way about Mister Moser."

"I can understand that," Hal said. "Escalante prides itself on allowing freedom, but there is a constant cloud over that. The so-called 'Fear Factor' is everywhere, even at Escalante. Moser rules by the 'Fear Factor' without realizing it. I understand all that and make sure that I always try to diminish the 'Fear Factor here.'

"I think I am understanding you, but I may need to think more about the 'Fear Factor'," Tommy said.

"I think I will spend the evening in the ceramics room. Do you want to join me there, or would you rather keep thinking about what you did in the woods?"

“You are right about the woods. I feel quite different from when I started out to go there.”

“I am sure you do,” Hal said, and got up from his chair. “By the way, I am going to visit Clara Anson on Saturday and Sunday. I can give you a ride home if you want.”

“I’ll take you up on that, Hal. It might be better to get back to my clearing by the stream than to wait around here for our next date.”

Hal and Tommy left The Escalante School by mid-morning the following Saturday. Along the way Tommy added to his supply of contraceptives. They arrived at Clara’s house where she listened to Tommy’s latest adventure with a girl friend. Later Tommy walked to the old farmhouse, and strolled down the trail to the clearing by the stream. He sat on the log as he talked to Ralph, telling him about Julie Branson, and how much fun he found with her. He went back to the house and visited with Bertha for a while before enjoying one of her special meals she always prepared for him when he came home. Bertha knew that Tommy had no desire to sit at the dining room table with his parents while they talked with garbled words about what he considered “nothing of any importance”. He escaped to his room before either parent realized that he was home for a weekend.

As he reclined on his bed thinking about Julie, he also felt happy that he would not have to tell his parents about her. Just before falling asleep for the night he determined that he would rise early the following morning and spend time in the clearing before meeting Hal for the ride back to school.

Arriving at Clara's house on Myrtle Lane, after spending the morning talking with Ralph at the clearing, he found himself listening to a long string of advice about girls that Clara felt that he needed to know. During the ride back to The Escalante School, Tommy thought over what Clara had said and began to wonder why, according to Clara Anson, girls were so different than boys,.

Tommy began writing an essay on "The Fear Factor", but got bogged down when he realized that he needed to know far more about it than he did. He asked Hal about any references that he might be aware of, but Hal could not remember any of the articles that he had read about the phenomenon. Tommy decided to postpone any further work on the subject until he knew more about it. His thoughts turned to meeting Julie at the old shack on Wednesday.

The day arrived and Tommy quickened his pace as he approached the curve in the trail nearing the old shack in the woods. He kept his eyes peeled to see if Julie had arrived.

Suddenly he saw some colors through the green leaves of the trees lining the pathway. He stepped quickly to the far side of the path and continued walking. Dressed in a colorful blouse over a bright red skirt, Julie stood on the path in front of the shack. She waved. Tommy waved back and began trotting toward her. Upon reaching her, he took her into his arms and kissed her repeatedly. Finally he stopped kissing her and held her out in front of him.

"I thought I would find you naked like you were last time," he said.

"I had so much fun taking off your clothes that time, I thought I should let you have as much fun taking mine off this time."

They laughed facing each other. Tommy took her hand and led her back behind the cabin where he saw she had already spread out the blankets for them.

"I never did this before, Julie, so tell me what button to start with," Tommy said.

"Last time you did just fine at what you had never done before, so start in back with the button at the top and work your way down. Once you get the blouse off you will see how easy the skirt is to pull away."

"All right, turn around, and I'll get this operation underway," he said. "While I am getting you naked, you can start stripping off my clothes."

They began getting each other naked. After struggling with the top button on Julie's blouse, Tommy found the rest easy to deal with. He slipped it away from her shoulders and tossed it onto the blanket. He stood trance-like looking at what he had had on his mind the entire week. He couldn't control his hands as they sought her breasts and he felt himself sigh as he moved his hands over her beautiful curvaceous body. Julie continued undressing Tommy and he stepped out of his Levis when they fell to his ankles. At first as they held each other on the blankets they were playful and laughed, but their desires for one another changed the mood to serious love-making that eventually brought both of them to the ecstasy for which they yearned.

During the aftermath of their lovemaking they chatted and caressed one another. Tommy pushed himself up to sitting with his elbows in back bracing him. He looked over to Julie.

"I was talking with Hal Cooper a couple of days ago and we were discussing what he called 'The Fear Factor'. He said that society is controlled by this in many ways."

"What is he talking about?" Julie asked. "I don't get it."

"Hal said that the government uses fear to control the people. Stuff like: if you don't pay your taxes you will be sent to jail, or if you don't pay the taxes on your house, the government will sell your house and you will have to leave your home."

"Oh, I get it now," Julie said. "It's like the pastor telling us that if we lead sinful lives we will go to hell instead of heaven. An even better example is my mother telling me that if I do it with a boy before I get married I will be a prostitute. I looked that up and a prostitute is a girl that gets paid for doing it. I got to thinking that since I like doing it, getting paid for it might be a perfect way to go for me."

"I don't know anything about that stuff," Tommy said. "I know when my father tells me that if I don't go to The Wharton School of Finance, I won't amount to anything. He is trying to scare me into going to the same college he and all the rest of the family went to. I have no intention of going to Wharton."

"What would you amount to if you did go to Wharton, or whatever it is?" Julie asked.

"I would amount to the same as my father, working at the family's Wall Street bank. I would be miserable from the first day I set foot in there. As far as I am concerned, I already amount to something and I didn't go to Wharton to amount to being a sculptor and I think I am getting to be a good writer, too."

"I haven't the slightest idea what I want to amount to yet. Maybe I never will know. All know is that I am having much more fun at Las Mujeres than I did at home. I don't even consider my parents' house home anymore. Who knows, I might become a prostitute. Would you pay me to do it with me?"

"Now I know what those guys were talking about in the recreation hall. They must have been talking about paying for doing it. One guy asked, 'Why buy the cow when you can get the milk free?' Does that answer your question?"

"That isn't the answer I expected from you, Tom Holmes."

Tommy paused, and changed the subject.

"You said you didn't like living with your parents. Why is that?" Tommy asked.

"They are evangelicals and they are constantly talking to Jesus."

"Is that the same as me talking to Ralph?"

"I think they would be better off if they were talking with Ralph. Jesus rules everything they do and they were always telling me what Jesus was telling me. And, I never spoke to Jesus. When you told me about Ralph, I got to wishing I also had a Ralph."

"Hal said that religion is a major way to control people using the Fear Factor. Hal seems to have figured out a lot of things I never even thought about," Tommy said.

"Hal is a lot older than you or I, so he has been around longer and has probably learned a lot that we have never even thought about," Julie said. "But, I will tell you what happened when my parents began getting close to yelling at me because I didn't know what adultery meant."

"I don't know what it means either," Tommy said.

"Well, I looked it up and it means doing it when the two people doing it are not married. Both my mother and father went on and on about adultery so I felt I should look it up. They said that 'Thou shalt not commit adultery' is one of the Ten Commandments. Then, of course, they gave me the same crap about not getting into heaven if I ever committed adultery. So, Tom, my lover, we will be together in Hell."

"My parents are drunk a good part of the time, but they never have yelled that kind of bull at me. Maybe they aren't so bad after all is said and done."

He leaned over to Julie and kissed her passionately.

"How about us committing adultery one more time before we have to go back to our schools?"

"That sounds better than talking about it," Julie said, and began taking Tommy into her arms.

After getting dressed for their walks back to the schools they stood and kissed good-bye.

"Next week, same place and time?" Tommy asked.

"Sounds great to me. See you then adulterer."

"Okay, my happy prostitute," Tommy said.

They both laughed before turning around to leave the old shack's grassy back yard.

The next month's dance between the two schools was held at The Escalante. Tommy stood at the entrance to the recreation building to meet the bus from Mujeres del Mundo. Julie was the last girl to step off the bus when it pulled up to the curb at the end of the sidewalk. Tommy was happy to see her and she stepped up to him and gave him a long hug and a kiss.

"That should give the chaperones something to chatter about," Julie said.

"Let them worry about us until the cows come home."

"How was your week?" Julie asked.

"I finished making a sculpture and Hal is going to show me how to wood fire it. I read a couple of books that were interesting. Both were novels. I like fiction better than all that real stuff that puts me to sleep."

They went into the building and sat next to one another waiting for the music to begin. Tommy leaned over to whisper into Julie's ear.

"Getting together once a week makes me wish we could meet more often," he said.

""I know what you mean, but if I sneaked off more often, someone might follow me and that would cause too much of a stir."

"I guess you are right. Nobody ever notices me when I slip onto the path to the shack."

Before they could continue the discussion, Charlie Rosas walked up and stood in front of Julie. Both she and Tommy looked up at Charlie.

"I would like to dance with you when the music starts," Charlie said.

"I don't think we have met before," Julie said.

"I'm Charlie Rosas, from Jamaica."

"I am Julie Bronson. I am from here, New York."

Julie glanced over to Tommy arching her eyebrows questioning Tommy what he thought about her dancing with Charlie Rosas. Tommy shrugged his shoulders and raised his eyebrows as if to say, "I suppose it is all right."

For a few minutes it was awkward for all three. Charlie stood where he had been talking with Julie. Julie and Tommy remained sitting on their chairs, but not speaking. The first of the dance music began coming from the sound booth, overseen by one of the Escalante students. Julie rose from her chair and Charlie took her by the hand and led her out onto the dance floor.

Tommy sat still in the chair watching every move Charlie and Julie made on the dance floor. He noticed that Charlie had pulled Julie in close when they had been on the floor for a few minutes. He also watched as they talked to each other as they danced. When Julie smiled at Charlie and then both laughed, Tommy wondered what they were talking about. The music stopped after the first dance. Charlie and Julie stood with the others on the dance floor, making no move to return to the chairs along the walls. The second song began and they went back to dancing. Tommy noticed, beneath his scowl, that they were dancing just as close as they had been during the first dance number.

"Ralph, what is going on?" Tommy asked, and then realized that he had not talked with Ralph for a long time.

"I don't know anything about this," Ralph said.

Tommy continued sitting on the chair against the wall. He felt helpless to do anything about the situation. He thought about getting out of the chair and leaving the dance hall, but decided that would not help. When the second song finished he was overjoyed to see Charlie and Julie walking arm in arm back to where he sat waiting.

Julie sat down next to Tommy again.

"Thanks for the dance, Julie," Charlie said. "I'm glad I learned how Americans dance."

"You dance very well, Charlie. Thanks."

Charlie left and walked to the other side of the room in front of all the chairs, some occupied, some vacant.

"What did he mean about learning how Americans dance?" Tommy asked.

"He told me that the reason he has never come to these dances is that they dance differently in Jamaica than they do here. He wanted to learn how we dance before coming to one of these monthly events."

"He sure was dancing close to you," Tommy said. "Did he learn that, too?"

"Don't be silly, Tom," Julie said. "You and I dance close, too."

"I know that, but Charlie Rosas is not me."

"I am glad you are you, Tom," Julie said. "I don't know Charlie Rosas at all compared to how I know you."

The next song began. Tommy took Julie out on the dance floor and began dancing with her closer than he ever had held her at the monthly dances. They continued dancing together until Charlie returned close to the end of the evening, and asked Julie for another dance. Julie got up from the chair and went out on the floor with Charlie as Tommy watched only them. In spite of what Julie had said, he was scowling again.

Tommy said nothing as he and Julie made their way out of the recreation building when the dance was over. Once away from the entrance, Tommy took Julie's arm and they stopped walking.

"Will I see you at the shack as usual?" Tommy asked.

"Of course," Julie said. "Why wouldn't we meet as usual?"

"It just seemed to me that you were having too good a time with Charlie Rosas out on the dance floor."

"Tommy, I told you I hardly know Charlie Rosas, and a couple of dances is certainly not enough for me to cancel our time at the shack. I think you are jealous. In one way you being jealous of me dancing with someone else is a compliment, but in another way it is bothersome. We don't have time now to talk about it so it will have to wait until we are at our favorite place in the woods. So, goodnight, my wonderful lover-boy, I am looking forward to our usual date."

Tommy kissed Julie and she went to the bus for the trip back to Mujeres del Mundo. Without waiting for the bus to leave, Tommy went to his room where he sat at his desk thinking about what had happened at the dance. He didn't bother to talk to Ralph about the situation since Ralph had told him he didn't understand any of it, so he sat alone with his thoughts about Julie and the Jamaican, Charlie Rosas. He contemplated talking with Hal Cooper about the problem, but then, thought better of it. He decided that talking with Hal about a lot of things was all right, but matters that concerned Julie were too personal to share with anyone. Without reaching any conclusions, Tommy went to bed and fell asleep almost instantly.

From the following morning until it was time on Wednesday afternoon to meet Julie at the shack, Tommy worked on writing an essay that he had started two weeks before. Thinking out what he wanted to write and how he wanted write the essay gave him enough of a distraction from the Julie/Charlie problem so that he was not bothered by it. However, when they met on the path in front of the shack, Tommy was not able to return Julie's usual happy smile.

"Is something wrong, Tom?" Julie asked. "You don't look your usual happy self."

"I can't clear my mind about how you seemed to be having too much fun with Charlie Rosas at the dance."

"I was having fun. I try always to have fun anywhere I am. Heavens, I have lots of fun with you every time we meet here. I think you are letting jealousy into your mind. That does you no good at all."

"What do you know about jealousy?" Tommy asked.

"I have seen it happen with other people just like I am seeing happen to you. It will eat you alive if you let it. Look at it this way. You and I have been having this adulterous fun here for months. You turned eighteen two months ago and I will be eighteen in another month. We were both seventeen when we began this love affair. Doesn't that tell you something?"

"I suppose you are right. I just didn't like the way he was holding you so close. I will try to forget that feeling from now on. By the way, we still have our clothes on," Tommy said, and smiled.

"That's better," she said. "Now let's see how fast we can get these clothes off and start doing what we came out here for."

It was not long before they were naked and entwined. Dancing with Charlie Rosas did not enter their conversation again. They continued their Wednesday meetings at the old shack. The following month's dance was at Mujeres del Mundo. Thoughts about Charlie Rosas re-entered Tommy's mind, but he decided that he would go to the dance and see what would happen. He also decided that Julie was right about jealousy, so he was determined to not allow any of those feelings that he had had the month before hamper the fun he hoped to have dancing with the girl that he had come to love. On the trip over he saw that Charlie Rosas was sitting in the front seat of the bus. Tommy sat in the middle of the bus. He was wondering if Charlie had taken his seat to be able to get to the building where the dance was being held sooner than anyone. As the bus moved out of the driveway Tommy thought that there was little use worrying about Charlie and Julie because after all he was doing "it" with Julie and Charlie wasn't.

The bus had barely come to s top at the Mujeres del Mundo recreational center when Tommy saw Charlie jump off and head for the entrance to the building at a fast pace. He arrived before any of the girls had managed to come out to meet the Escalante boys. Tommy joined the line of boys getting off the bus, and walked to the building without hurrying. As he approached the entrance with a bevy of girls crowded around, some giggling, some arching their necks trying to spot some boy they were waiting for, he didn't see Julie.

Once inside he spotted Julie and Charlie Rosas sitting together. He also noticed that the chairs to either side of them were occupied. In spite of the knotted feeling in his stomach, he went to another side of the room and sat down on one of the empty chairs. He had barely gotten seated in the chair when a girl that he had noticed at other dances came over and sat down next to him.

"Hi, I am Gretchen Shafer, do you mind if I sit with you?"

"I don't mind at all," Tommy said. "I am Tom Holmes. I've seen you at dances before."

"Yes, I have been here at Mujeres for four years and I am about to get out of here and go out West to New Mexico to college."

"Where in New Mexico are you going to go to college?" Tommy asked.

"New Mexico A and M. I want to be a farmer."

"That's a great idea. I wish you good luck. I don't know when I will leave Escalante. I am a sculptor, and haven't given much thought to going anywhere. My parents think I am going to The Wharton School of Finance, but I have news for them. I will never walk on that campus."

"Julie Bronson is your girl friend, isn't she?"

"You might say that," Tommy said, and squirmed slightly at Gretchen's question.

"I have wanted to dance with you since I got here, but you were always dancing with Julie."

"I guess you're right."

"I see she is sitting with Charlie Rosas tonight. Is she still your girl friend?"

"She hasn't said anything to me to make me think differently. Is there something you are trying to tell me?"

"Actually, yes," Gretchen said. "You seem like a really nice fellow and I think there is something you should know in case you are getting too close to Julie Branson."

"That sounds serious," Tommy said.

"Well, it is serious. You need to be aware that Julie Branson has a lot of boy friends."

The music for the first dance began and interrupted their conversation.

"Would you dance this one with me?" Gretchen asked.

"Sure, let's show them all how."

They stood up and began to dance to the music, a medium paced number that made for a good first dance to start off with. Tommy brought Gretchen close to him as they danced. He could tell that she was not built the same as Julie, but as they chatted while dancing, Tommy understood that Gretchen seemed to have more depth in her conversation than Julie. He listened closely to what she said. Her blonde hair grew straight, and as it moved with her movements Tommy found it had a beauty of its own. During the third dance of the evening Tommy and Gretchen danced in the vicinity of Julie and Charlie. Tommy caught Julie's eye, and winked at her. Julie not only did not wink back, she also turned her head away. Tommy wondered what was going on with Julie, but chased those thoughts away as he spent the evening dancing and talking with Gretchen. Toward the end of the dance Tommy walked across the room and stood in front of Julie.

"I would like the next dance," he said.

"I would like that," Julies answered, and rose from her chair.

Turning to his right, Tommy said, "Hello Charlie."

"Hi there Tom. Nice dance tonight."

The music started and Tommy took Julie by the arm and led her onto the dance floor.

"I didn't think you would ever ask me to dance tonight," Julie said as they danced.

"You seem to be having a good time with Charlie, so I stayed out of your way," Tommy said.

"You seem to be having a nice time with Gretchen. You two have danced every dance except this one."

"Are we still up for Wednesday as usual?" Tommy asked.

"Of course," Julie said. "Why wouldn't we be?"

"Just wondering," Tommy said.

When the music stopped, Tommy escorted Julie back to her chair next to Charlie Rosas and then returned to sit next to Gretchen Schafer.

"What did Julie have to say for herself, Tom?"

"Nothing much. We didn't talk about anything in particular."

"Just be careful, Tom. I am telling you for your own good, and in case you are wondering, I am not doing this with any ulterior motive in mind."

"Thanks, Gretchen," Tommy said. "I appreciate your thoughts very much. I can also say that I have enjoyed dancing with you tonight and hope we can do it again."

"I agree with that," she said.

The music began for the last dance. Tommy stood up with Gretchen and they danced. Gretchen kept her eyes closed the entire time. When the music stopped and the dance was pronounced over, Tommy said goodnight to Gretchen, walked to the bus and boarded it. All the way back to The Escalante, Tommy pondered what Gretchen had told him about Julie. He continued thinking when he was back in his room getting ready for bed. Sleep came easy as he shifted his thought to Gretchen Shafer, wondering what she would be like naked out by the old shack in the woods.

The following Wednesday Tommy walked down the path to the shack in somewhat of a quandary, because he didn't feel the same as he had before Charlie Rosas began chasing Julie. Tommy couldn't figure out if he was surrendering to Charlie or whether he was disappointed that Julie had not been completely honest with him about her many boy friends. He also wondered if Gretchen was telling the truth about Julie in trying to lure him, Tommy, away from his girlfriend that he had been making love with for such a long time.

He was happy to find Julie waiting for him at the shack, and smiled at her before taking her into his arms for a kiss. Neither he nor Julie mentioned the dance or Charlie Rosas or Gretchen Shafer. They both disrobed and enjoyed one another. Before they went their separate ways to their respective schools they assured one another that they would meet again the next Wednesday. Back at The Escalante, Tommy smiled as he ate supper in the dining hall and went to his room contented and satisfied with the day's happenings.

Everything in his life seemed normal to Tommy. He continued his sculpting and spent most mornings working on his writing which he enjoyed discussing with Joe Eager, his mentor. Joe told him that he had a unique style that could possibly be commercial if he chose to send his work out to prospective editors.

The meetings at the shack with Julie continued as usual, and Tommy was able to hide or disguise what he thought about her and Charlie Rosas.

One Friday noon, Tommy was walking around by the tool house after returning a shovel he had used to dig clay. He caught the sight of Charlie Rosas entering the path that went to the old shack. Tommy noticed that

Charlie walked into the woods like he knew exactly where he was going. Tommy stopped in his tracks, and suddenly wondered if he should follow the Jamaican to the shack and see what was going on. But, he thought better of that and went back to the ceramic studio, assuming that Charlie was heading out to meet Julie at her favorite spot to make love. Tommy decided that his times with Julie would be short-lived at best.

The big news for Tommy was when he received the letter from the National Endowment For the Arts notifying him that he had been awarded a two-year fellowship to pursue his work as a sculptor. The letter also said that he would be getting a check for twenty-five thousand dollars in the mail. Hal had convinced Tommy to apply for a fellowship based on photographs of his work as a sculptor and a recommendation by Hal. Both he and Hal kept the news to themselves because neither wanted any publicity, nor did they want the school to use it as a promotional vehicle. Most of all, Tommy did not want his parents to know that he had received the fellowship. Hal drove him into Newburgh where he started a bank account. As they were leaving to get back to The Escalante, Tommy held up his right hand.

"Hal, if you have time, I would like to show you the old family farm that I told you about once. It is not too far from here. The nearest village is Walden and the farm had the Wallkill River for one of its borders. My uncle took me there many years ago but I know I can find the way back."

"How do you know you can find your way back there after all these years?"

"Well, my uncle never took me anywhere else so I remember that time very well. To me it is almost yesterday that we went there. I still remember the apple trees and the barn. Nobody was living there, and my uncle told me that he was showing the place to me because my father didn't care about it and was far too busy stacking up his money to be bothered showing it to me."

"Then, let's go. I have nothing to do for the rest of the day."

Walden was not far from Newburgh so they arrived after an hour's drive. Tommy directed Hal right to the entryway, an old overgrown dirt road that led to a small cabin and a small barn that had a roof that was half caved in. The cabin looked in good shape. Hal remarked about the two buildings.

"My uncle told me that when he was a boy, the family had used the cabin as a hunting lodge where members of the family went to hunt deer in the fall."

Hal pulled up to the cabin and they got out to look around. Tommy walked over to the barn and saw that the roof would have to be rebuilt if the building was ever to be used again. The cabin was another story. Tommy remembered that his uncle had taken an old iron key out from under a flat rock by the side of the cabin and had opened the door with it. Tommy walked over to the only flat rock next to the cabin, lifted it up and found the old iron key. He took it out of its hiding place and went to the door and unlocked it. After opening the creaking door, Hal and Tommy went into the cabin and looked around. It was furnished with rustic furniture and had a bed with a mattress that looked too rotten to be of any service.

I guess I will have to get a new mattress for that old bed," Tommy said.

"Are you figuring on moving here?" Hal asked.

"I'm thinking this will be a good place to live and work because there is nobody around here to bother me. And, I know my parents will never think that I came here."

"When are you planning this move?" Hal asked.

"I am not sure, but I think it will be fairly soon. I know I will come here once my father knows for sure that I have no intentions of going to The Wharton, as he calls it."

"Well let me know when you want to move in so I can help you bring in a new mattress and any other stuff you think you will need."

"Thank, Hal. I appreciate that very much. You are truly a good friend."

Just before the next dance was to happen word flew around The Escalante that Charlie Rosas and his cousin Tack Sing had returned to Jamaica on family business and would not be coming back to The Escalante.

The dance was at The Escalante and Tommy wondered how Charlie Rosas' departure would affect Julie. As was his custom, Tommy went to the recreation hall to meet the bus from Mujeres del Mundo. When the bus was about half unloaded he saw Gretchen step off the bus and walk toward where he was waiting.

"Hi Tom, I am so glad you are here," Gretchen said.

"I am glad to be here. How are you, Gretchen. It is sure nice to see you."

"I don't know if you are waiting for Julie or not, but she will not be at the dance."

"Why is that?" Tommy asked.

"Julie is no longer at Mujeres del Mundo. Step over here away from the others."

She and Tommy moved over away from the entrance to the building. Tommy turned toward Gretchen.

"Tom, Julie went home. She is pregnant."

"For heaven's sake, that is serious to be sure," Tommy said. "Who is the father? You told me she had lots of boy friends."

"I didn't get to talk to her because her mother and father came to get her and her things. There wasn't time to even say good-bye."

"I'll bet her parents are raving mad at her. Julie told me all about how they are, being evangelicals and all. I hope she is all right."

"You might be the father, Tom. Are you aware of that?"

"Gretchen, me the father of Julie's child is impossible."

"Why not, I know you and Julie have been intimate for a long time."

"We have, Gretchen, but I have always…how do you say it? I have always worn a raincoat. I guess that is the best way to say it."

Gretchen laughed at Tommy's way of describing wearing a condom during sex.

"I guess that is one way of describing it. So if you are not the father it must be one of the others."

"Let's go in to the dance. I am not going to give Julie and her predicament another thought," Tommy said.

Tommy and Gretchen danced every dance that evening. They became rather lost on the dance floor, conversing and keeping to the music at the same time.

They complemented one another nicely, and Tommy felt comfortable with Gretchen in his arms. When the dance was over they went outside with the others and Tommy kissed her goodnight. It was not a long passionate kiss like he was used to with Julie, but he was happy that it had happened.

"Tommy, thanks for a nice evening. You are a very nice guy and I enjoy your company very much," Gretchen said as they walked to the bus. I am happy to have you as a friend," Tommy said. "Can I reach you by telephone?"

"Yes, I'll give you the number."

Gretchen took a small pad and pencil from her purse and wrote down her telephone number at Mujeres del Mundo. It was the one telephone in the sleeping quarters so she told Tommy that he would have to ask for her when he called.

Tommy went to his room. He sat at his desk for a while thinking about Julie and her leaving school because she had gotten pregnant. Then he remembered how Charlie and his cousin Tack had left Escalante suddenly and gone back to Jamaica. He wondered if Charlie was the father of Julie's child.

The following day Tommy was working on his latest sculpture in the ceramics studio when Hal came in with a worried look on his face. Tommy looked up from putting a short slab onto an animal he was making.

"What's bugging you, Hal?"

"George Moser, the director called me to his office three hours ago and I just now got out of there. Tommy, I think you are in for some trouble."

"How do you figure that, Hal?"

"When I got to Moser's office Julie Branson's mother was there ranting and raving at Moser, telling him that The Escalante School was responsible for getting her precious daughter pregnant. I sat down and waited for the tirade to end and learned that your girl friend Julie is pregnant and she is accusing you of being the father. Is there any truth to that? I thought you were using condoms like I advised you."

"I always used condoms. When the ones you gave me were used up, I went to town and bought more. You were even with me one time when we were going to Clara Anson's house. Julie Branson is not telling the truth. I met another Mujeres girl and she told me that Julie has lots of boy friends. In fact, Charlie Rosas was one of them until he went back to Jamaica."

"Well, Tommy dear friend, Julie's mother was threatening to take you to court so that you would have to pay all the costs of Julie's pregnancy and child support until the kid is eighteen."

"What should I do, Hal?"

"For starters, Moser wants to see you as soon as you can get over there. I think he is determined to expel you from The Escalante. If that is the case, I think you will be lucky because you can go home and face your father and mother because they already know about all this crap. I am saying this because if Moser knew that I had advised you to run away and hide, I would lose my job just as fast as he expelled you. I am not thrilled to be stuck here, but I have no money to get established anywhere else."

"I have that twenty-five grand. You can have that," Tommy said.

"Tommy, I cannot thank you enough for that gesture, but you will need every penny of that, and probably more, to live on while you work on your sculptures for the art show. You do understand that you are obligated to have a piece ready for the show next spring."

"I already have something in mind for that show."

"That's good. I am anxious to see what you come up with."

"I think I should go home and face the music that they have in mind. Then I want to escape to the old farm, get settled in for the summer and start to work on sculptures. Do you have time to drive me and my junk to Walden?"

"No problem. I think you are thinking in the right direction. Get out of Escalante as soon as possible, touch base with your parents, and then go to Walden without telling them or anyone else but me where you are. That way you won't have any interruption to your work. Your work will be even better than it has been here. I am thinking that I should do my best to get away from Escalante also, because there are far too many distractions. I don't mind the students; it is the administrators that are the biggest interference problem. Tell me when you are ready to go home and I'll take you there so I can see Clara."

"I will be ready as soon as I get through being expelled and get my stuff packed."

Tommy walked over to the administration building, reached George Moser's office and knocked on the door. Moser came to the door and opened it. Moser said. "We have quite a bit to talk about. Sit down."

Moser stepped to the rear of his desk and sat in the leather office chair. Tommy sat in one of the chairs at the front of the desk.

"Holmes, I have spent the entire afternoon listening to your girl friend's mother tell me that you have fathered her daughter's child that will be born in seven months. She was not clear about the projected birth date, but she has missed two periods. Missus Bronson also threatened to take you to court if you don't agree to pay all her daughter's expenses and then child support until the kid is eighteen years old. What do you have to say to that?"

"I have only one thing to say. I am not the father of Julie's child to be."

"How do you know that? Her mother was certain that it is you. She is a good Christian woman and she wouldn't lie."

"Her daughter is a liar."

"How can you say that, Holmes?"

"Because every time I did it with her I used a condom."

"Can you prove it?"

"I am afraid not, Mister Moser. I did not save the used rubbers."

"Then it is her word against yours, Holmes."

"I suppose it is and if you believe her I have a giant cake of ice called Greenland I will sell you."

"You are talking stupidly, Holmes. I am afraid you have given me only one alternative and that is to expel you from The Escalante School. I want you out of here by tomorrow morning."

"Well, I hope you find out who the father of Julie's kid is, but it sure as hell is not me."

Tommy rose from the chair, left the director's office and hurried back to the ceramics studio to tell Hal what had happened.

"That doesn't surprise me at all," Hal said when Tommy finished the story of his encounter with George Moser. "What are you going to do now?"

"I don't have too many choices since Moser told me to be out of here by tomorrow. He also told me that my parents had been informed about me getting the boot from the famous Escalante School for problem kids. This place has been my only home since I was seven, and now I have to leave on his orders, not my choice."

"Where are you thinking of going?" Hal asked.

"I am going back to where I came from, but I need a ride. If I dilly dally around here my mother will probably show up, if she can leave her Scotch alone long enough to get into her car. I don't need to listen to her crap all the way back to the old farmhouse."

"Are you figuring on staying with your parents?"

"Hell, no! Tommy said abruptly. "I am going there to have it out with them, because I know damn well what my father is going to say. But, I need to do this. I have been living with feeling his scorn all my life even here away from both of them. I thought about this while Moser was giving me all that crap about it being my word against Julie's that I am the father of her kid. Why should I stay around anywhere there are people that don't believe me or think I am stupid enough to become a father with a girl who does it with any man she can lure. I am going to that old family farm where nobody except you will know where I am. I hope you will keep that a secret, because I don't want anyone intruding on me and my work, especially some lawyer trying to get money out of me for a kid that is not mine."

"As I said, I'll drive you there as soon as you are ready, Tommy. I understand your need to get away quickly and your need to get things settled with your parents."

"I appreciate your help, Hal," Tommy said. "I can get all that I want to take with me in five minutes. And, by the way, I hope I can stay at Miss Anson's tonight, because when I get through with my parents, I doubt that I will be welcome there, and it is still too chancy for rain to sleep at my clearing. On the way back, tomorrow, you can let me off in Newburgh because I know I am going to need a vehicle to haul supplies and groceries, so I need to look for something suitable to buy."

"You seem to have thought everything out quite well, I must say," Hal said. "I would be happy to go around Newburgh looking for a vehicle with you. I know a little about car values. You were smart to learn how to drive with the old school pickup a few years ago. I remember when that happened. You learned quickly. That was fortunate because when they caught you driving, they never left the keys in the ignition again."

"I remember that, too. That was the first time I almost got expelled."

Tommy went to his room, packed his clothes in a suitcase and his writing materials in his briefcase. He returned to the ceramics studio. Hal and Tommy left the school grounds and headed down the road to the old farmhouse where Tommy had once lived with his parents.

"It's Sunday so my father should be home when I get there. Hopefully he and my mother won't be drunk yet. The car places will be open tomorrow so I can buy a car, and you can go back to that concentration camp."

"I thought about that. Everything is going to work out just right. I hope that the time you are with your parents won't be too bad for you. Does your father ever get violent?"

"I have never seen him get that angry. At least he has never tried hitting me or my mother, just Ralph when he broke my friend on the rocks in the stream. He generally limits his anger to screaming at us when something doesn't go his way."

"That's one thing you won't have to worry about unless what you have planned might be crossing some line with him. So you need to be on your guard and watch out for anything out of the ordinary."

"I have thought a little about that, but I haven't been round them for so many years I don't really know what they are like these days."

Hal drove up to the old farmhouse at three o'clock. Tommy got out of the car, but left his things on the back seat. Hal drove away as Tommy walked up to the front door. Jason Holmes was standing in the open doorway when he climbed the four steps up to the entryway.

"Your mother drove up to the school to get you," Jason said. "Why the hell didn't you wait for her?"

Even after the many years away from his father, Tommy could tell he had had a few drinks.

"Nobody told me she was coming, Tommy said. "Are you going to let me in?"

Jason moved back from his position that had been blocking the doorway.

"Go sit down in the living room. I want to talk to you."

"I think that it is past time when we need to talk to each other," Tommy said, as he walked into the living room, and sat down in the chair he knew would be opposite from where his father would sit.

Jason came into the room, went over to the bar and filled his glass. Then he walked to his chair and sat down.

"What is all this bullshit about you getting some girl knocked up and then expelled from The Escalante School?"

"It is bullshit about getting Julie Bronson pregnant, but they did expel me from The Escalante. I was ready to leave anyway. I need to go out into the world by myself."

"Well let me tell you something you may not be aware of," Jason said scowling and raising his voice. "It will be tough getting you into The Wharton after getting tossed out of The Escalante, but I will try my best. I still have influence there because my bank gives them a substantial amount of money every year."

"You don't have to bother about getting me in to your Wharton because I am not going to The Wharton."

"What in hell do you mean, you are not going to The Wharton? Every Holmes man goes to The Wharton whether he wants to or not."

"Not this Holmes. I have no interest in finances and banking. I am a sculptor, and have been for a long time. Money breeds greed and I want no part of the quest for money every day including weekends."

"With that attitude and no degree from The Wharton where do you think you will fit in at my bank?"

"I don't fit anywhere in your bank or anyone else's bank. You have never bothered to try to understand me.

I am your son and you don't know me at all. You know your bankers better than you know your own son."

"I think I know you very well. I know one thing; that you are too lazy to go to The Wharton where they make you learn about finances. You would rather sit on your ass and talk to some imaginary person named Ralph."

"For your information, I talked to Ralph because neither you nor my mother would talk to me. All I heard from you two was a snoot full of booze talking bullshit, as you would say. As for a job at your bank, you couldn't pay me enough to work there one single day. You can go there forever, stack your money and count it ten times a day, but you will never get me inside that mausoleum you call 'YOUR BANK'. It has been a prison around your mind since you walked in there holding your father's hand. Maybe you would feel more comfortable if I changed my name from Holmes to something else seeing how I will be breaking the family tradition of being slaves to a bank."

"I must say you are getting to be quite a smart ass talking to me that way."

"I have to tell you that I think this is the first time in my life you have spoken more than one short sentence to me. And, I will also say that I didn't realize that I was better off with your silence than I am with all this crap you are handing me now."

"Then why are you still here?" Jason asked with a sneer. You don't have to sit there and listen to me, go talk to Ralph, your best friend."

"Very good suggestion," Tommy said. "I guess this is as good a time as any to say good-bye."

Tommy pushed himself up from the chair and walked to the kitchen where he chatted with Bertha for a few minutes just to tell her some of what had just happened. She gave him a big hug before he left and walked to Clara Anson's house to tell Hal all the details of his meeting with his father.

Both Hal and Clara watched Tommy and listened closely while he told them about the confrontation he had had with his father. Hal interrupted with a comment or two during Tommy's story, and when Tommy finished, Hal smiled.

"I don't think you need to worry about him chasing after you," Hal said. "From what you say, I think he must be glad to get rid of you,"

The three of them enjoyed the evening chatting about clay and ceramics, and what the possibilities might be to have their own gallery. Tommy could feel the bond between Clara and Hal and it made him feel good that his two friends cared for one another.

The following day after breakfast, Hal and Tommy left for Newburgh. As they entered the city, Hal told Tommy that he knew where the used car lots were and drove to the street where most of them were lined up on both sides. Hal parked the car at the curb next to a used car lot with a large sign announcing "CAR CORRAL". Hal and Tommy ambled onto the lot looking around at the various vehicles. A man wearing a black cowboy hat with the brim curled up, a bolo tie over a flowery shirt, a white belt and a white pair of shoes came out of a small shack that served as an office.

"Good morning, fellers. Which one of these beauties can I put you behind the wheel of?"

"We are just looking," Hal said.

"What do you have in the way of pickup trucks?" Tommy asked.

"Come with me, young feller, I got three of the best pickups in the entire county. One's a Ford, one's a Chevy, and the other is a little Toyota."

They followed the man to the rear of the lot where the three pickups were parked together.

"Mister, uh," Hal said.

"Just call me 'Tex'", the salesman said.

"Whereabouts in Texas are you from, Tex?" Hal asked, grinning.

"I'm from Columbus, Ohio."

"How much are these pickups?" Tommy asked, after almost laughing at the man from Columbus, Ohio named "Tex".

"The Ford is seven fifty, the Chevy is eight ninety-five, and that little Toyota will run you a thousand dollars."

Hal and Tommy spent the next half hour looking over the three trucks both inside and under the hoods. Tommy had no idea what he should be looking for, but Hal made a few remarks, especially when they read the mileages on the speedometers. Hal took Tommy to one side.

"I think the Ford is the one to try for. The paint is terrible but you are not driving paint around. The other two have a lot of miles on them. I would offer him four fifty for the Ford and see how that price strikes him.

Tommy walked over to "Tex" and put his hands in his pockets.

"Tell you what, 'Tex', I'll give you four hundred and fifty bucks for the Ford. The paint looks like it has gone through a forest of bramble bushes."

"Now young feller, that Ford is one helluva good truck. You should get in and drive it around the block."

“I think you have made a good suggestion,” Tommy said. “Come on, Hal, let’s go for a spin in the Ford and see if the rest of the paint peels off.”

He looked over toward “Tex”.

“The keys are in it,” ‘Tex’ said.

Tommy and Hal got in the pickup, Tommy in the driver’s seat. It started up quickly and they left the lot. Tommy had driven only one other car, so it took him a little while to get used to the Ford.

“How does it steer?’ Hal asked.

“Seems fine to me,” Tommy said. “I don’t have any idea how the motor should sound, but it sounds all right to me.”

“I’m not good with motors either, so I suppose we will both have to guess at it,” Hal said. “I think you should stick to your offer. I’ll bet this paintless wonder has been on his lot for a while.”

Tommy drove the pickup back into the lot and he and Hal got out. “Tex” strolled up to where they were standing.

“Ain’t she a piece of cake? Tell ya what I’ll do since she needs paint. You can have it for six hundred. Now that’s a cream puff deal.”

“‘Tex’”, you are a nice guy and I like the truck, but I will give you four fifty and not a penny more. I’ve got groceries to buy.”

“Now, come on feller, you are trying to steal that Ford. Six hundred is the best I can do.”

“Then I guess we will look somewhere else today,” Tommy said. “Let’s go, Hal. ‘Tex’ thinks the Ford’s tires are spun out of gold.”

Tommy and Hal turned and walked toward Hal’s car at the curb. They opened the doors to get in and “Tex” came trotting up waving his hat with the curled up brim at them.

"Awe right, young feller, you win. You can have the Ford for four fifty. Come on back and I'll get the paper work done on it."

Tommy and Hal went to the office and sat in the folding metal chairs that "Tex" unfolded for them. As Tommy was writing the check, Hal told "Tex" a story he had heard once.

"Two cowboys were watching a dude walk down the street of Tombstone wearing a black hat with the brim curled up just like yours. One cowboy said to the other, 'Butch, don't that there dude feller know better than to curl up the brim of his hat and make it worthless to keep the sun and rain off his face?'

'I don't guess he does, Sundance. He does look a tad funny.'

'I know one thing, he ain't no cowboy, he just found the hat.'

Hal grinned at the end of his story

"That's a good one," "Tex" said.

Hal raised an eyebrow knowing that "Tex" had no idea about the point of the story.

With the paper work done, Hal and Tommy walked to the Ford and Tommy got in behind the wheel.

"Am going to the bank and get some cash," Tommy said. "I need to buy some groceries and fill the gas tank on this pickup."

"You would make a really good horse trader. The next time I have to buy a car, I hope you will come with me to bargain with the salesman. By the way, you may have forgotten this, but you will need to get a driver's license, and maybe insurance."

“Thanks for telling me about the driver’s license. I have read about insurance companies and I am not sure whether or not I want to deal with them.”

“The law requires you to have insurance,” Hal said.

“Rules, rules, rules forcing me to deal with people I want no part of,” Tommy said

“You won’t be driving a helluva lot once you get settled in and working. I suppose I should get back to the ceramic studio in case someone wants something, so I’ll say good-bye and good luck. I’ll be out to see how you are getting along one of these days.”

“So long, Hal. Thanks for everything. You are a true friend. I look forward to your visit.”

Tommy waved, started the truck and drove off for the bank.

# Part Three

Having been insulated from what most take for granted for the first eighteen years of his life, Tommy found himself at somewhat of a loss when it came to taking care of details that were routine for others. When he finally remembered what Hal had told him about getting a driver's license, he asked a bank teller where he needed to go to apply for it instead of opening a telephone book to look for the address. He spent his first month at the cabin meandering around what had once been a small farm, walking along the Wallkill River that was one of the farm boundaries, or walking into the village of Walden to visit with Roy Johnson, a blacksmith that Tommy had made friends with during his first week in the country.

He found the rural setting peaceful and calming. He was glad that he was no longer forced to live with the fifty boys that attended The Escalante School. During all the years that he was forced to be there, Tommy sought ways of avoiding others as much as he could because he had never learned how to get along with people. The only exception was Hal Cooper. Sitting by the river thinking about his current situation, Tommy found that he was perfectly content to sit and watch the current of the river carrying fallen leaves from the trees downstream. He didn't miss Hal. He thought about Julie and wondered why she had accused him of being the father of her child when she must know the real truth. He thought about Gretchen Shafer. Gretchen was not like Julie physically or in her personality. But, Tommy liked her long face with the slender nose between her eyes that sparkled in a totally different way than any of the other girls at Mujeres del Mundo. He wondered if Gretchen had ever made love with any of the boys at Escalante. After pondering that point for a short while, he realized that whether or not she had didn't make any difference to him. However, he was curious about what that would be like with her. He felt that he could trust Gretchen to be honest with him. That was more than he could feel about Julie.

On one such day by the river, Tommy began, for the first time since the day he had arrived at the cabin, thinking about his father's attitude, and how he sided with the people that believed Julie Bronson's accusation. As he watched a previous year's oak leaf float down the river he finally had the words to describe his and his father's relationship.

"Ralph, look at that oak leaf floating away. It is just like my father floating away from my mind. I'll tell you something, Ralph. I really appreciate your friendship all through these years."

He stood up from his seat on the old dead log by the river and walked back to the cabin thinking about the time when his father had heaved his ceramic Ralph onto the rocks in the creek by his clearing.

"It is weird, Ralph," Tommy said as he walked. "I have been angry with my father for many years for tossing you into the creek. For some reason, I am no longer angry with him. It is not that I have forgiven him for doing that. I don't even think about forgiving him, I just accept it. I suppose the reason for those feelings is that he no longer matters. When I walked out of the old farmhouse that has been home to the Holmes family for several generations, I walked away from the Holmes family in addition to the old farmhouse. All that stuff doesn't matter anymore, Ralph. I don't even wonder how my father feels about me, or anything about me. I do feel sorry for my mother so addicted to booze and her shallow social life, if you can call it a life. At least she drove to the school to get me after they told her that I had been expelled. But, I am glad I was gone when she got there or else I would have had to listen to her sermon on chastity all the way back to the old farmhouse."

A month had passed since Tommy had moved to the cabin near Walton before he felt settled. He had had a number of things that he had to accomplish, but finally, as he sat on his log by the river, he decided that he wanted to spend some time with Roy Johnson because during the few times he had dropped by Roy's shop he had watched Roy work iron, making decorative wrought iron gates and other items. Working with metal piqued Tommy's interest. He walked the mile to the village and stopped at the shop with "Blacksmith" painted on the gable that faced the only road through Walden.

"Hello, Roy," Tommy said when Roy put down the hot iron rod held by his tongs.

"Well, Tom, it's nice to see you again. Are you settled in the old Holmes cabin yet?"

"I would say I am as settled as I'll ever be. I am sure I have forgotten something or else there is something I haven't done that should be done and I am not aware of it."

"The last time you were here you said that you were going to start work on a sculpture. How is that project coming along?"

"To tell you the truth, Roy, I am still trying to figure things out. Originally I was going to use clay for the sculpture, but after watching you working with iron, I am in a quandary as to what material I want to use."

"Have you ever worked iron?" Roy asked.

"No. Up to this point I have only worked with clay. But, after watching you bend and shape your iron, I am thinking that I would like to try working with copper for my sculpture."

"Copper is an interesting metal to work. It bends easier, but it sure as hell melts quicker than iron. I did some work with copper a couple of years ago, but I decided that iron and I are better off together than me and copper."

"As you say, copper melts quicker than iron. Maybe you were too used to working iron before you started your project with copper."

"When you put it that way, I think you are right," Roy said. "I remember having a terrible time not heating the copper to melting point, especially with my acetylene torch. I can heat iron on the forge and I can see when it is ready to work. Copper is very different."

They chatted while Roy worked. Every once in a while he put down what he was working on to emphasize something to Tommy. Tommy felt grateful to his new friend for his attention and willingness to explain various things about working with metal.

The following day Tommy drove to Newburgh to look for a book about copper. Roy had told him about a used bookstore a block north of the main street where he might find a book that could tell him what he wanted to know. Roy's directions got him right to the curb in front of Bob's Books. The vast number of shelves surprised Tommy. Bob greeted him after he walked in. Bob asked if he could help find something.

"I am looking for a book that will tell me all about copper. Not where it is mined or that sort of information, but what can be made from copper and how to work the metal."

"I think I know just the book you are looking for," Bob said. "Follow me. It is in the next room with other arts and crafts volumes."

Tommy followed Bob through an open doorway into the next room where Bob went directly to the place on a shelf where he took the book down and handed it to Tommy.

"Do you know where every book is?" Tommy asked, amazed at Bob's ability to go to the book he was searching for without looking up and down the rows of shelves.

"I am alone here, and shelve all the books that are here. After fifteen years of living with these volumes, I have become quite familiar with all of them."

Tommy stood looking through the book entitled "Art With Copper". Bob went back to the front desk. Tommy looked through half the book and was happy to see that it contained the information he wanted. He returned to the front desk and paid for his book plus a pad of drawing paper and some pencils. He asked Bob a question.

"Is there a place in this city where I can buy copper sheets and tubing?"

"Four blocks toward the river and a block north you will find O'Toole's Metals. They carry about any metal you want plus a lot of tools."

"Thanks, Bob. And thanks for the help finding this book. It is exactly what I was looking for."

"Come again. As you can see, I have a great selection of books here."

Tommy found the building where they sold metals of various kinds. The salesman showed him where all the copper was stored and where he could find the prices of each size and shape. After getting a good idea what the different shapes cost he went to a large room where all sorts of metal working tools were displayed. He left without any further conversation with the salesman because he needed to read the book to figure out what he would need to begin with. As he drove away he was happy that he had bought the pickup rather than a car because he would need the Ford to haul copper in.

Back at the cabin, Tommy sat down and with deep interest began reading his book to learn all he could about copper. He spent a considerable amount of time looking at illustrations depicting lots of things that coppersmiths had made from copper. He had spent little time looking at the prices for the various shapes he had written down when he had walked through the warehouse in Newburgh. He finished his first read of the book after he had fixed supper and had gone outside to sit on his log by the river to think about using copper for his sculpturing.

Tommy had been thinking for some time about what he wanted to make as a sculpture, a requirement that came with the grant he had received from the government agency fostering art and literature. He returned to the cabin, left the book on his desk and took the pad of drawing paper and the pencils back to the log by the river. He began sketching his ideas for a sculpture. Squinting as he looked at the first sketch, he folded the page over and began another.

The following day he spent all morning sketching his ideas for sculptures while sitting on the log next to the river. At one point he dropped the pad onto the grass by the log, stood up and began walking toward what was once an apple orchard. Now the trees held more dead branches than live ones. As he passed by the old derelict trees he noticed that they were starting to bloom. Walking around in the old orchard he saw that there were more blooms on some of the trees than on the others. He made a mental note to ask Roy Johnson about the orchard the next time he went to the workshop. Back with his sketchbook and pencil, he began a new drawing and like a streak of lightning illuminating the sky, an idea for a sculpture took over and conquered his mind. With free strokes he moved the pencil over the paper, first forming the basic pattern and then filling in at intervals the rest of what he wanted to make from copper. He looked at the finished drawing with satisfaction. "Now if I can learn how to make this from copper I'll have a great sculpture to take wherever they want it to go." He glanced around to make sure nobody had heard him talking to himself.

After looking at the drawing a few more times, his thought went to looking around the area near the cabin for a place to build a small shelter for a workshop. A level piece of ground between the cabin and the old falling down barn caught his eye. Then, as he glanced toward the barn he saw that there were a lot of old gray wooden boards that had once been the barn. He realized that most of the materials for his workshop would come from those planks. Tommy scratched his head as he pondered building the workshop. He did not know the first thing about construction, so he hoped that Roy Johnson could tell give him enough information about building a workshop so that he could start the project.

Just as he started to go back inside the cabin, Tommy's thoughts began swimming around in circles. The idea for a workshop converged with his ideas for making copper sculptures. He stood still trying to get his mind to focus on one thing at a time. He scratched his head again, and looked out over the field that ended at the bank of the river.

"Ralph, I just realized that even after reading all about copper and sketching my idea for a sculpture, I don't know the first thing about actually working with copper because I have never done it. I know a lot about clay because Miss Anson told me all about it and about all the different kinds there are. Then I learned how to throw clay pots and stuff on the potter's wheel. Then I guess I taught myself how to work the clay into slabs to make things without using the wheel. But, Ralph, I have never done anything with copper except look at it in a warehouse. I think I need to find a coppersmith who will let me work with him so that I will get a feel for copper just as I got a feel for clay. I guess there is a lot more involved with changing mediums than I knew when I decided to work with copper instead of clay. I wonder why Hal didn't warn me about this."

Tommy walked down the graded country road to Roy's workshop. Roy was in the midst of welding some ornamental pieces to the gate struts. Tommy sat down on the barrel Roy had for guests to use as a chair. Having finished welding the iron leaf, Roy shut off the acetylene torch and hung it on the wire hook that was on the dolly that carried the acetylene and oxygen tanks.

"Hello, Tom, what's going on today?"

"I've been going around in circles but I think I have figured out why."

"That's always a sign of progress," Roy said.

"I was up there planning where I should build my workshop and I suddenly realized that I have read all about copper but I have never worked with it. I think I need to find a coppersmith somewhere and see if I can work with him to get the feel for it. I know a lot about how clay performs when I am working it, but I haven't a clue about copper. Do you know of a coppersmith around here?"

"George Haskell just outside of Wllkill does copper. He's been there for years. He does mostly decorative stuff for houses like stove hoods and light-switch plates. The last time I saw George he was complaining about getting too old to be climbing around kitchens and roofs. I'll bet he would hire you to help him."

"I don't want to get stuck with a job once I learn what I need to know about working copper."

"You wouldn't get stuck with George. He has about the same attitude toward life that I have. We both take things as they come and either do something about it or put it out of our minds."

"How long has George been working with copper?" Tommy asked.

"I imagine longer than I have been alive. He's probably old enough to be my father."

"I think I would like to go and meet George Haskell," Tommy said.

"Take 208 to Wallkill and then 18. George's place is a half-mile up 18. His name is on the mailbox."

"Thanks Roy, I guess I might as well drive up there today."

"Tell old George I sent you and he'll be more likely to listen to you. He is getting a bit strange in his old age. He never has cared much for people, especially strangers."

"Thanks for that advice. I'll let you know how it goes with him."

After driving the Ford pickup over the Wallkill River and finding George Haskell's place easily, Tommy stopped and walked over to the workshop where he saw George at work. Tommy was a bit reticent to approach George after Roy's description, but after George greeted him with "Hello, young feller, what can I do for you" in a pleasant tone of voice, Tommy relaxed and began the conversation that led to him getting a job with George Haskell to learn about copper. Tommy didn't mind that George could not pay him on any regular basis because all he wanted was chance to study how George worked the metal and how the metal responded when Tommy attempted to work it. He was impressed by the multitude of different tools that Haskell had around the workshop, and Tommy wondered at that point how many he would have to acquire in order to complete his sculptures.

When he got out of the pickup at Roy's he wore a broad smile when he told his friend about his success with the old coppersmith.

When talking with George about the hours he could devote to the work, Tommy told George that he wanted to build his own workshop from the old barn lumber so that might eat into the time for working with George until it was finished. George was totally agreeable, mentioning that since he wasn't paying Tommy on any regular basis, he didn't expect Tommy to work in the Haskell workshop on any regular basis. But, Tommy knew he would spend most of the time for a while learning about how it feels to work copper.

Tommy's arrangement with George Haskell not only saturated Tommy with the way the metal behaved under various circumstances, but also allowed him enough time to build his own workshop in between the cabin and the old barn. The latter got demolished for the most part during the construction of the workshop. Tommy had very little in the way of materials to buy in order to build a sturdy shelter in which to work on his art of sculpting copper. He found that he could build the roof of the workshop out of the old somewhat rusty sheets from the old galvanized tin roof from the barn. The winter weather and the few snowstorms that blew in slowed his progress temporarily but he learned how to work with the weather instead of against it.

Tommy found George Haskell to be friendly and very interested in showing him all that he thought was important in working with copper. George also showed Tommy what brass was like to use for various applications. By the time the winter melted into spring Tommy had become satisfied that he had chosen the right medium for his sculpting and the right person to introduce him to the vagaries of its behavior when worked and manipulated. He had become close to George Haskell and appreciated George's paternalistic approach to him. One day when he was driving home he was talking to Ralph about how he enjoyed working and talking with George Haskell.

"Ralph, the difference between my father and George Haskell is mind-blowing," Tommy said. "George would never throw you onto the rocks in the stream. George would never send me away because I liked talking with you and myself. Why is my father the way he is? Will he ever change and become human?"

Tommy watched the weather that spring. Roy had told him about planting a garden and pruning the apple trees the previous fall. He harvested quite a few apples in the three crates he found in the old root cellar. He was still enjoying the apples on occasion when he remembered to get some out of the cellar.

Roy had warned him about over planting his garden so Tommy was careful to plant what he thought he could consume. He still commuted to work with George Haskell, but he was beginning to feel that he was ready to work the copper by himself. He also wanted to take advantage of the spring, summer and fall to work in his workshop before winter set in again with its freezing temperatures. He had installed a small butane heater in the workshop, but he wasn't sure if it was large enough to keep the workshop comfortable enough in which to work. It was too early in the year to test the heater, but he wanted to get it installed before fall brought chilly temperatures to the old cabin.

After Tommy spent some time on his log by the river thinking about the work he was doing with George and the plans he had formulated for sculpting, he decided to talk to George about spending fewer hours with him so that he could start working at home.

George encouraged Tommy when he spoke about his working hours.

"Tommy, I am anxious to see what you come up with using copper to make statues," George said. "Take as much time as you need. Don't worry none about me. I was alone working here when you came by."

"I might ask to borrow your long shear to cut some strips from copper sheets."

"You can use any of my tools anytime. Just come over and I'll get out of your way. What you are doing is more important than these light switch plates and stove hoods."

"Those are important to you and to the people for whom you make them."

"I suppose you're right there. But, don't hesitate to come by and use what tools I have."

Tommy was happy that George was so accommodating. He appreciated all that George had taught him and the time he had spent doing so. He also appreciated George's friendship. After the conversation, when Tommy was ready to leave, he felt like giving George a hug out of affection, something he had never experienced with his father. But, with both his hands he took George's hand and let his affection pass to George in that manner. He drove home with a broad smile on his face.

The following day he left for Newburgh after breakfast. It was an exciting day for Tommy because he was heading for the city to buy a supply of copper. This would include copper sheets as well as various sizes of copper tubing and some rigid copper pipe. He already had collected the tools he thought he would need as well as tanks, gauges and torches for brazing. He also intended to get some new pieces of lumber and some screws and nails from which to make jigs to use in making various shapes in sizes that he wanted for his designs. After loading all of his purchases, he found a small restaurant where he could think about what else he might need and have lunch to satisfy his hunger.

He sat at a table for two and gave his order to the waitress. As he was going over in his mind the amount of copper he had bought, including the tubing and pipe, he looked up to see Gretchen Shafer standing next to him. He almost jumped up from his chair to greet her.

"Gretchen, what a great surprise!" What in the world are you doing here in Newburgh?"

Tommy put his arms around her and gave her a hug and a short kiss on her left cheek.

"I might ask you the same question. I had no idea where you had disappeared to after you left The Escalante in such a hurry. I live just outside of Newburgh. I finished school at Mujeres and now I work in a real estate office a block from here. This is where I have lunch every day."

"Wonderful," Tommy said. "Sit down and join me."

Gretchen sat down in the chair opposite Tommy. The waitress arrived.

"What'll it be today, Gretchen?"

"I think a ham on rye will be just right."

The waitress walked back to the ordering window.

"What are you having, Tom?"

“I ordered a roast beef sandwich.”

“They do that well here. Now tell me what you have been doing since I saw you last.”

Tommy reached over and ran his index finger down the ridge of her nose.

“It is so good to see that beautiful nose of yours. I missed it and you. I am all excited today. I bought a bunch of copper and I am starting a new sculpture using copper instead of clay like I used to. I have been working for a really nice coppersmith who lives in Wallkill. He has taught me all about working copper and now I am ready to work it in my own workshop that I built where I live.”

“Where do you live, Tom? Are you close to Newburgh?”

“When I tell you where I live, Gretchen, you and Hal Cooper will be the only two who know. I have been kind of hiding out since all that crap came from Julie and the school. I also caught a bunch of hell from my father. Nobody believes me when I say that I couldn’t possibly be the father of Julie’s kid. Gretchen, I always used a condom with her.”

“I believed you, Tom. Are you going to tell me where you live so I can visit”

“I live in a cabin next to the Wallkill River in Walden. It is a little over ten miles from here. It is a cabin that someone in my family on my father’s side built for a hunting lodge way back when my family went there to hunt deer. My uncle showed it to me a long time ago but he doesn’t know I am living there. Nobody in my family goes there and I even wonder if my father remembers that he owns it. The Holmes family never sells real estate even if they don’t use it. In this case I guess they don't sell it even though they can't remember that they own it."

"Someone must pay the taxes on it," Gretchen said.

"I suppose my father has someone that takes care of such details as taxes. He is far too busy running his big-assed bank on Wall Street to be bothered by such minor things as taxes on an old cabin he never sees."

"Since I work in real estate, that sounds strange to me," Gretchen said.

"Strange is a good word to describe my father, too. I can't say that I miss him, or my mother for that matter."

The waitress brought their lunch plates.

"I still live at home and my father owns the real estate business. But, he is easy to work with. I am glad that I am in that situation. I am not sure if I have the temperament to work with anyone else."

"I could never work with my father. I couldn't even work in the same city as my father. I have never really known him because he rarely talks to anyone except my mother until she gets a snoot full of booze. Then they both eat supper and go to bed."

"I would love to see the cabin where you are living, Tom," Gretchen said. "Are you going back there after lunch?"

"I am finished buying supplies so that is where I am heading. Are you busy with work this afternoon, or can you follow me out to Walden?"

"This isn't one of those telephone answering days, so I am free to go anywhere. I would love to follow you. And, I do have a car that my father bought for me when I got done with Las Mujeres. It's a Toyota."

They sat at the table chatting between bites from their sandwiches until they finished and Tommy paid the waitress. Outside, Tommy pointed to his Ford pickup.

"That's my in-need-of-paint pickup," he said. "Where are you parked?"

"I am just a block away. Why don't you go to the west end of town and I will get behind and follow you?"

"Sounds good to me. I won't be driving fast with this load of copper I am hauling."

Gretchen followed Tommy to the cabin. Tommy parked the Ford so that he could unload the copper into the workshop without having to carry it far. Gretchen parked her Toyota in front of the cabin. They met at the door to the cabin.

"So this is your hideaway?" Gretchen asked.

"I like living here better than any other place I have been. Let's go inside and you can see that I am not a fussy housekeeper."

They walked into the cabin and Tommy went to the stove, lit it and put the coffee pot on to warm the contents.

"I hope you don't mind coffee left over from breakfast."

"I do the same thing. Sometimes it has a better taste than fresh. This cabin has more room than it looks like from outside."

"When I first got here I thought I might want to put on an addition, but I have since gotten used to the space and I built a workshop instead."

"Tell me more about what happened at The Escalante," Gretchen said.

"I think I have told you just about everything. You were right about Julie having a lot of boy friends. One of them got her pregnant and it wasn't me. I still can't understand why she accused me of being the father. I thought we were having a wonderful time together. Then all of a sudden I get hit with that crap and get expelled from that school that claims to be for its students. What a joke that turned out to be. Julie's parents are evangelical religious nuts. How in the world did Julie get to be such a runaround?"

"I know Julie quite well from Las Mujeres del Mundo. Julie is rebelling against her parents' attitudes toward just about everything."

"Then why the hell did she accuse me of knocking her up?"

"I don't know. She never said anything about being pregnant to me." Gretchen said. "I can only guess that she was desperate because her parents probably threatened her for just about everything. Just because she came across as a woman of the world to you doesn't mean she wasn't scared about what her parents would do if she got pregnant."

"I just hope nobody finds me here. But, I am glad you are here," Tommy said, taking her into his arms and kissing her. "Welcome to my humble cabin."

"It is a great place. I like the cozy feel to it. I still live with my parents in Newburgh and their house is huge. My father bought it years ago when a bank threatened the owner with foreclosure. Banks are sometimes unmerciful. Being in the real estate business I see a lot of things I don't like about banks."

"I don't know anything about banks except that I have an account in one of the banks in Newburgh. I wonder if I should take my account somewhere else in case Julie's parents start trying to find me and find my bank account. They may be evangelicals and talk to Jesus all the time, but they seem intent on getting money by any means they can by accusing me of fathering a child that could not happen under the circumstances that I told you about."

"I can't advise you on that matter, "Gretchen said.

Tommy put his arms around Gretchen again and pulled her close to him.

"How about having some fun in bed before I warm up the beef stew for our supper?" Tommy asked.

"I'm afraid I would rather just talk the way we have been talking. I am hesitant to be intimate with you right now. I guess I am afraid you might be substituting me for Julie instead of just making love to me, Gretchen Shafer."

"I think you are afraid of something that will never happen. I think of you as Gretchen and only Gretchen. Julie has not been any part of my life for a long time and I know she will never be a part of my life ever again. But, I am not insisting on doing it. I will put it this way; I will leave that decision completely up to you."

"I hope you are not upset with me, Tom. I don't know why I have that feeling, but I am sure that in time I will get over it. I like you a lot. I remember when I approached you at that dance. I had watched you and saw that you were a gentleman with Julie and she never really appreciated that in you. I talked to her about you and I got the impression that from her point of view, you were just another of her conquests. I was surprised at myself when I found that I became angry with her for her attitude. I guess that I liked you more than I knew."

"I am glad you did approach me. I also appreciate your telling me what kind of a girl Julie really is. One day after that evening I saw Charlie Rosas heading down the path through the woods to the old shack where Julie and I always met."

"I think that is enough about Julie," Gretchen said. "Let's keep her out of our conversation. We could spend the night in bed with our clothes on. How does that strike you?"

"Gretchen, my dear girl, I know what it is like being intimate with a woman. If I had never done it before I might think differently, but if I was next to you in bed with all our clothes on I would be asking for torture."

"I can understand your point," Gretchen said. "I did it once, but it was terrible. That was two years ago, and I don't think about it. It just came to mind after what we are talking about.

I really like you, Tom. I hope this doesn't cool you against me. Heck, I might come here in a couple of days, rip my clothes off, and jump into bed before you could get through the door to say hello."

They both laughed. Tommy took her face into his hands.

"I am fine with just seeing and talking with you. I enjoy your company. I am sure that we will know when the time is right if we decide to jump into bed together. In the meantime I will just wonder what it will be like to make love with you."

They enjoyed the warmed over beef stew. Gretchen sat in the only chair. Tommy had moved the table next to the bed. He ate sitting on the bed. They talked about all sorts of subjects, both expressing their dislikes for the schools they had been sent to by their parents.

My parents sent me to Escalante because they thought I was crazy after they heard me talking to myself and to my imaginary friend, Ralph. The Escalante, a school for boys with special needs, ha! Why did your parents end you to Mujeres?"

"They thought I would get a better education there than at the local high school. All the years I was at Mujeres del Mundo, I was isolated from the world. I had no clue what was happening away from that place. Once in a while we watched the news, but those programs never tell you all about what is happening."

"I was stuck at The Escalante from the time I was seven until I was eighteen," Tommy said. "Since I got booted out I have been amazed at what life is really like away from that place. If I ever have any children, I will never send them away to school. I liked it there at first, but I guess I grew out of it and the feeling of being incarcerated that they call freedom."

"I cannot agree more. I knew quite a few girls at Mujeres that were bitter at their parents for sending them there. I understood my parent's motives for my being at Mujeres, and I think I learned more than I realized at the time."

"Look at it this way, Gretchen," Tommy said. "If neither of us had gone to those schools, we wouldn't be sitting here wondering what the other looked like naked."

"You are just too much fun, Tom Holmes. I don't think it will be too long a time before we will be looking at each other's nakedness and exploring it."

"All right, let's talk about world affairs or something other than our naked bodies because I can feel myself getting far too curious for right now."

The sun disappeared over the horizon. Tommy got up from the bed and took a match from the box on the shelf above the kitchen sink and lit the gas lamp that hung down from the ceiling over where the table usually was.

"This is so rustic and homey," Gretchen said. "Not many people these days get their light from a gas lamp. This is so much nicer than just flicking a switch with your finger and an electric light pops on."

"I inquired about getting power to this place when I moved here. The power company told me that I would have to pay three thousand dollars to get electricity as far as the boundary of this old farm. That was all I needed to hear. So when I went into town I found a store where they still sold gas lamps. There it is lighting up the entire cabin. I can even write stories at night with it turned on."

Finished with the stew, Tommy got up from the bed and moved the table back to its usual place under the gas lamp. Gretchen moved the chair and sat next to the table. They continued their conversation after Tommy sat back on the bed. Gretchen tucked her legs under her as she sat looking at Tommy as he spoke.

"I have been thinking lately that having to stay at The Escalante all those years gave me the opportunity and ability to appreciate this place. I feel like I have finally found a home. I didn't feel at home when I lived in the old farmhouse with my parents. The only person that ever showed me any love was Bertha, the cook, and she is very important in my life. I can feel her big black arms around me bringing me to her huge bosom that was such a comfort to me whenever I needed to get away from my parents when they talked about stuff I had no clue about. My father talked Wall Street banking and my mother, slurring her words, told my father all the gossip from all the groups in which she was a member. He didn't give a damn about her gossipy tales and she paid attention to her drink rather than to what he was telling her about his banking exploits. Bertha said just enough for me to know that I could always count on her."

"We never had a cook. My mother did all that except when my father got things together and cooked Sunday breakfast. We never went to church on Sunday, or any other day. I'll never forget the Saturday evening when we were all sitting around the table after the meal. My father told us, my mother, brother and me, that some man had come to the real estate office and told him that he would sell more real estate if he went to church on Sundays. My father told the man that if his business depended on him going to church on Sundays, he would sell the business and move to Florida where he could work as a beachcomber. My father told us that the man turned and left without even a smile at his joke about Florida."

"We never went to church either. I think they were both suffering hangovers every Sunday morning so church would not have been a good idea for them. I suppose that if you have never been to church, you don't miss it."

"I now you were friends with Hal Cooper," Gretchen said. "Have you seen him since you left The Escalante?"

"He helped me move out here. He even helped me buy the Ford pickup. Hal is a good friend. I don't know how long he will stay at The Escalante. I know he is not very happy with those in charge of things there.

"I never could understand why anyone would work at places like those schools," Gretchen said. "It was bad enough being a student there. But, if you are working there you stay until they drive you bonkers."

Their conversation stopped as if someone had turned off two faucets at the same time. They looked at one another. They smiled in unison. Gretchen fluffed her hair with both hands. Tommy scratched the back of his head. Their eyes did not leave the stare that both shared. They smiled again. This time Gretchen wrinkled her nose and Tommy leaned further toward her. Their eyes remained focused on each other.

Gretchen reached up to the top button on her blouse and undid it. Tommy raised his eyebrows in disbelief at what he as seeing. She undid the second button. Tommy squirmed slightly, but enough so that Gretchen caught the movement out of the corner of her eye. They continued looking into one another's eyes. She reached lowly up to the third button on the blouse and undid it. Tommy opened his mouth slightly and followed that by reaching up to the top button on his blue chambray work shirt. He unbuttoned it quickly and went right down the line of buttons until they were all unbuttoned and his shirt opened to show his chest covered with light brown curly hair. Gretchen saw what he had done and quickly unbuttoned her blouse all the way and took it off, tossing it on the floor.

Tommy dropped his eyes from hers and stared at her breasts, moving his eyes from one to the other. He directed his eyes back to hers, and raised his head in a movement meaning a question.

"Yes," she said. "We both know it is time."

Both hurriedly removed the rest of their clothes and lay on the bed with their arms around each other. They ran the palms of their hands over each other.

Tommy took her breasts into his palms.

"You are absolutely beautiful, Gretchen Schafer. I saw the love in your eyes and knew you had decided it was time."

"Oh yes, Tom, it is definitely time. I am tingling all over and I don't want to stop kissing you and feeling you with me."

"Gretchen, I am so happy that we met again in that little restaurant. I had to tell you that before I go crazy over you."

Their lovemaking lasted until they both fell asleep in each other's arms. In the middle of the night Tommy was awakened by a dream. The gas lamp still lighted the cabin. He looked over at Gretchen and felt his entire body relax as he remembered the way she felt as he made love with her. He didn't want to make any comparisons between Gretchen and Julie, but he couldn't help himself. Gretchen gave herself to him but Julie just wanted him for her own pleasure. That was a huge difference. As he thought about that he wondered if he should tell Gretchen how he felt since she had expressed fears that he was substituting her for Julie. He knew that was not the case. Then after their time together he was completely certain that it was Gretchen that he loved. He also decided that he didn't need to tell her about the big difference between her and Julie Bronson. He leaned toward her and took her face in his hands. She stirred as she sighed. Tommy kissed her lips with a tender touch, but he felt his passion passing to her. Gretchen opened her eyes, blinked twice and put her arms around Tommy's shoulders.

"That was such a beautiful kiss, Tom. You have me tingling all over again."

"You are so beautiful, I cannot believe how close I am to you. It is as if our minds converged with each other to where there is a single passion. It is no longer a matter of my passion or your passion it is our passion."

"Yes, yes, you say that so well," she said. "I would say that it is that time again."

Their lips met and they shared the passion.

The sun announced mid-morning as they ate a breakfast of scrambled eggs and bacon that Tommy cooked with a smile on his face. When they finished, they went outside and unloaded most of the copper that Tommy had purchased. He left two sheets in the bed of the pickup, explaining to Gretchen that he had to take that copper to George Haskell's to cut strips from it on George's six foot shear.

"I would love to go with you and watch you work, but I had better get back and go to work with my father. I know there are two closings due tomorrow and there is a lot of paper work I need to do for them."

"What will they say to you being gone all night?"

"I stopped by the office when I went for my car to come out here. I told my father not to expect me home. My parents are good about letting me live my own life."

"You are lucky that way. I'll bet my father is still fuming because I didn't go to his beloved Wharton School of Finance to go to work for him at his bank. What a drag that would have been. Will you come back here this evening?"

"I would like that," she said, and put her hands in back of his neck. "Tom Holmes, I enjoy every minute I am with you. Now I am going to kiss you."

Tommy stood and watched Gretchen get into her car, start it and drive away toward Newburgh. He watched until the car disappeared after rounding a curve beyond the limits of Walden.

The lovemaking with Gretchen seemed quite different that he had experienced with Julie. He stood there and thought about that. With Julie he made love to her body. The preliminaries were fun and sometimes playful. The aftermaths were a sense of physical satisfaction. But, with Gretchen the entire experience was far more than just physical, he had a deeper feeling and by the ways Gretchen reacted, he knew she felt the same. Their minds were joined and their bodies expressed what was in their minds about one another.

"Well, Tom Holmes, you now know what real love is all about," he muttered as he opened the door of the Ford.

He got into the pickup and drove to George Haskell's. George was in his shop working when Tommy arrived. When Tommy explained what he needed to do with the copper sheets, George helped Tommy maneuver the sheets onto the shear for cutting strips. They cut a variety of widths, from a half-inch to two inches.

"What do you aim to do with these?" George asked.

"These strips will be part of the sculpture, I hope," Tommy said.

"I don't understand how those strips fit into a sculpture, so I reckon I'll have to wait 'til you are finished with it to find out."

"George, that's a good idea because I am not sure how or where they will fit either. I am just hoping that it will all fall into place somehow."

Tommy drove back to the cabin with the strips of copper he had cut and unloaded them, placing them by width in bundles on a shelf he had made for them. Then he took some of the boards that he had bought and began making jigs for bending the copper strips uniformly so that eventually they could be braised together with the figures he planned to cut from other sheets of copper.

He drilled one quarter inch diameter holes a half an inch deep into the lumber in a pattern he had previously drawn on his sketchpad and transferred onto the board. After the holes were drilled to the desired depth, he cut dowel rods into uniform lengths of two and a half inches and pushed them into the holes in the lumber.

With the first jig done, he took a strip of copper one inch wide, and bent it around the dowels and found that with a clamp on the starting point he could bend a curve in the strip that would remain bent without springing back. He was glad that he had bought the small clamps along with some other tools.

Once he had bent a strip to the shape he strived for, he cut it to the length that he had drawn on his sketchpad. Taking it in his hands he examined the figure with its curve and tail, and was satisfied that the jig he had made would do what he wanted it to do. Next, he took a two-inch wide strip and repeated the process. He was happy that the jig worked just as well for the two-inch wide strip as it had for the one-inch wide strip. He clapped his hands enjoying the accomplishment.

He proceeded, making more jigs for various sizes until he had made a dozen different sized jigs, but all with the same pattern. By mid-afternoon he had bent a dozen strips of ten different sizes. He decided to stop with that number and wait until he had built the framework. Then he would determine how many more of each size he would need as he assembled them onto the frame. He was not quite ready to begin the frame. He still had some thinking to do about the frame design, since that basic component would determine what the sculpture would look like when it was finished.

He looked down the road when he left the workshop to take a break from his labors. He knew it was probably too early for Gretchen to arrive, but he was anxious and felt the need to check anyway.

Inside the cabin, Tommy began getting things together for supper. He assembled a box of spaghetti, a jar of sauce and took some ground beef out of the picnic cooler containing a block of ice that he used as a refrigerator. After lighting the gas stove he put a pot of water on for boiling the spaghetti and on another burner, he put the frying pan with the ground beef to cook before adding it to the sauce. He planned it so that he could finish cooking the meal once Gretchen had arrived at the cabin. He stepped outside and checked the road from town again. Back at the stove, he stirred the ground beef so that it would cook evenly. The sputtering of the frying beef caused him to miss hearing the Toyota drive up and stop. The next thing he knew Gretchen had opened the door and was coming into the cabin.

"How was your day, my man?" she asked.

Tommy dropped the spatula onto the frying pan, turned and took her into his arms.

"My day with copper went well, but my day without you was miserable," he said, and laughed.

"Stay here for just a minute," she said. "I have to get something out of my car trunk."

Tommy took the spatula out of the frying pan and put it on the counter.

Gretchen left the cabin and went out to her car, opened the trunk and took out a wooden chair with a pillow tied to the seat. Tommy looked through the door as she did this and was walking back to the cabin.

"Wow, you think of everything," he said. "Now we can both sit at the table to have supper. You are very thoughtful, Gretchen Shafer. It is a small wonder that some man hasn't married you by now."

She shook her head slightly and closed her eyes.

"I have had lots of chances, but none of those boys were men. Now I have found a real man who appreciates a real woman."

"You've got that right," Tommy said. "Are you hungry yet?"

"Hungry for what? She asked, and gave him an impish smile.

"I'll have either one ready for you in seconds," he said, and reached down to his belt buckle.

"What has been on your mind all day? Did you spend all day thinking about copper?"

"In spite of a major distraction, I got a lot done. I took two sheets of copper over to George Haskell's place and cut them into strips on his shear. Then I came back, made jigs for bending the strips and then bent a few to see how the jigs work. All went well, so I am now ready to think more about the frame. That will take some time, but that is what sculpting is all about."

"How about showing me what you did today. I would enjoy knowing what it is you do and how you find it so compelling."

"Then, follow me to the workshop and you will see a bunch of copper of various shapes and sizes. I won't be able to tell you much, because I won't know what it will look like until it is finished. That will most likely be months from now."

Gretchen followed Tommy out to his workshop. He told her what was happening as well as what he hoped would happen as he progressed to the finished sculpture.

Back in the cabin, Tommy finished cooking the spaghetti. They sat at the table and ate the meal.

"I forgot the Parmesan cheese when I was at the store in town," he said.

"Don't worry about that. This is good spaghetti without it. You're quite a cook, Tom."

"I watched Bertha a lot. She can cook anything."

"It sounds to me like you are very close to Bertha."

"I am closer to her than I am to my mother. Some day I'll take you over there to meet Bertha. I know she would appreciate meeting you."

"I have to tell you that I talked with my mother today. We talked about you. Dad was out of the office at the courthouse doing the closings so Mom came over to help out in case I got busy. Nobody came in so we had a great talk. She is quite excited about us, and started giving me motherly advice. I let her ramble on because I do appreciate her interest in me and in us."

"What did she have to say about us?" Tommy asked.

"She wanted to know if I was going to move in with you, and I told her that question would have to be answered by you. Then she wanted to know if we planned on getting married. I told her that we had not discussed that yet. I don't think she understands that we are just at the stage of realization about each other."

"Well, what about moving in with me?" This cabin is small, but we seem to get along well enough so we would consider the cabin cozy instead of small or cramped."

"I will bring my few clothes out tomorrow when I get off work. How does that sound to you?"

"That sounds perfect to me," Tommy said. "If this place proves too small, I can build an addition to it out back or on either side. But, it won't be from logs. The forests around here don't have trees the right diameter for log buildings. George Haskell told me that one day when we were talking about houses and cabins."

"I figure to leave all my stuff where it is. I only need some clothes to wear to work. By the way, where do you take a shower?"

"There's a washtub under the floor of the porch. I bring it inside during the winter but in summer I take it out to the old barn, what's left of it. There is no way to heat the water so I had to get used to cold showers."

"I suppose cold showers are better than no showers," she said, and laughed.

"When I get done with this sculpture I will see what I can do to make a bathroom off the back of the cabin. We have propane so we can get a gas water heater and have hot showers."

"I can always go to my parents' house for showers. For that matter, you can join me there. That might be quite the fun taking showers together."

What would your parents say to that kind of an adventure?"

"They probably took showers together when they were young. I know you don't know my parents, but, believe me, from what you have told me about yours, my parents are superb by comparison.

Just after sunset Tommy lit the gas lamp and they sat at he table discussing all sorts of things, mostly about what they believed. They both felt that it was close to miraculous that they thought about things close to the same with every topic. Once again the conversation stopped abruptly and their eyes focused on each other. Tommy reached over and ran his index finger down her nose.

"I have never seen a more beautiful nose in my life," he said, and began unbuttoning his shirt.

A month after Gretchen moved into the cabin, she and Tommy were sitting outside taking a break from working with the copper. On Sundays, Gretchen was used to going to the workshop and being there for errands when Tommy needed something.

A car approached on the road from Newburgh. They watched it as it turned into their yard and stopped. Hal Cooper and Clara Anson got out of the car and walked toward Tommy and Gretchen. The two rose from their chairs.

"Hal, Miss Anson, what brings you way out here?" Tommy asked.

"Cooper and Anson stopped in front of Tommy and Gretchen.

"We came out here to bring you some good news. We are on our honeymoon."

Tommy held out his hand and shook Hal's and then went to Clara and gave her a hug.

"That is wonderful news, just wonderful."

He turned to Gretchen.

"You know Hal Cooper from The Escalante, don't you?" he asked. "And this is Clara Anson, but I guess we call her Clara Cooper now."

"This is a pleasure," Gretchen said. "Tom has told me about both of you."

"When did all this happen, Hal?" Tommy asked.

"Yesterday afternoon. That was Saturday. Friday was my last day at The Escalante. I am finally free from that crap hole."

"Come on in and tell us all about it," Tommy said and picked up the chairs to bring into the cabin.

The four of them went in. Hal and Clara sat at the table on the chairs. Tommy and Gretchen sat on the bed.

"You remember when I brought you out here, I told you that I was not happy at that school. Well, the shit hit the fan last week. Moser called me into his office and started telling me that Loring Lincoln, Clara's principal, had called to tell him that someone in your home town was complaining about me spending nights with Clara. I have no clue how they found out my name and where I worked. These people are religious freaks. Moser forced Loring Lincoln to tell him the names of the complainers and he said it was a woman that lives a block down the street from Clara. She attends the same evangelical church as Lincoln.

I held up my hand and told him to shut up. He stopped his tirade and I told him to write me my last paycheck. That lard ass asked me why I was quitting, so I told him that I was tired of working in a place where there were no brains in working order. He wrote the check and even added a small bonus. I suppose he doesn't want me to tell everyone what The Escalante is really like."

"So you two just decided to hell with all the crap and got married," Tommy said.

"That's about it," Hal said, and turned toward Gretchen. "Now I know where I have seen you. It was at one of those dances and you were dancing with Tommy."

"That sounds accurate," Gretchen said.

She got up from the bed and went over to heat what was left of the morning coffee.

"How's the sculpting coming along, Tommy?" Hal asked.

"Good progress. I am getting the parts cut out so soon I will be starting to braze the stuff together."

" Hal told me that you had changed from clay to copper," Clara said. "You were really good with clay."

"I like clay very much and think about it still. But, this sculpture calls for, and even begs for copper. When it is finished I think you will agree with me."

Gretchen asked how they all took their coffee. Then, she proceeded to pour, fix and serve.

"You seem like you live here, Gretchen," Hal said.

"I sure do. I am the happiest woman in the world."

"I may have to call you on that one," Clara said and laughed.

"Are you two married also?" Hal asked.

"In our hearts and minds we are married forever," Tommy said.

"That's all that matters," Clara said.

"By the way," Hal said. "Clara will retire early the first of the year. She is fed up with Loring Lincoln and this latest thing is just too much."

"I want to quit right now," Clara said. But, that would make a hundred dollars a month less on my retirement."

"I am interested in knowing why you two got married, Tommy said. "You were doing just fine before."

"You are correct," Hal said. "We were doing fine before all that crap came down from Loring Lincoln. Lots of couples live together these days without the benefit of marriage. Most people accept that and leave them alone. But there are these evangelicals who seem to think they are on earth to mind other people's business. They intrude where they don't belong and cause unrest in communities. Clara and I decided to get married so that Loring Lincoln could have no complaints about us being in the same house together. Also, being married is what we have been for several years. We just never bothered to pay for a license."

"I think Gretchen and I are lucky to live here away from all that evangelical nonsense," Tommy said. "We will probably end up buying a license some day. But right now, we are content with our situation. By the way, you said you were on your honeymoon. Where will that be?"

"Niagara Falls of course. Where else is there for a honeymoon? We are now conformists by getting married. But, we know that we have been on a honeymoon for quite a few years. And, speaking of our honeymoon, we should get going. We drove by here to tell you the news. Now we should continue to our destination."

Hal and Clara left the cabin after the well wishing from Tommy and Gretchen. Tommy and Gretchen went back inside the cabin. They sat at the table talking about Hal and Clara. Tommy told her about the times he spent the night in Clara's house to avoid his parents. He also mentioned that it was to Clara's house he went when he ran away from home.

"Clara probably did more for my sanity than I realize. I could always count on her for a safe haven and someone to talk with when all I got at home was silence. I suppose I must thank both Clara and Ralph for a lot that I would otherwise have missed."

"She seems like a down to earth nice person," Gretchen said. "You certainly had your share of bullshit growing up."

"That's a good word for it. I feel lucky that my parents sent me to The Escalante even though as I got older, it was damn near a prison in many ways."

"I am glad they sent you there," Gretchen said. "I would probably never have met you if you had been somewhere else. And, by the way, I am in no hurry to get married. Nobody in my family would ever pressure me to do that. My mother told me that she and Dad lived together for five years before they got married and they did that because she was pregnant with my brother."

"You know all sorts of things about your parents, and I know practically nothing. But, as things have turned out, I have strong feelings of not giving a rat's ass about their life before or after my arrival. I do wonder, at times, if I am the product of a broken condom or a miscalculation of her cycle. Even that makes no difference because I am quite happy that I am here regardless of how I happened to get started.

They had been talking for an hour when they heard a car drive up and stop in front of the cabin. Tommy went to the door, looked at the visitor and turned back to Gretchen.

"It's Hal and Clara back again," he said. He turned around and walked over to the car and spoke through the open window on the driver's side.

"Did you forget something?" he asked Hal.

"Yes. We got to talking and I forgot one of the things I came to see."

"What is that?"

"I am curious about your sculpting progress. Do you have anything you can show me?"

"Come with me and I will show you my workshop and a bunch of the stuff I am working on. I can tell you somewhat about the design plan, but there is a lot about it that even I will not know until I arrive at certain stages."

Hal and Clara got out of the car and followed Tommy to the workshop. He showed them the copper strips bent into the shapes he intended on using for the sculpture, and explained his design plan.

"These heavier copper pipes and tubing will eventually form the base framing, and from them I will attach the segments I have already begun to make. I am at the stage of brazing the segments together to make the symbols I am speaking through."

"You are telling me that your sculpture will also be an essay?"

"I cannot help it," Tommy said. "There is one question that has plagued my life in many ways, so I am attempting to show that in my art. I may include some writing as well."

"You have certainly come a long way since I was teaching you how to throw pots," Clara said.

"I remember when I wanted to work with clay slabs instead of throwing and you seemed perturbed at that idea," Tommy said,

"I got over that when I saw the sculpture you called Ralph."

"Ya know, Miss Anson; I mean Missus Cooper, I still talk to Ralph sometimes."

"I knew how important Ralph was to you, Tommy. That is why I left you alone to make him into a sculpture. I will never forget the day you came over and told me that your father had thrown Ralph into the creek by your clearing. I wanted to go to him, slap his face, and tell him what an ignorant ass he was."

"Back to your current sculpture," Hal said. "When you first told me about this idea that you had thought about in a very slight way, I was not sure about it. I, being a ceramic artist have difficulty visualizing forms other than those made from clay. I have realized today, after your explanations, that you have that unique adventuresome spirit that is so necessary for pure and true artistry. I am anxious to see more of the progress of your project and hope you will keep in touch."

"We don't have a telephone and do not expect to get one, so just come out here whenever you find the time and have the inclination to see what I have been doing. You know you are always welcome, my friend."

"Without a telephone how do you and Gretchen contact one another when she is in town working?" Hal asked.

"If we ever had an emergency she could call Roy Johnson, a blacksmith friend of mine here in town. I never had any reasons to have a telephone when I was growing up. I suppose when you are not used to something, even if it is mundane to others, you can get by without it. I had hot water at home and at The Escalante, but we take cold showers in an old galvanized washtub out here. I guess adjustment is what happens."

"Whatever is your lifestyle, you seem to be thriving with it," Hal said. "I guess we will head back. When I realized I had forgotten to see what you are dong we decided to go on our honeymoon to Manhattan and look at art galleries and museums."

"I am glad you came back," Tommy said.

"So am I. I am happy with my newfound freedom. I wonder why I didn't tell Moser to shove it long ago. That school at the start had great possibilities, but through the years too many so-called educators sneaked in and their philosophy floundered. The entire country needs more of that attitude that was with The Escalante at its beginning and less of this memorization crap that chains minds instead of opening them."

"I must say I am glad I was there. You were a good mentor and let me explore things. I am realizing the result of all that as I work on this sculpture. It is a grand adventure for me. Once in a while I think about what a boring time I would have had at The Wharton school of Finance thinking about money all the time and how to grab it from the rest of the world. That is all bullshit in my opinion."

"We have talked about all this before and we got into discussing what I call The Fear Factor and the dangers of it to society. I have thought a lot about that, Tommy, and I can see no end to that type of control unless we can change our education system."

"I agree with that, Hal, but that system is mired in too much tradition which has become obsolete and even dangerous to freedom if there is such a thing."

"Well, Tommy Holmes, I will be back sooner than you think," Hal said. "Keep up the good art!"

Hal rolled up the window and drove off toward Newburgh. Tommy stood where he was for a few minutes digesting what Hal had said. Then he went back inside to talk more with Gretchen. They sat across from each other at the table with cups of coffee that Gretchen had heated.

"Hal came back to talk about my sculpting," Tommy said. "They gave up going to Niagara Falls. They are a nice couple and have been good friends of mine for a long time. Hal has connections with the art world in Manhattan. He was instrumental in my getting that big grant, so I suspect he has something in mind for my work in copper."

"How will you know?" Gretchen asked.

"I am sure I won't know anything until I get the sculpture finished."

"I think you shouldn't think about what Hal might be able to do and concentrate on your work. I have noticed that you do not need distractions."

"I know that, too. But there is one distraction I enjoy so much that I don't care when it comes and stops me from working."

"We both agree on that one," Gretchen said.

Every morning after breakfast, Tommy went to work in his workshop doing what he needed to do for his copper sculpture whether it was cutting out pieces for different parts or bending strips in the jigs. Brazing soon became close to automatic in that he didn't have to ponder the process as he had at the beginning.

Gretchen began working at her father's real estate office mornings and getting back to Walden shortly after noon to have lunches with Tommy and then help him with the copper during the afternoons. When she wasn't shelving the various parts for easy access, she helped cut out parts according to Tommy's instructions.

One day, a month and a half after Hal and Clara's visit, Tommy suggested that they take a break from the copper and drive to Manhattan to visit some art galleries and museums to look at what other sculptors were doing.

"I don't want to copy anything, I just want to see what others are doing. I would not change what I am doing for any reason. While we are there we could go down to where the ocean-going ships dock and look at them. I used to like reading sea stories and the descriptions of foreign lands."

"I agree that we can use a break, even though I can see that we are making good progress. Am I right in saying that you are close to putting the framework together?"

"You are right, and that is one reason I would like to take a break. Once I begin all that assembly work I don't want to quit before I am completely finished. I will need to keep my mind focused all the time except when I am sleeping."

"There might be some distractions that you accept," she said.

"That goes without saying," Tommy said.

"Then, let's start out in the morning," Gretchen said. "We will get there in time to find a reasonable hotel. I think my father told me once that there is a good and reasonably priced hotel in the Tribeca section of Manhattan. We can stop at the real estate office and tell my father that we will be gone for a few days."

Gretchen drove and Tommy sat in the passenger seat of the Toyota smiling all the way to Newburgh and then down along the Hudson River into Manhattan. They had stopped at the real estate office in Newburgh to tell Sam Shafer that his daughter would not be at work for a few days. Sam and Tommy had met and they greeted one another warmly.

"I found your cabin and farm on a plat map. The deed on that piece of ground goes way back," Sam said. "It has been in your family for well over a hundred years."

"There's a saying that nobody in the Holmes family ever sells land, because it is a limited resource."

"That's an old economic principle," Sam said. "Anyway, if you ever need the legal description to get some permit or other, I have it for you here in my folder."

"Thanks, Sam. I'll keep that in mind," Tommy said. "I guess we had better get going to the big city."

"Have a good time, and by the way, Tom, I am glad that Gretchen is with you."

Tommy patted Sam on the shoulder.

"So am I," he said.

They didn't say much during the drive along the Hudson River, and when they reached Manhattan they continued their silence as Gretchen maneuvered through the heavy traffic to The Tribeca Hotel. Neither had much experience driving in the city so there were a few close calls as taxicabs weaved in and out of traffic to maintain their speed.

They spent three days at various art galleries and museums. During the last afternoon they went to the bowery and looked at the ships that were docked.

"Did you ever want to go on a cruise?" Gretchen asked.

"I would rather go out in a sailboat and feel the waves throw spray on my face. Those cruise ships look like floating hotels, not titans of the sea. I guess I have read too many sea stories when all the ships had masts and sails to deal with the wind."

The drive back to Walden brought them home when the sun had dipped close to the horizon. Tommy went out to his workshop to make sure nobody had come by and disturbed anything.

The following day at mid-morning, Roy Johnson drove into the yard just as Tommy stopped brazing to take a break with a cup of warmed up coffee. He invited Roy to have coffee with him, and the two went into the cabin and sat at the table.

"Where's Gretchen?" Roy asked.

"She works mornings in Newburg. We got back from the city last night so she had to go to her office early to get caught up with business."

"I knew you were away somewhere because some man who called himself the caretaker of your cabin came by to ask me if I knew who was living in the cabin."

"Did you catch his name?"

'Here's his card." Roy said, handing a business card to Tommy.

"Robert Clausen. It gives his address as Goshen."

"He said his father had been the caretaker until he died a few years ago. This fellow said he had taken over the job that means coming by about four times a year to see if all is well with the cabin. He asked if I knew who was living in the cabin. I told him you were and I gave him your name when he asked. I didn't tell him anything about Gretchen in case he is some kind of church person prone to make trouble.

When I told him you were Tom Holmes, he looked kind of funny, but didn't say anything. He said his family used to live here in Walden but went broke farming. They moved to Goshen and worked for some farmer over there. He said his father kept the caretaking job because the family needed the extra money."

"I have never seen anyone come by saying they were a caretaker of this cabin," Tommy said. "He must work for my father."

"He said he had not been by for quite a while because his wife has been sick," Roy said. "Anyhow, I thought you should know about this jasper so I came by to tell you. Now I gotta get back to the forge."

"Thanks for the information, Roy. I appreciate you keeping your eye out," Tommy said.

Roy left the cabin to return to his blacksmithing, and Tommy sat in the chair wondering what the caretaker business was all about. The big question that loomed was; for whom was this caretaker working?

Gretchen returned from town just before noon and the two had lunch together in the cabin while discussing the news that Roy Johnson had brought to Tommy.

"There is nothing you can do about it even if you knew the man's employer," Gretchen said. "Don't worry about it until something happens that you have to deal with."

"I suppose you're right, Gretch, but I hate being in the dark about this. I reckon I had best get back to the shop and get some sculpting done. I'll meet you there when you are finished in here."

Tommy went back to his copper. Gretchen joined him after she cleaned up the kitchen and sat for a few moments digesting what Tommy had told her about the mysterious caretaker.

Three days later, Gretchen returned from Newburgh earlier than usual. She went directly to the workshop without going into the cabin. Tommy shut off the acetylene torch when he saw her approaching.

"How come you're back so soon?" he asked

"Come with me," she said. We need to sit down and talk," and turned to go to the cabin. Tommy followed her.

When both were sitting down in their chairs, Gretchen began her story.

"When I got to the office, my father called me over to his desk. I sat in the client chair next to him and he tilted his head like he does when he has something important to say.

"'Gretchen,' he said. 'I got the multiple listings in this morning and one caught my eye. It is that land where you and Tom are living in the cabin. The listing is for sale at fifty thousand cash. The listing owner is Jason Holmes. That is Tom's father is it not?'"

Gretchen ran her hand over her forehead and cleared her throat.

"I told him that Jason Holmes is your father. And my father wanted to know why Jason was suddenly selling the property while you are living there. 'Are you two planning to move?' he asked me.

"I described a little about your father and he seemed to understand what might be going on. He got real pensive and stopped talking about the listing. After a while he did ask me to tell him more about your father so I told him all I knew from what you have told me. My father's final remark was a mumble about your father not being a very nice father. I agreed with him and then I said I was going home to tell you what was happening."

"Now I have figured out what that so-called caretaker was doing out here, and I'll bet my bottom dollar that he went right over to tell my father that I was the one living in the cabin. The listing for sale is so we will have to move. It is just my father's method of getting his own way."

"I have a little money saved from some of the commissions I've earned, but not close to fifty thousand dollars," Gretchen said.

"I have quite a bit left from the fellowship, but nowhere near fifty thousand either. That bastard doesn't even know about that fellowship I got. He thinks I must be working somewhere to be able to eat. I feel like going back to the old farmhouse and giving him a real piece of my mind and pour a bucket of wet bullshit on top of his head. And, here we are without a bull."

"I think we should try to keep calm and wait to see what might happen. Let's get our butts out in the workshop and get some copper made into some good stuff."

"You're right, Gretch. But why the hell can't that son of a bitch leave me alone?"

They worked with the copper until it was past suppertime, expending their nervous energy onto the work. Finally, as it was getting close to dark, they went into the cabin and made sandwiches to eat. Before going to bed, Tommy put his head in his hands.

"Why, oh why?" he asked. "Why did those two turn into such mean bastards?"

"Look at it this way, Tom," Gretchen said. "Had they treated you like a son, they would still have a son. My parents treated me with love and caring and I am still their daughter."

Gretchen drove to work after breakfast, and stayed at the office until the normal time for her to come home. When she arrived back at the cabin she went directly to the workshop with a smile on her face.

"Tom, my father has solved the problem of your father," she said. "We had a nice talk as soon as he got back from an errand this morning. He told me that he had already done enough research on this property to discover that it is worth quite a bit more than fifty thousand, and guess what he did?"

Tommy held the lighted torch in his hand.

"What did your father do?"

"He submitted his offer to the listed owner, your father, and guess what else?"

"Your father accepted the offer of forty thousand dollars cash. This all happened via email, and it is as good and final as if they had been together. My father told me that he was glad that your father didn't know my last name or even that I was living with you."

"So what do we do know, pay your father rent?"

"Heavens no," Gretchen said. "Daddy said that he would sign it over to us jointly once we are married."

"Suppose we don't get married?" Tommy asked and laughed.

"Then I will get my father to sign the place over to me and you can pay me the rent," she said and laughed harder than Tommy.

They took each other into their arms and held on for a long time. They finally kissed and sat down at the table again to chat about what had happened.

"Did your father say when this deal would close?"

"Next week, because the title will be easy to search since there has been one owner for over a hundred years and there never has been a mortgage on it."

"That sounds great to me even though I know nothing about real estate nor money in general."

"Maybe you should have taken your father's advice and gone to The Wharton, as he calls it."

"You could have gone all year without saying that, Gretch. It's a good thing I know that you are joking."

"I am glad you know me well enough to know that I would never tell you to regret anything you have done or not done."

They returned to the workshop and continued working the copper into the desired shapes for the sculpture. They had been working on the basic framework for a week. Tommy modified the angles, changed diameters, and lengths of segments as he proceeded to braze the framework together. Gretchen had brought him the pieces of copper and various tools he called for every afternoon. After the event of her father's purchasing the cabin and the acreage surrounding it, the work with the copper resumed as before. Two days after she had come home with the real estate news, she came back at mid-day. After their lunch and when they had gone to the workshop she stood with her arms akimbo looking at Tommy with her eyebrows forced upward.

"Tom, I must tell you that ever since I have been helping you with this project I have been wanting to ask you what it is going to be because I haven't a clue about that and I don't understand if you have some concept that you are following. Can you fill me in?"

Tommy put the unlit torch on the workbench and faced her.

"I have thought about that, and have tried to think of some way to explain what I am striving for with this sculpture. There are times when I have wondered about it myself. What this will end up being is sort of a tower of question marks that will be different sizes and not all the same shape. They will be attached so that there will be variation in how they will appear to the viewer. All those pieces that we cut from the strips and bent on the jigs will be brazed to the question mark cut outs that we made in different sizes. They will end up as square copper question marks that when polished, will sparkle and hopefully send out the message or messages that I am concerned about."

"That certainly clears things up in my mind. How tall will this tower be?"

"I don't know. I guess I will go as high as my thoughts go while I am making this framework that we are working on right now."

Satisfied that he had answered Gretchen's question as best he could, he picked up the torch and was about to light it to go back to brazing the framework together. They saw a car drive up and park at the front door of the cabin. Tommy dropped the torch onto the workbench and hurried to the back of the shop.

"Come back here quickly," he said to Gretchen. "That is my mother's car."

Gretchen joined him at the back of the shop.

"She is bound to come looking for you since it is obvious that she knows you are here," Gretchen said. "Let's see what she wants, but don't say a word about my father buying this place from your father for us."

"Don't worry about that. I will probably not get a word in edgewise with her motor mouth going full speed."

They heard Blanche knocking on the cabin door as they approached. Catching them out of the corner of her eye, Blanche turned toward Tommy and Gretchen.

"Well, you are home after all," she said. "How are you, Tommy? I have a lot to tell you, can we go somewhere to talk?"

Tommy walked up to the door and opened it.

"Come in and have a seat," he said. "This is Gretchen. Gretchen, this is my mother, Blanche Holmes."

All three went inside of the cabin. Blanche and Gretchen sat in the chairs at the table. Tommy sat on the edge of the bed.

"I remember this cabin years ago when your father and I were newlyweds. He brought me out here twice, then he got too busy with his damn bank to take me anywhere."

She reached into her large purse that looked more like a knitting bag than a purse. She withdrew an almost full bottle of Glenlivet Single Malt scotch and put it on the table.

"I brought this because I know you don't drink. Do you have a glass and some ice?"

Tommy got a couple of pieces of ice from the cooler that they used to keep food from spoiling and put them into a water glass he took from the sink.

"Who are you, Gretchen? Have you ever been to our old farmhouse that is Tommy's home?"

"I have never been there Missus Holmes. Tom and I met when he was at The Escalante and I was at Mujeres del Mundo."

"You are not the girl that claimed Tommy fathered her child?"

"No, Missus Holmes. That was Julie Bronson, and I know very well that Tom is not the father of her child. I don't even know where she is these days."

"My husband and I haven't heard anything about it and hope that we don't. Tommy, I wish you had never gotten mixed up with that girl."

"Me, too. I would just as soon change the subject, Mother. Why did you come out here and how did you know we were here?"

Blanche took her bottle and filled the glass half full of Scotch. She put the bottle back on the table and lifted the glass to her mouth. Staring at Tommy, she took a gulp from the glass.

"I have some bad news for you, Tommy. You took off after you were expelled from The Escalante and we had no idea where you had gone. You haven't contacted us to tell us where you are or what you are doing. Your father is furious with you for not going to The Wharton. He thinks you will become a derelict and worthless as a Holmes. I think you should go home and explain things to him and somehow get back on his good side."

"Mother, I have never seen my father's good side, so how would I ever get back on it?"

"Well, it is probably be too late for that. And, after I tell you what he has done you will not want to see him. The caretaker, Robert Clausen, who took over after his father passed on, came to report that you were living here in the cabin. He came by here for his seasonal inspection, but you had gone somewhere. He found out you were the one living here and came to report that to your father."

"I know the man who told your caretaker his information," Tommy said. "So what if we are living here? According to Uncle Ben it belongs to the family. Oh, I forgot what Dad said when I got booted out of The Escalante. I suppose he doesn't consider me family because I will not obey him and go to his dream school, The Wharton. Let me say something about all that crap. When I see what The Wharton did to my father I wouldn't walk on their campus."

"Your father always wanted you to follow in his and the rest of the male Holmes's footsteps."

"My father has no respect for individuality. He is a pea in a giant financial pod and I want none of it. What did he do, send you out here to give me one of his lectures? That is all I ever heard from him when he wasn't on Wall Street or at Winged Foot playing golf with that "shrink". He should have sat on the "shrink's" couch instead of playing golf with him.

"Tommy, I don't think you realize how much we have done for you. Sending you to The Escalante was quite expensive you know."

"Mother, both of you hardly ever talked to me. I felt like I was always in your way. I started talking to Ralph, and you sent me to that "shrink" because you thought I was crazy. Maybe I am crazy, but I am happier living here crazy than I ever was in the damned old farmhouse. The only one that ever showed me any love was Bertha."

"Bertha is still there. She is getting on a bit, but she still comes to work. She doesn't talk much."

"Did you ever wonder why she doesn't talk much?"

"Now Tommy, get me some more ice so I can have another drink."

Tommy got another chunk of ice and put it into her glass. She took the bottle and filled the water glass almost to the top. After taking a gulp, she put the glass down on the table.

"All right, I am going to tell you what happened when Bob Clausen told your father that you were living here. Your father flew into a rage. I have never seen him in such a state. He called you every nasty name I have ever heard and yelled out that he was going to 'kick your skinny ass out of the cabin'.

After he calmed down and Clausen had left, he called a realtor friend of his and told the man to sell the cabin for fifty thousand cash and to kick you out of here so that the place would sell easier. Then I heard him say, 'Be sure to put it into multiple listings so it will sell quickly'.

When he got home from the bank the following day, he told me that the cabin had sold and that would fix you good. I must admit that this entire thing has upset me greatly."

Tommy and Gretchen looked at each other from time to time as Blanche told her story, and smiled without commenting about the sale.

Just then, Roy Johnson stopped by and came to the cabin door.

"Tom, I'm going to town to buy a little steel. Do you need any copper?" Roy asked.

"Thanks for asking Roy. I am all set for now. But wait just a minute. I have a present for you."

Tommy grabbed the bottle of Glenlivet from the table, and handed it to Roy.

"Have a good time tonight," Tommy said.

Roy turned and quickly left as Blanche gave out a yell that Roy said later, "Was enough to curdle milk."

"What the hell are you doing with my bottle?" she asked Tommy.

"Mother, you have a long drive home and you sure as hell don't need to be drunk behind the wheel of that Town and Country. By the way, I see you have the latest model."

"By Jove, I am mad now. You have no right to steal my whiskey. I am leaving. I can see that I am not wanted here. You had better get your stuff out of here because the new owner wants to move in right away."

Blanche got up, walked a little shakily to the door and left the cabin. Tommy got up from the bed to watch her get into the Town and Country, start it and drive off toward Newburgh. He turned around to Gretchen who was still in the chair, but laughing so hard the tears had formed in her eyes. Tommy joined the laughter. When they had gotten over the humorous happening, they both breathed deeply.

"You were brave to grab that bottle of whiskey, Tom," Gretchen said. "From what you have said about her drinking habit, she would have finished that entire bottle if you hadn't given it to Roy."

"Maybe I should have let her finish the booze. The only problem with that is that she could have killed someone on the road. Even now, with what she already drank, that could happen."

"All that stuff she told us about your father getting into a rage and selling the cabin was hilarious because we know what really happened."

"Something tells me that sometime or other my father will find out who bought the cabin and who is still living in it. Too bad the caretaker won't be around any more or he would be the ideal one to enlighten my father about who is still living here. What a joke all this has become. My father will birth a baby alligator when he finds out what happened."

"Your mother didn't give me the time of day except for wondering if I was Julie Branson. I must say, I don't blame you for talking to Ralph and I don't blame you for getting away from them. I haven't met your father, and I am not sure that I ever want to meet him from what you have told me and from what your mother just described."

"As I watched her drive toward Newburgh, I hoped that I would never have to see her again. And that goes for Jason Holmes, the Wall Street banker."

"Let's get back to the shop and do some more with copper," Gretchen said. "That is if you are not too riled up to light your torch."

They finished the afternoon working and were having supper when Roy Johnson stopped by to thank Tommy for the Scotch.

"That is good hootch," Roy said. "Who was that old broad that was drinking it?"

"That was my mother, and you don't need to apologize for calling her an old broad. She has a definite drinking problem."

"She sure did look mean when you grabbed that bottle away from her."

"If I hadn't taken away that booze she would have finished it sitting there and driven off to hit something or driven into the Hudson River."

"Sounds to me like you did your mother a big favor. And, thanks to you I also profited by that favor. Thanks for the gift."

Roy left and Tommy turned back to Gretchen.

"I need to go down to my log by the river, Gretch. There are some things I need to straighten out in my mind."

"I'll be here when you get back, Tom."

Tommy sat on his log listening to the sound of the river as it traveled along with a peaceful murmur. He talked to Ralph about his mother and father. He got lost in thought as he imagined his father ranting and raving when he found out he didn't accomplish what he wanted to by selling the cabin. He told Ralph all about the cabin deal with Sam Shafer and how he and Gretchen were able to keep quiet about the deal when his mother was with them in the cabin. He took a circuitous route back to the cabin because he wanted to check out the apples to see if any had ripened since he had last seen them.

The first tree he came to yielded two ripe apples. He picked them and put them in his pockets. He glanced around at the other trees and saw more fruit that looked ripe, and he was glad that he had taken the advice to prune the trees. He decided to come back the next day with a sack in which to put more apples.

"Well, Gretchen Shafer, you have now met my mother and together we were able to keep straight faces while she told us almost what we already know. I wonder what she will tell my father when they have their "Happy Time" before supper. I suppose all that doesn't matter. I will feel better when the sale closes and my father no longer has anything to say about this place."

"I now what you mean, but I refuse to worry about something I have no control over," she said.

The sculpture progressed rapidly once Tommy was satisfied with the framework. The morning that the framework was complete, he walked around it until noon, making sure that it was exactly the way he had envisioned. He was still looking at it when Gretchen arrived from town. She went straight to the workshop and joined Tommy as he looked over what he had created so far. He put his arm around her shoulders as their eyes digested the framework with its branches and most of the copper question marks attached at various angles and positions.

"What does it tell you, Gretch?" Tommy asked.

"To me it says that life is full of questions to be answered. Some questions are crucial and beg for answers while others can remain unanswered but lurk, waiting for attention. Then there are some questions that are not worth the time and effort to deal with because, as you have said, if you cannot control something, there is no point in worrying about it because it will remain beyond your reach. Am I reading this right?"

"I would say you will probably be one of the few who know me well enough to understand what I am saying with my art. There will be those who may find this concept beyond their thinking and too challenging for their imagination. But, the work does not have to be lost for them. They can look at it as a puzzle, and that can be their challenge."

"Does all that mean that you have created this so that there is something for everyone in it?" Gretchen asked.

"Exactly," Tommy said. "I am really glad you came home when you did. I have been walking around this jumbled mass of copper for a couple of hours trying to decide if I am on the road to accomplish what I started out to do. What you have just told me confirms that I am going in the right direction. From now on, and until the moment I can say that it is finished, I will be able to maintain my freedom of thought and design, because thus far that freedom has allowed me to use my imagination and a depth of thinking that I may not have been totally aware of. Let's go to the cabin and chase away our hunger."

"Is that hunger for food?" Gretchen asked.

"Dear girl, hunger for food can be satisfied with our clothes on."

Three days later at ten o'clock in the morning, Hal and Clara drove into the yard. They got out of their car and walked directly to the workshop where Tommy was busy with his torch. He saw them approach, turned of the torch and put it on the hook by the tanks of oxygen and acetylene.

"Good morning." Tommy said. "What brings you out to the country so early in the morning?"

"I figured you must have made enough progress on your sculpture so that I can see what it will be when you are finished," Hal said. "I got a good idea about it last time we were here, but now I see you have made great progress. You concept has bloomed. I am impressed."

"I am glad you like it, Hal."

"I think it is outstanding," Clara said. "When I saw what you were doing last time we were here, I wasn't sure. I suppose I am much too used to clay. But, as I look at it today, I can really see it and feel what it is saying."

"That makes me happy," Tommy said. "Let's go to the cabin and I will warm up some coffee for us."

Hal and Clara sat at the table. Tommy busied himself with heating the coffee in the blue enameled coffee pot he had bought at a yard sale for fifty cents. He took three cups from the shelf near the stove and put them on the table. He filled the cups and sat down on the bed.

"Tommy, I need to talk to you about your sculpture. I must tell you that I have been hired by the Museum of Art in Manhattan to scout upstate New York and New England for potential entries into the various shows at the museum. There is a sculpture show coming up in March. That is five months from now. Will you be finished with this by then?"

"I am sure I will get it done before then. In fact I will be ready to sell it by the time winter arrives."

"Would you be willing to hold off selling it until during or after the spring sculpture show at the museum?"

"I suppose so, why?"

"I want your permission to enter this in the Spring Show. I am convinced that this piece will catch the eye of the judge or judges and you will have a good chance for recognition. Let me say this. There are lots of sculptures of people and animals and even landscapes that are beautiful in every respect, and they are technically done to the utmost details. But, your sculpture is not only beautiful with its balanced gleaming copper. It also speaks. It has heart. It becomes part of the viewer's mind in that it makes those minds think. I'll tell you that I think this creation of yours goes far beyond a piece of art. Do I have your permission to enter it?"

"Wow, what a treat your words are. Of course you have my permission and my eternal gratitude."

"Good," Hal said. "I brought my camera and I need to take a few photographs to accompany the entry application, so let's go out and get that done before we go back. By the way, Clara got a red ribbon for one of her fancy pitchers in this summer's craft show."

"Congratulations, Clara. That is so nice to hear."

Hal took several photographs of Tommy's sculpture after they had carried it outside and used the wall made of the old gray barn wood for a background.

"I will get the application in as soon as I get prints of these photos made. I almost forgot, do you have a title yet?"

"Yes," Tommy said. "I am calling it, "WHY?".

"Perfect," Hal said. "I understand that better than most will."

Hal and Clara drove off toward Newburgh. Gretchen came home a half an hour later. Tommy told her all about Hal and Clara's visit and about the show in Manhattan. Gretchen was impressed and happy at the same time.

"You had better win, or I'll kick the judge's ass," Gretchen said, and laughed.

"I have read a lot about art shows and what it all boils down to is that the winners and losers are the result of one person's opinion, no more no less. If there is more than one judge, the results are a combination of opinions. The results are therefore irrelevant to what others may think about any piece of art in the show."

"My mother paints landscapes and I have heard other artists at meetings in our house saying that entering shows gives an artist exposure," Gretchen said.

"I would say that an artist can get better exposure by wearing a short sleeved shirt in the sun."

"That might be," Gretchen said with a smirk on her face, but what about sunburn?"

"I never wear short sleeves."

Tommy continued working on the sculpture. Gretchen joined him every day when she came back from her job at her father's real estate office. One afternoon they went to see Roy Johnson. Tommy had a question about using something heavier than the copper for a base. He was afraid that the lightness of copper would not keep the sculpture standing should someone brush against it.

Roy took off his blacksmith's cap and scratched his head as he contemplated the problem. After a while he went outside to his scrap pile. Rummaging around the pieces of iron and steel, he took out a large round disk that was once on a plow used in farming. The disk, about eighteen inches in diameter was curved, and there was an inch diameter hole in its center.

"If you could cover this old disk with copper and braze the copper pipe you are using for your frame, I think this disk is heavy enough to keep that whole outfit standin', even in a windstorm," Roy said, holding the disk with both hands as he handed it to Tommy.

Tommy took the disk and hefted it.

"That is sure enough heavy," Tommy said, and turned toward Gretchen. "And, by golly, I know just how to make it work to blend in perfectly with the rest of the sculpture. I can braze it around the edge, and then braze the copper pipe on the frame on the inside of the disk. Then I'll attach small copper question marks over the curve covered by copper."

"Looks to me like the problem is solved," Gretchen said.

"How much for the disk, Roy?" Tommy asked.

"It's yours for the taking. I'm no farmer and I have had that in my scrap pile for five or ten years. If I haven't found a use for it by now, I never will."

"Thanks Roy, I appreciate it."

"I wish I hadn't told your name to that jasper who said he was a caretaker. Your mother didn't waste any time gettin' out here."

"My father sent her, and he will be surprised very soon. By the way, I hope you enjoyed that Glenlivet Scotch."

"I still have some. That stuff is smooth."

While they were walking back home, Tommy stopped abruptly.

"I just had a wonderful idea for the base," he said. "It will take more time than just covering this disk with sheet copper, but it will serve another purpose that I have been puzzled about."

"Well, let's hear it,'" Gretchen said. "I haven't a clue what you are talking about."

"I know that because I have never mentioned it. At any rate, we both know that question marks on paper have a dot at the bottom. The question marks that we have made from copper have no dots because I haven't been able to figure out how to attach then so that there is a space between the question mark proper and the dot at the bottom. Now I have a solution. Cover the disk base with brass and then cover that with round and square dots that would normally go at the bottom of the question marks. I can sweat those circles onto the brass. These dots can be square or round and of different sized dimensions like the question marks are. And, I will put them in a scattered arrangement , some on top of others so that it looks like fallen dots."

"I still don't understand what you are trying to accomplish by putting all the dots onto the base," Gretchen said.

"I admit I am going to the edge with this, but all the dots could have fallen off the question marks when the one questioning and trying to answer "WHY" has concentrated to such a degree that the dots fell off onto the base. That explains why there are no dots near the bottoms of the question marks that constitute the sculpture. Of course, not everyone viewing the sculpture will have the imagination to fully understand this."

"Why are you making it so difficult for the viewer?" Gretchen asked.

"I believe that any art should not only be unique and perhaps beautiful, but also a challenge for the viewer to think about," Tommy said, arching his eyebrows.

"All right, now I see what you are getting at," Gretchen said. "That sounds absolutely ingenious."

"I don't know about that, but it sure as hell solves the challenge I have been facing since I started this."

They left the steel disk in the workshop and went into the cabin for coffee. Tommy took his sketchpad, drew the disk in for the base and then sketched in the dots that had fallen from the question marks. He showed the sketch to Gretchen.

"Can you see the concept better with this sketch?" He asked.

"Now it is clear. I think that it is better than I thought before," she said. "It looks like it will take a lot of time to get that completed."

"What else do we have besides love and time?"

The following morning Tommy began work to make the old plow disk into a base for his sculpture, and by the time Gretchen returned from Newburgh, he had it covered with sweated on pieces of brass that he cut out in various shapes and sizes. He had decided that brass would make a good contrast with the copper question mark dots. Before sweating on the brass pieces he had secured the main vertical shaft of the framework through the hole in the disk and then braced it with heavy copper piping that he attached to the inside of the disk and the shaft with the piping placed at forty-five degree angles. He had just finished the last of the brass pieces when Gretchen returned.

"That looks very strong and sturdy," she said after looking at the work he had done. "I have good news. The property deal between my father and your father closed today. My father has the deed and all the rest of the legal stuff. So now we don't have to worry about your father discovering who my father is in relation to you."

"That is good news. Now I can erase those thoughts from my mind. It is so sad that a son cannot trust his father."

"I am lucky to have the loving parents that I have. My dad was beaming with joy when he got those papers. I have told him a lot about your father, so my father has been careful about not telling anyone about that property business."

"I would like to be a fly on the wall when my father finds out about how his plan to make us homeless backfired."

Progress on the sculpture was steady. Tommy enjoyed placing the copper question marks at the locations on the framework that he chose. He wanted to end up with them pointing upward for the most part, but every once in a while he attached one that came close to upside down. He avoided placing them at same or close to the same angles. This, he had in his mind, that such differences portrayed the difference in the topics of the many questions. At all times he maintained what he wanted to say by speaking through the sculpture, and at the same time create art and beauty with such an obscure message.

Two weeks after they had received the good news about the purchase of the farm by Gretchen's father, Hal and Clara arrived with more good news. The approval letter of Tommy's submission of his sculpture to the Museum of Art had arrived at Hal's and Clara's, so they drove to Malden immediately.

Hal explained that he had sent the submission letter along with the photographs he had taken with his return address for the reply. He used his own address because Tommy had had no address as long as his father owned the property. Hal and Clara were happy that their friend and former student had been accepted for such a prestigious exhibition.

Hal took his camera back to the workshop and took more photographs to send to the museum for their show catalogue. One photograph included Tommy standing next to the sculpture.

"Your sculpture looks like it is very close to being finished," Hal said. "How much more time are you planning to spend on it?"

"I suppose that basically, it is finished," Tommy said. "There are some minor details that ask for small changes, but what you are looking at right now is probably, with one or two very minor exceptions, what you will see in New York."

"I am sure you remember what both Clara and I have told you about being careful not to overwork your art, no matter what that art might be."

"Hal, I am quite mindful of that. I even have that in mind with my writing."

"What are your plans to work on while you are waiting to go to New York?" Hal asked.

"I have quite a lot of small scraps of copper left from the sculpture. I am thinking of trying to figure out something...what I can make out of them that can be called art."

"That should keep you busy enough. The first snow is due any day now, so you will keep warm with your torch in your hand.'

"As long as I have some warm gloves on," Tommy said, and smiled. I have already been thinking about making copper flowers. Most of the scrap has points that can be shaped into either leaves or flower petals."

"It sounds to me like you are way ahead of the game," Hal said.

"That sounds like something you can sell at these country fairs around here," Clara said.

"We can use the money after buying all that copper," Tommy said.

"For heaven's sake don't starve to death. Let me know if you need some help," Hal said.

"Hal, my friend, you have helped me more than you will ever know. So have you, Clara."

"We need to get back home," Hal said. "We have pots to trim and it is getting late. I'll keep you posted on any news or instructions from the Museum of Art."

"Thanks for the good news. One of these days, I suppose we should get a telephone. But, I think that the ringing would drive me crazy."

"You could always turn it off when you weren't using it," Hal suggested.

"Then why have it to begin with. I have no reasons to talk to anyone that I cannot see."

Tommy went back to the workshop as soon as Hal and Clara left. He looked at some of the question marks closely and then stood back to look at them again with a critical eye. Finally he nodded his head slowly up and down affirmatively. One procedure that he insisted of himself was once he had attached a question mark, it was where it would be. He vowed never to remove any or move them once they were attached. This method, in his mind, forced him to be meticulous as he placed them over the framework. While looking at the sculpture with Hal and Clara, he thought he saw two of the question marks too close to each other, but when he inspected them after the visitors had left, he saw that the two he had wondered about were in truth at different angles and one was lower than the other. He sighed as he stood up and went about lighting the torch in order to attach a few circular dots to the base onto the others already in place.

Two weeks later, just after Tommy told Gretchen that he felt that he had finished the sculpture the first snow fell. When the storm ended its gift of eight inches of fluffy white to the land, Tommy went out to the workshop to give another once over look at his creation. He walked around it several times, climbed a step ladder to see the higher regions, and lastly crouched on the floor of the shop to look from the bottom up to see if that view was what he wanted. Gretchen arrived as he was looking upward from the floor.

"Are you figuring that some people will be on the floor looking at 'Why'?"

"The chances are almost none that anyone will take this position to view 'Why'. I am here close to ground level, because I want it to be exactly the way I designed it, otherwise I would be cheating."

"Cheating?" Gretchen asked. "Cheating who?"

"Cheating myself. If it is not what had been in my mind for a sculpture as I progressed and I just let it slide I would be cheating myself because it is my work, my art. Should it ever be on display somewhere, and I walk by it, I want to be able to say to myself that my sculpture has integrity because I have integrity."

"Thank you for explaining that. I now have a better understanding about you and your art work," Gretchen said. "You have finished just in time to enjoy winter without having to work in a cold workshop."

"I'll put on more clothes so I can keep warm enough to work. I have decided to make copper flowers from all the scrap I have accumulated while making 'Why'. I am going to visit George Haskell now to see if he has any scrap he wants to get rid of."

"Don't you think you should wait for the snowplow to plow the roads clear?"

"I might have to wait for a week for that plow to get here, so I will give the Ford its head like a racehorse and I will bet I make it without a hitch."

"Suit yourself. If you're not back in two hours, I'll come looking for you in my car," Gretchen said.

"And, suppose you get stuck in the snow?"

"Then we will be stuck together," she said.

Tommy made it to Haskell's without getting stuck in the snow. George had a substantial pile of scrap copper in the corner of his workshop.

What are you planning to do with all that scrap, George?" Tommy asked.

"I haul it to Newburgh and sell it by the pound," he said.

"I can save you a trip if you sell it to me. I can put it with my scrap and make some stuff I have in mind."

"I haven't got a scale here, but I would say from times past there's around ten bucks worth in that pile."

Tommy reached into his pocket and took out a small roll of bills. He took a ten-dollar bill out of the roll and handed it to Haskell.

"I'll give you a hand loading all that scrap. I've got a #12 pitchfork that I use."

Between the two of them the Ford had almost a full bed of copper scrap on top of the snow that had fallen into it previously. Tommy drove home happy with his purchase, especially since Haskell's scrap was mostly cut in straight lines rather than all the curved lines on his scrap. Arriving home, he backed the Ford up to the shop door and parked. He got out of the Ford, opened the shop doors and began unloading the copper scrap into the corner of the room where his other scrap was piled. He put the Haskell scrap in a separate pile because of its different shapes. As he unloaded the scrap he thought about what possibilities besides flowers he might make from it.

Some of the Haskell scrap looked long and wide enough to save for small sculptures, so he put those pieces in another separate pile.

Gretchen came out to the shop as Tommy was unloading, and looked at the scrap he was sorting into piles in the corner.

"I was wondering about what to make from the scrap while I was washing the pots and pans, and I got to thinking that there is probably a market for sculptured wall hangings," she said. "I see that some of this scrap is big enough for that sort of thing."

"That's amazing that you were thinking the same thing that I was as I was unloading this stuff. I got all of this for ten bucks, which is sure enough a bargain. There's too much snow for me to go down by the river and sketch designs, so tomorrow I'll try sitting at the table or on the bed to sketch some ideas."

"You might think about getting a larger heater for the workshop, Tom. Winter has barely started and I can feel the chill inside the building. Do you want me to look for another heater when I am in town tomorrow?"

"That's probably a good idea," Tommy said. "If you find one, I'll drive the Ford in and pick it up. We could probably use that small heater that is in the shop over here in case we have an unusually cold winter."

"That's a good idea," Gretchen said.

Gretchen found an adequate heater for the shop and Tommy picked it up the following day. For several weeks he worked on flowers and sculptured wall hangings and made a substantial amount of items that he planned to sell at an artisan sale in an old warehouse in Newburgh. A group of craftspeople and artists held annual sales events in the warehouse bringing things that they advertised as "Holiday Gifts". Tommy came close to selling out of everything he had brought and took home close to a thousand dollars for his efforts.

After the holidays which Tommy and Gretchen spent with her parents, He used up the remaining pieces of scrap on the same kinds of things he had sold at the Holiday Gifts sale.

Hal and Clara paid them a visit during the last week of January. Hal had the final list of information about the exhibition at the Museum of Art, and talked with Tommy about hauling the sculpture into the city. Hal knew the traffic patterns in the city and they planned to arrive when traffic was the least crowded. Hal agreed that he would meet Tommy in Ossining at a gas station on the outskirts that Hal knew about.

The museum had planned a cocktail party for the opening night, the tenth of March. According to the instruction for exhibitors they would be due on the sixth of March, allowing time for setting up the exhibition and to be ready for the judging on the seventh. That schedule meant that Tommy would start from Walden early in the morning of March sixth. If all went well he would meet Hal in Ossining in the early afternoon. With that timing they would miss the late afternoon traffic in Manhattan and get to the museum well before dark.

"It seems to me that we are way ahead of time with all this planning," Tommy said.

"This is your first exhibition, Tommy," Hal said. "After this first one you will understand the necessity to plan ahead of time to make things go smoothly."

"I am planning to build a large crate for the sculpture. It will take a while and some lumber, but I think I need to do it."

"I agree wholeheartedly," Hal said.

Hal and Clara left for home. Tommy and Gretchen sat at the table discussing the plans for the museum exhibition.

"I have the design for a crate in which to haul "Why" to Manhattan. I am going to town tomorrow and get some lumber, screws and cardboard. I also need some Bubble wrap," Tommy said.

"If you get finished shopping before noon, stop by the office and we can go out to Mollie's Café for lunch."

"That sounds like my incentive to hurry with the shopping," Tommy said, with a grin.

The following noon, Tommy had all the materials for the crate bought and in the back of the Ford pickup. He and Gretchen enjoyed lunch together at Mollie Ingram's restaurant in the middle of town. Gretchen suggested that he should buy some better clothes than he had to attend the exhibition because the Museum of art had a reputation for well-dressed attendees of receptions and openings of exhibitions.

"I can wear what I have and keep out of sight," Tommy said.

"Suppose you have to get up and speak. You might be a bit embarrassed to do that in the clothes that you have right now."

"Hell's fire, Gretch, I wouldn't know what the hell to buy if I spent an entire day in a men's store."

"I'll go with you this afternoon. We aren't busy today, so Daddy really doesn't need me there."

"If you say so, but I am really not much in favor of this," Tommy said. "After the show, all the new clothes will be in the closet because, as you must know by now, I always wear my work clothes."

"I have a notion that you will be exhibiting in a lot more museums and galleries after this one," Gretchen said.

From Mollie's Café they walked to Carl's Men's Shoppe that was a half a block away from the restaurant. Gretchen looked around as Tommy talked with Carl, the owner of the store about the winter weather, and how it looked like we might have an early thaw. After a few minutes, Gretchen stopped and faced Tommy, suggesting that he join her to look at something that she had found.

"I think this sport coat and these dress pants would be just right for the occasion. With a new blue oxford cloth shirt and a tie, you will look like the handsome sculptor that you are."

"All but the shirt. That is the kind my father wears all the time because that is what he wore at The Wharton. Make it a plain blue shirt and a dark blue necktie."

Carl approached.

"Have you decided on something?" he asked.

Gretchen showed Carl what they wanted. Carl measured Tommy's waist and the length of his legs. Carl shifted through the dress pants and came up with the size he was looking for. Then he measured Tommy's neck and got a blue shirt from the shirt display shelf.

"How about a nice leather belt to go on the trousers," he said. "You don't want the trousers to fall down to the ground, do you?"

Tommy chose a black leather belt with a brass buckle. He went into the dressing room and put the outfit on to check on the sizes. Everything fit, but before he came out of the room the thought came to him that he would probably have to get some new dress shoes and socks. But he was tired of the clothes ordeal so he decided to say nothing about shoes.

He paid for the clothes and left the store. Gretchen returned to the office. Tommy drove home with the new outfit in a package on the front seat of the Ford. After unloading the materials he had bought for the crate, Tommy consulted his sketches with the measurements and began making the crate. A major feature of the assembly was the use of screws to join the panels. Tommy incorporated this feature so that the crate could be disassembled easily at the museum and could be used again whenever the sculpture needed moving to new locations. However, in the back of his mind Tommy hoped that his creation would attract a buyer so that moving the sculpture would be someone else's chore, not his. He had purchased a cordless drill to make the pilot holes for the screws and, with a change of bits, could be used on the screws. The cordless drill would not only be a time saver, but would set the screws to make a tight fit of the panels.

By the time Gretchen arrived home from the office, he had everything laid out to start sawing the two by twos to the needed sizes and the cardboard cut to enclose everything. He had put the roll of "bubble wrap" on a shelf to put around the sculpture before closing the crate with screws. Gretchen changed her clothes and went to the shop to help Tommy build the crate. Between the two of them they got everything cut and all of the pilot holes drilled for the screws. Tommy told Gretchen that he wanted to wait until the exhibition date was closer so that he could continue to inspect the sculpture for any minute flaws it might have.

Besides visiting the sculpture every day, Tommy spent his time writing. He had thought about a novel about a sculptor that had created a massive statue from granite rock, but had to leave it where he had finished it because of its weight and size that nobody would attempt to haul. The man had given up his art and moved to the city where he became a bartender in a bar in the Bowery that catered to seamen.

Tommy spent an entire day thinking about where he wanted the story to go and therefore where the bartender could end up with a life sculpting smaller statues than the one he had done but couldn't move.

By the end of February he had written two hundred pages, but the story was not finished by any means. However, one day Hal came by and made arrangements to return in three days to help Tommy finish crating "Why" and loading it onto the Ford for the trip into Manhattan. Clara arrived the day before they were scheduled to leave. She and Hal spent the night in a hotel in Newburgh.

All four friends were packed and ready to drive to Manhattan by five o'clock the following morning. Hal and Clara were in Clara's car. Tommy and Gretchen climbed into the Ford Pickup. Clara followed the Ford until they were close to Ossining when she passed the Ford and followed Hal's directions to the gas station.

Tommy followed Clara into the gas station, and filled the Ford's gas tank before Hal joined him and Gretchen changed vehicles to Clara's car. They left with Tommy in the lead. Tommy enjoyed driving on the highway that occasionally came close to The Hudson River. The traffic increased as they entered Manhattan. Hal gave Tommy directions to follow Fifth Avenue south until they came to Central Park. Then Hal told Tommy to slow down because he needed to turn left on 97th Street so that he could take an alley to the rear of the museum. Hal explained to Tommy that he would need to back up to the loading and unloading area at the rear of the building. Clara followed them and parked her car in a designated space for exhibitors only.

Once Tommy had parked and shut off the Ford, he saw two men come out of a wide doorway. They approached the Ford. Tommy and Hal got out of the pickup and waited for the men.

"We are here to help you unload," one of the men said.

"Thanks," Hal said. "Do you have a dolly large enough to take this inside?"

The men looked at the crate in the bed of the pickup.

"Is it heavy?" the same man asked.

"It took the two of us to load it into this pickup," Hal said.

Tommy stood watching what was going on. This was all new to him and he was impressed that not just one man had come to help, but two, and they looked like they were strong enough to lift the crate easily.

One of the men went back inside and quickly returned with a dolly on which to carry the crate inside.

"That should work fine," Hal said. "I think we should take it to the exhibition hall before uncrating it because it is difficult to carry without the crate."

"I'll have to call the exhibition director for permission. Most things get unpacked here and carried in later," the man said.

"Tell Wendell that it is Hal Cooper with Tom Holmes."

"All right," the man said, and went back inside the building.

Five minutes later, the man returned to the pickup where Tommy and Hal waited.

"They had to find Mister Gallagher. He said to bring it on in to the hall. He also said to welcome you both to the museum."

"Thanks," Hal said.

With the dolly in place to receive the crate, the two men lifted it out of the pickup as Tommy watched carefully to see that they didn't drop it or bump into the sides of the pickup bed. The dolly was a perfect size for the crate and the men maneuvered it through the door with ease. Tommy and Hal followed the crate and the men to the exhibition hall. Tommy carried his cordless drill to take the screws out from the crate's framework.

Tommy's eyes widened when he and Hal followed the men into the exhibition hall. He looked up at the ceiling that was thirty feet above him. The room was wide and long. He had no idea about the measurements, but he figured he could put at least twenty-five Ford pickups on the floor of the hall.

Wendell Gallagher arrived and greeted them.

"Hal, it's good to see you. I am glad you got here a little early. That crate will take a while to take apart."

"This is the sculptor, Tom Holmes, Wendell."

"A pleasure, Tom. Hal has spoken well of you and your work."

"It's nice to meet you, Mister Gallagher. The crate will not take much time. I designed it so that with a few screws taken out, the sculpture will be ready to place. If you can tell us where you want it stood, we can move the crate while we still have the dolly."

"Very good," Gallagher said. "I think it should be in the middle of the hall about fifteen feet from where it is right now."

Tommy walked out from where they were standing and stopped where he thought was the spot where Gallagher had described.

"How is this?" Tommy asked.

"That should be perfect," Gallagher said.

The men, still waiting patiently, moved the crate to where Tommy stood and took the dolly out from under the end of the crate.

"Do you need our help with the uncrating?" The man that had done all the talking thus far asked.

This won't take long. Maybe you could wait and take the crate panels out back wherever you store such things."

"You got it," the man said.

Tommy took the cordless drill to the screws and removed them, taking away the panels as they came loose. When all the panels were off, he had the men hold the sculpture as he removed all the "bubble wrap" from "Why". The men carried the crate panels back the way they had come.

Hal and Gallagher were chatting nearby. Tommy joined them.

"Tom," Gallagher said. "Hal sent me a copy of your poem "Why" and I think it goes perfectly with your work. I took the liberty of making some fancier copies to have available to any visitor that wants one. Is that all right with you?"

"That's very nice of you to do this. Thank you."

"You are multi-talented, Tom," Gallagher said.

"Isn't everyone? Tommy said.

"Stay here a moment, I'll be right back with your catalogue and exhibition program."

"Where do we go now?" Tommy asked.

"When Wendell gives us all the paper work, we can go to the hotel and have supper. I have stayed there before and the food is good. Tomorrow morning we will have a few hours free before the reception and opening because the judging will be going on in the morning and afternoon. We cannot be around while that is going on."

Wendell Gallagher returned with the catalogue, the program of events for the following day, and four exhibitor badges so that they could come and go as they pleased during the exhibition. Hal got permission to park the Ford and Carla's car out back for the duration of their stay.

"How are we going to go to the hotel without transportation?" Tommy asked when Wendell had left to guide other exhibitors to their spaces.

"The subways are far easier than trying to drive in the traffic," Hal said. "You saw how it was as we came in. Just think what it will be like during rush hour. There will be more taxis racing on the streets than you think there are in the entire world. Subways are the only way to get around Manhattan, believe me, so let's go back and get the girls and our luggage. We can lock the vehicles and walk a half block to the subway entrance. If I remember correctly, we will catch the train that will take us all the way to Tribeca, where our hotel is."

Getting the small amount of luggage they had and putting the cordless drill in one of the suitcases, the four of them walked to the subway, went down the stairs and paid their money to ride the famous Manhattan subway system. Tommy and Gretchen had been to Manhattan, but had never ridden the subway, so it was with a little hesitation that both stepped aboard the train when it stopped in front of them. Hal smiled as he watched the look on Tommy's face.

They enjoyed supper at a nearby restaurant rather than at the hotel because Hal knew the restaurant had lobster on their menu, and he knew Tommy had a special taste for lobster. On returning to the hotel, they retired early to be ready for the long day that waspromised for the following day.

Hal took everyone to breakfast at a small standup restaurant that he said he preferred over any other in the city when he had lived in Greenwich Village after graduating from college. There were no tables, chairs or even stools at the counter. Everyone there stood at the counter to eat whatever they had ordered. Tommy thought that it was the best restaurant idea he had ever heard of and he enjoyed his generous platter of ham and eggs with a toasted English muffin smothered with butter. Riding the subways, Hal took them on a small tour of the city, during which he showed them where he had once lived in Greenwich Village, and where he had maintained a ceramics studio for two years before he took the job at The Escalante School.

Hal took them to Times Square where he knew about a restaurant that served interesting lunches. After lunch they returned to the hotel so that Tommy could change into his new clothes. Gretchen had insisted that he stop in a shoe store that was near the hotel to buy a pair of dress shoes for the opening.

By three o'clock in the afternoon Hal announced that they should start heading to the museum in order to be early for the opening in case the director needed information or anything he wanted to know about the sculpture.

Hal didn't say anything about the judging, but he was anxious to know how Tommy's work stood in the judge's eyes. When they were close to the museum Hal stopped and turned to Tommy.

"When we get there the judging will have been completed unless something happened to delay things. I need to tell you in case your sculpture didn't receive any recognition, the results of the judging do not mean that you did not do a masterful piece of work. It only means that the judge has his own opinion and it may not apply to your work. These art shows and literary contests are not like horse races. Entering art shows is really a crapshoot. In a horse race, the horse that crosses the finish line first is the winner and that's that. There really is no winner of an art show because the judge or a few judges give the ribbons and acclaims. In another show the piece that won the first show might be ignored in the other show's judge or judges. Keep this in mind once we go back to the exhibition hall at the museum. As I looked around at the pieces on display when we were uncrating 'Why', I couldn't see any that came close to 'Why'. But, that is only my opinion."

With their exhibitor badges pinned onto their coats and sweaters the four walked past the guards at the front entrance of the museum. Hal stepped out in front leading them to the Exhibition Hall. They walked through a large arched entry that had its doors opened and swung around to the adjacent walls. Hal suddenly stopped, waited for the others to catch up.

"Look," he said. "They have moved 'Why' up to the front and there's a small table in front of it. Hurry, I think we are going to be surprised and pleased.

The four walked faster and kept looking at Tommy's sculpture at the front of all the rest. Hal stopped and quickly turned around.

"Tommy, see that purple ribbon hanging on that plaque on the table. 'Why' is 'Best of Show'! Congratulations a million times."

Tommy walked cautiously up to the table and looked at the purple ribbon and the card announcing that "Why" had been judged "Best of Show". Next to the plaque was a stack of the fancily printed copies of his poem with the same name as the sculpture "Why". He turned, wrapped his arms around Gretchen and hugged her a long time before kissing her.

"Wow, my darlin' what a nice feeling I have," he said.

"Me too, my love; you have accomplished a great thing with your mind and your hands. I am very proud of you."

Hal and Clara came to him with their congratulatory hugs.

"I owe you lot, Hal. 'Why' would not even be here if it wasn't for you leading me to do all this," Tommy said.

"That is because I have believed in your talent and imagination since you first went to The Escalante."

"I have believed in you longer than that," Clara said, and hugged him.

Wendell Gallagher strode up with his congratulations.

"That is the most imaginative sculpture I think I have ever seen, Tom. Your poem is also perfectly appropriate. I am sure you have read what this award involves besides the purple ribbon"

"I am sorry, Mister Gallagher, I don't know what you are talking about."

"You have also won a ten thousand dollar prize for being Best of Show. The museum director will present that to you during the award ceremony. You might start thinking about what you will say."

Tommy turned toward Hal.

"You didn't tell me much about this stuff when I agreed to enter the show. Don't get me wrong, I am not in the least bit angry, I am just wondering about the secrecy,"

"I didn't want to get your hopes up and distract you from your sculpting. I was hoping earlier this evening that you wouldn't know about the ten thousand dollar prize money until the director of the museum handed you the envelope, and you opened it."

"It is probably better that I have found out now instead of later at the ceremony because I might have wet my new trousers."

Tommy laughed along with the others including Gallagher. He and Gretchen had been holding hands since he had learned about the prize money. All of a sudden a girl pushing a baby carriage approached them. Tommy nudged Gretchen.

"Look who came to the show," he said to her.

Gretchen tilted her head and looked around Tommy at the girl with the baby carriage.

"Julie Branson, what brings you to this museum?" Gretchen asked.

"Hi Gretchen. Hi Tom. Congratulations for winning the show."

"How did you know I would be here?" Tommy asked.

"I saw the announcement in the newspaper. I must say that I was surprised. I had no idea what had become of you since you left The Escalante."

"You had a lot to do with my leaving. Now I have the opportunity to thank you. I wouldn't be here had I stayed at that school."

"Gretchen, do you mind if I talk to Tom alone?" Julie asked. "I have some explaining to do. By the way look at my little boy. He is Charlie Rosas' son. I named him Billy and call him Billy Boy. He is a really good baby."

Tommy and Gretchen looked into the carriage and saw the baby boy that they both knew had to be Charlie Rosas' baby because of its dark color and very curly black hair.

"I don't mind at all if you speak with Tom alone," Gretchen said.

"Are you sure?" Tommy asked.

Gretchen shook her head and smiled.

Tommy and Julie walked a short distance away, Julie pushing the baby carriage.

"Why the hell did you accuse me of being your baby's father? You must have known that it was from Charlie."

"That's what I need to explain," she said. "I knew I was pregnant with Charlie's child and when I told him that I would need some support because of the way my parents are, he took off for Jamaica along with his cousin Tack. They were both at school on a full ride scholarship. Charlie had no money to support me so he took off. I accused you because I was desperate for two things: I wanted a father for my child and I needed support. Then all that blew up and we both got kicked out of those schools."

"What have you been doing, Julie. Do you still live with your parents?"

"Heavens no," she said. "Do you remember that I told you that my mother told me that if I did it with men before I was married, I would be a prostitute? Well, since I like to do it so much I decided to become a prostitute. And, guess what? I really enjoy what I am doing, although some guys get rough at times."

"Do your mother and father know what you do for a living?" Tommy asked.

"Yes," she said, and scowled. "I got to dislike them both very much when I had Billy Boy and they came to the hospital. When they saw Billy Boy they got angry and called me a whore and other names. They also showed their terrible racism. I told them to leave and never try to find me. They haven't looked, thank God."

"How did you live while you were pregnant?" Tommy asked.

"I told you about my profession. I have learned a lot since I left Mujeres del Mundo. Now I am a real woman of the world. I do have one more thing to tell you."

"What now?" Tommy asked. "You have already told me more than I could have ever imagined."

"I work at Demitri's, a small bar and grill just off Wall Street. I am a waitress and, of course, that is where I pick up my johns. It is a favorite place for certain bankers. I remember you telling me about your father wanting you to go to The Wharton School of Finance. Well, Tom, most of my clients are from your father's bank, and that includes your father!"

"Good grief, are you bull-shitting me?"

"No," she said. "He tips me better than any other client. He has told me that his wife is so constantly drunk that he no longer desires her. Incidentally you make love better than your father."

"I don't think I need to know any more about your favorite client. It was nice seeing you, and I wish you and Billy Boy the best of luck."

"Just one more thing that might interest you; I told your father and Demetri Pappas about this exhibition. They may attend this opening. And, Tom, I told your father about Billy Boy and about you and me. He is okay with that, and other stuff."

Julie took the handlebar of the carriage and pushed it toward the entrance. Tommy went back to Gretchen, Hal and Clara. Gallagher had left for the cocktail party in the back of the hall.

"Do you want to join the others at the party?" Hal asked.

Tommy looked over at Gretchen and saw that she was open for it.

"Might as well celebrate the crap-shoot," Tommy said.

They took their drinks from the small serving bar and stood apart from the crowd that had gathered and was busy chatting away in the middle of the large room adjacent to the exhibition hall. Tommy had just finished telling Gretchen about his conversation with Julie Bronson when Wendell Gallagher approached them, accompanied by a man in a gray pinstriped suit. He stood at around five feet four inches and was bald except for a salt and pepper ring of hair just above his ears. Wendell introduced him to Hal, Clara and Gretchen, then to Tommy.

"Demitri Pappas this is Tom Holmes, the sculptor whose work you have purchased. Tom, Mister Pappas owns and operates a Greek restaurant off Wall Street and he tells me that he is acquainted with your father."

"It is a pleasure meeting such a talented artist as yourself," Demitri said. "One of my waitresses told me about this exhibition and showed me the photograph of your work in the newspaper. I took her advice and stopped by a little while ago. When I saw your sculpture, 'Why', and looked at its entirety, I knew I had to have it to my restaurant for my customers to see and perhaps understand. You see, when I was a young man in Greece, I wanted to become a philosopher. A lot of young Greeks want to become philosophers like Aristotle and the others. 'Why', to me, is the essence of my own philosophy and I have purchased it so that I can share it with others."

"That makes me happy to know that 'Why' will be available for others to see and contemplate. Thank you for your interest,"

"By the way, I have known your father for many years. He is one of my best customers."

"It has been a pleasure meeting and talking with you, Mister Pappas. I hope that Gretchen and I can enjoy your restaurant soon and see 'Why' there."

"I already have a plan and a place for 'Why' with lighting that will have it observable from every table. Thank you so much for your talent and philosophy."

Gallagher and Pappas left to wander around among the other guests. Hal raised his eyebrows and looked at Tommy with a look of amazement.

"What a day!" he exclaimed. "First you get the Best of Show ribbon and ten grand. Then you sell you sculpture for twenty-five grand. I would say you should be up there on cloud nine."

"What do you mean, twenty-five grand for 'Why'?" Tommy asked scowling in disbelief.

"Haven't you looked in the catalogue? For Sale Prices are listed there for each piece that is in the show. The price for 'Why' price is twenty-five thousand dollars."

"Where did they get that price?" Tommy asked.

"That's the price I put on it in the application I sent in," Hal said with a wide grin spread from ear to ear.

Tommy raised his arm and nudged his forehead with the heel of his hand.

"For heaven's sake, Hal Cooper, you have done so much for me, I would like to know what I can do for you."

"Tom, you have done plenty for me just by doing what you do so well. Your talent and work returns to me as a reward for recognizing both. And, besides, your friendship goes right along with the rest."

Tommy turned to Gretchen who stood next to him.

"I guess 'Why' has made it easier for us to afford that addition on the cabin for the baby," he said and smiled at her and over at Hal and Clara.

"Wow, that is quite the good news," Hal said.

"It sure is," Clara said. "It makes me feel like I will be a grandmother."

Gretchen stepped over to Clara and hugged her closely.

The four had come close to finishing their drinks when Tommy turned toward Gretchen.

"Gretch, my father is here and saw me. He is walking this way."

Gretchen stood there with an anxious look on her face, but said nothing in reply.

"Hello, Tommy, it has been a long time," Jason Holmes said as he stopped in front of Tommy.

"Hello, Dad. It has been a lot of years to say the least. How are you?"

"I am fine, I guess. Your mother couldn't make it, or I should say, I didn't tell her to come to the city for this opening. I read about it in the newspaper."

"Dad, I know who told you about this event. It was Julie Bronson. She came by a short while ago."

"I guess you are right. She did tell me when I was having lunch at Demitri's where she works."

"Julie told me a lot, Dad."

"Tommy," Jason said. "Is there somewhere we can be alone to talk? I need to tell you a lot of things."

"We can probably go to the rear where they store things. It is where I came in with my sculpture when we got here."

"That sounds fine, I'll follow you,"

Tommy stepped over to Gretchen and told her that he was going with his father to have some sort of conversation. Then he started for the back room with his father at his side. The door was open so they went in. Tommy closed the door behind them. He was glad that the lights were on as he spotted a stacked line of folding metal chairs. He grabbed two of the chairs, unfolded them and put them on the floor opposite each other. Father and son sat down. Jason sighed and began talking.

"I guess I would like to start with Julie. I know all about you and her and I also know about why she accused you of being the father of her child. I also know about Billy Boy. I must tell, you that Julie opened my eyes about you. She told me things that I never realized as you were growing up."

"I remember telling Julie a lot about my feelings growing up."

As I look back, I was married to that bank. The bank was also my child. I was a lousy father to you, but I was a good father to the bank. Julie told me about you and Ralph. I am ashamed of what I did with that sculpture. I often question what in hell was going through my mind when I did that. I hope that someday you will be able to forgive me, Son."

"I must admit that all that stuff comes back to my mind every so often, but I am not bothered by it like I once was," Tommy said.

"By the way, I no longer drink booze. I am sure you remember how I would come home from the city, sit down with a couple of drinks before supper and talk with your mother but never with you. Your mother's drinking made her into serious drunk. I thought I should drink with her for some reason. I can thank Julie for making me understand why I was drinking and for encouraging me to quit. Your Julie is very important to me, Tommy. I know that your mother needs someone to take care of her so I have convinced myself to stay with her. Julie was also influential in that matter, too. She may be a so-called "Lady of the Night", but she has a good and tender heart."

"I am glad that everything has worked out the way it has. I am very happy with Gretchen, the girl I was standing with. She and I will make you a grandpa in a few months. When we go back I will introduce you to her and to Hal and Clara, my dear friends. You may remember that Clara was Miss Anson, my ceramics teacher in grammar school."

"I think I remember hearing your mother talking about her. I saw Demitri as I was getting here. He told me about buying your sculpture. I was going to buy it for the bank lobby, but he beat me to it. However, I am glad that he got it. He told me about his plan for its place in the restaurant. I will be able to tell all those Wharton boys that a man who refused to go to The Wharton created it. After seeing 'Why', I fully realize that you made the right decision."

Jason paused as if he was trying to think of something else to say. Finally he reached across and patted Tommy's knee.

"I guess that is about all I needed to tell you. I hope you will understand that I do love you and I am very proud of you. And, I look forward to meeting my grandchild."

"Dad, this has been a wonderful and heart warming conversation. When you see her, thank Julie for me.

And, give Mom a hug from me. I hope she can find herself somehow. I guess it's time to go back to the others."

They rose from the metal folding chairs. Tommy folded them up and returned them to the row where he got them. Father and son went back to the cocktail party. Tommy introduced Jason to Gretchen, Hal and Clara. Tommy and Jason hugged each other tightly. Releasing from the long hug,Tommy watched as his father walked away toward the entrance of the museum.

"I see people moving toward the exhibition Hall. It must be time for the awards ceremony," Hal said. "We might as well go there and try to get good seats."

Tommy held up his hands.

"Before we go over there, I want to tell you that my father and I had a great conversation, and we got everything straightened out. This really made this a day to remember."

Tommy picked up one of the few copies of his poem still left on the table and read it to Gretchen and his friends.

WHY?

Why can't young understand old
Why can't old understand young
Why the gap
Why the chasm

Why is there love

Why is there hate
Why is there war
Why can't there be peace

Why is there certainty
Why is there doubt
Why are there friends
Why are there enemies

Why is there corruption
Why can't honesty prevail
Why is there fear
Why does fear rule

Why must there be war
Why can't there be talk
Why can't understanding happen
Why does ignorance kill

Why do some lives flow like a stream
Why do others rampage like a hurricane
Why do tempers boil
Why does self-doubt simmer

Why are there rebels
Why are there sheep
Why is there fury
Why are there tears

Why is life a tower of question marks
Why are they intertwined
Why is there no summit
Why does it grow

Why is the ultimate rebel always the summit
Why is it the adventurous rebel
Why is it the courageous rebel
Why not?

END

## About the Author

John Duncklee has been a cowboy, rancher, quarter horse breeder, university professor and award-winning author of thirty-three books and two hundred articles, poetry and short stories. He is a Western Writers of America Spur award winner and was awarded a $5000 unrestricted fellowship for writing excellence by the Arizona Commission on the Arts.. He lives in Las Cruces, N.M. with his wife, Penny, an accomplished watercolorist.

26893807R00150

Made in the USA
Charleston, SC
24 February 2014